SPECIAL MESSAGE TO READERS

This book is published under the auspices of

THE ULVERSCROFT FOUNDATION

(registered charity No. 264873 UK)

Established in 1972 to provide funds for research, diagnosis and treatment of eye diseases. Examples of contributions made are: —

A Children's Assessment Unit at Moorfield's Hospital, London.

•

Twin operating theatres at the Western Ophthalmic Hospital, London.

•

A Chair of Ophthalmology at the Royal Australian College of Ophthalmologists.

•

The Ulverscroft Children's Eye Unit at the Great Ormond Street Hospital For Sick Children, London.

You can help further the work of the Foundation by making a donation or leaving a legacy. Every contribution, no matter how small, is received with gratitude. Please write for details to:

**THE ULVERSCROFT FOUNDATION,
The Green, Bradgate Road, Anstey,
Leicester LE7 7FU, England.
Telephone: (0116) 236 4325**

In Australia write to:
THE ULVERSCROFT FOUNDATION,
c/o The Royal Australian College of
Ophthalmologists,
27, Commonwealth Street, Sydney,
N.S.W. 2010.

Valerie Kershaw was born in Lancashire and now lives with her husband in Gozo, Malta. They have three grown-up children.

She has been a newspaper and radio journalist, and with her fourth novel, *Rockabye*, won the £5,000 Lichfield Prize.

MURDER IS TOO EXPENSIVE

Hours after Jon Stanton has dined with an attractive girl, his corpse is found at the wheel of his old beetle. It looks like suicide. Could it be murder? The sudden death of the wealthy, young researcher sends shock waves through his colleagues at Birmingham's Radio Brum. Raunchy, middle-aged investigative journalist Mitch Mitchell — while fighting to keep her job in the face of younger opposition — begins to probe Stanton's private affairs. A substantial legacy to a cousin; photographs mailed to a close friend, late of MI5; a break-in at Mitch's house — all lead her inexorably to another corpse . . .

Books by Valerie Kershaw
Published by The House of Ulverscroft:

ROCKABYE
THE SNOW MAN
ROSA

VALERIE KERSHAW

◆

MURDER IS TOO EXPENSIVE

Complete and Unabridged

ULVERSCROFT
Leicester

First published in Great Britain in 1993

First Large Print Edition
published 2000

The moral right of the author has been asserted

Copyright © 1993 by Valerie Kershaw
All rights reserved

British Library CIP Data

Kershaw, Valerie
   Murder is too expensive.—Large print ed.—
Ulverscroft large print series: mystery
1. Detective and mystery stories
2. Large type books
I. Title
823.9′14 [F]

ISBN 0–7089–4289–X

Published by
F. A. Thorpe (Publishing)
Anstey, Leicestershire
Set by Words & Graphics Ltd.
Anstey, Leicestershire
Printed and bound in Great Britain by
T. J. International Ltd., Padstow, Cornwall

This book is printed on acid-free paper

To Lizzie and Peter Roberts,
without whom . . .

IN MAY

Trinity Sunday
When I went to All Saints' Church this
morning I almost walked into a puddle just
beyond the lych gate. It came into my mind
that he could drown. Unfortunately, he's a
strong swimmer. The big toe on his right foot
is webbed to the next. I must say that his
froggy foot always made me shiver though in
the beginning I pretended to adore his little
abnormality and covered it with kisses.

I keep staring at pictures of him. I can't
keep my eyes off him. I'm always wondering
how I'm going to do it. I keep thinking, he
wouldn't smile like that if he knew what he
was in for.

My head's awhirl. This morning when I
looked in the bathroom mirror I began to
wonder at what I saw. Is this the face of evil?

I rather think it is. Though one must be
tentative. I've always thought evil is a very big
word. Not to be used lightly.

Tuesday
Such wild thoughts. I've been toying, among
other things, with the idea of his appearing to

1

have drowned. In other words, could he be dead before he hit the water? On investigation — oh yes, I did a little homework — this didn't prove at all feasible. The weight of water in a drowned man's lungs would drag him under. A man who died before he went into the sea — actually, I didn't have the sea in mind, but the lake in Cannon Hill Park — would float. And then there is the problem of the tiny aquatic organisms a pathologist would expect to find in the tissues of a man who had died by drowning.

The amazing thing is that I feel quite sprightly now. No. Very sprightly. That doesn't describe it. I feel . . . good heavens, I jolly well feel wonderful. Like, like . . . like I was when I was a teenager and fell in love with Barrie Southern and my flesh tingled at unexpected moments and I spent hours and hours planning how I'd get him in my arms. I succeeded, too.

Friday
I have visualised him dead. I thought that would put me off killing him.

When I've killed him he'll look younger because when someone dies his muscles relax and grow looser. Death irons the creases out. After an hour red patches will begin to appear all over his body. I wonder what sort of

2

chemistry produces that? About three hours later all his muscles will grow hard as rigor sets in. It even affects the tiny muscles around hairs. He'll have goosebumps all over. Even on his webbing.

If flies get to his body they will lay maggots between his eyelid and eye and between his lips.

Did this knowledge — and there is more and worse — put me off for a moment? The truth is that it did not, though at the time I pretended to myself it did — I still see myself as a decent person, you see. I made a great thing about getting myself a good stiff gin.

Later I laughed so much inside I almost spilled my G and T.

Vengeance is mine, says the Lord.

A He naturally.

I'll think about the Lord later. When I've done it.

Saturday
I really will have to try and calm down. My mind is almost on fire. Such wild, wild thoughts. One finds oneself going into the ins and outs of cutting him up and putting him in ham and cider pies, bedevilling his brains, making a nice fricassee of sweetbreads. But it is not only the practical problems which beset one. One has to think of the aesthetics of the

thing. Really. I feel one must try and overcome one's worst instincts and bring to the situation the sense and sensibilities of a Miss Jane Austen. One is not, after all, an animal. One should try to aim for a nice, clean, neat, understated job.

I've found out that a good dose of lilies of the valley will wreak havoc in a chap's heart. Mother, for one, always relied on flowers. She found they nearly always answered when one was faced with any kind of social difficulty.

If one were to mix some *Convallaria majalis* in a chap's gentlemen's relish, for instance, he would first get hot flushes. He'd become very irritated, too — quite menopausal, in fact. This would be followed by hallucinations, cold clammy skin, vomiting, stomach pains, and a slow heartbeat. This, in theory at least, would culminate in coma and death.

But it is a bit late in the year for lilies of the valley. Or am I thinking of snowdrops? Both have little white flowers.

Dear me. The cat's still out.

Sunday
Well, in the end I did go to morning service. This is how I squared it with myself. I decided that as I was planning to kill him — and enjoying the choosing so much — I

4

must be mad. This led me to thinking I won't be responsible for my actions. That seems to make it all right with God. Therefore, one trotted off to All Saints as usual.

But I've had to put the Sunday joint back in the freezer. I just couldn't look at that lump of dead flesh. I felt so jolly peculiar. That could be him, I thought.

Perhaps I'm not mad. If I'm absolutely perfectly sane . . . what then? Bridge tonight. Bridge. Imagine that. Life goes on just as normal. As if I'm not going to kill him. But I know I'm going to do it. Every now and then I shake all over.

1

Mitch Mitchell was half-way through the front door when the phone rang. She hesitated. 'Oh shit.' She dumped her jumbo-sized patent leather handbag next to a Tesco bag bulging with spools of tape, newspaper clippings, a play list, peep-toe shoes and a hat. In the distance a police siren began to wail.

'Hello.' She was panting slightly as she picked up the wall-mounted phone.

'Is that my favourite crumblie? Darling, I caught your show last night. Loved the package on the skate-boarding duck. You'd never have thought something like that would work on radio. I practically saw that duckiwuk whizzing across the farmyard.'

'Oh, it's you . . . ' Mitch, blinded by sun which poured through the kitchen window, turned to face the hall. 'Don't call me a crumblie, Digger. It's not funny. But I'm glad you liked the duck.'

'Blossom, I didn't mean to upset you. Not for the world — '

'Of course you did. You enjoy being a shit.' She noticed the bright red ring round next

7

Friday's date on her calendar. The start of her summer holidays. She turned her thumb up. Then she saw that morning's date. Friday the thirteenth. 'Look, I'm going to be late. What do you want, Digger?'

'To check the time of Jon's funeral. I never realised he was one of *the* Stantons. Did you?'

'What Stantons?'

'The tractor Stantons who sold out to that Japanese firm a few years back. Of course, he obviously came from a classy background.'

'Listen, Digger, I'll have to dash. Shaun's off and I've got landed with an interview he fixed up. Some footballer for the sporting memories spot. I don't know anything about it. Football, I mean.'

'You're already about to make the first mistake. Never interview a footballer.'

'Why not?'

'They only say er. And that's on a good day. By the way, are you going to wear black? I mean for Jon's service.'

'I'm in it already. A black polka dot dress. The best I could do. I've put a hat and stuff in my bag. It's all right for women. Some of them can even look tasty in black. It turns most men into waiters or out-of-work violinists.'

'I suppose our beloved programme organiser is coming too?'

8

'I can't imagine Freya Adcock missing it.'

Digger sighed. 'Not a fun day. See you later, blossom.'

Mitch collected her bags and went out into the bright sunlight. She lived in a terrace of Georgian-style houses built right at the beginning of the Victorian era; each was double-fronted, their shady front gardens dropping sharply to the dual carriageway beyond stone-capped gateposts. The red fibreglass TVR sports car stood nose down towards the road. Mitch knew that, at fifty, she was too old for a car like that but as she'd been driving sports cars since she was twenty she was damned if she was going to give up now.

Four lanes of traffic met her at the bottom of her dipping drive. She edged her way across, turning right to the broadcasting centre. She started to whistle and then, horrified, stopped. It was poor Jon Stanton's funeral in three hours. And yet she couldn't help feeling happy. It was a sunny day in June and soon she'd be off to see her daughter in Washington. They'd go shopping and talk of hairstyles and Cassie would entertain her by using more American expressions — 'swing by for lunch', 'let's snack on brownies' 'the cheese has slid off the poor guy's cracker'.

The broadcasting centre was built between

two parallel main roads on the south side of Birmingham. A central strip of grass divided the dual carriageway; beech and sycamore trees cast shivering shadows on the pavements. A few days ago she'd been shocked when a grey squirrel had dropped off its perch on to the roof of her TVR. The security man on the gate had removed the corpse for her. He was there this morning and when she showed him her identity card he winked at her. She parked behind the seven-storey building, dug out the straw hat and shoes from the Tesco bag, and left them on the passenger's seat.

As she straightened up she saw Freya Adcock emerging from lines of parked cars on to the tarmac apron at the back entrance to the building. Though Mitch had been working for Radio Brum for almost a year, the station's progamme organiser still had the power to disconcert her. Freya Adcock was so horse-boned that it seemed more natural to measure her height in hands than in feet. She ought to wear tweeds over those fetlocks and her voice ought to register somewhere in the baritone range. But Freya decked herself in little girl gingham pinafores and sailor-collared outfits which saucily hinted at something-up-the-mainbrace; she alarmed with skittish buttons and bows and coloured slides in baby-soft hair. And when she was really excited Freya squealed, though this was something she heroically fought to control. Brought to such a pitch she was apt to lose her voice. Jon Stanton's death had silenced her. Today she was in one of her sailor outfits; perhaps navy blue was the deepest shade in her wardrobe. She carried a briefcase which was so full it wouldn't shut, as befits a programme organiser who was acting as station manager. A temporary state of affairs, Mitch prayed. The former manager, Reggie Brown — the man who had given Mitch a job — had gone off to higher things within the organisation. A new manager had not yet been appointed. If Freya did get the job Mitch thought it would be unlikely that her contract would be renewed.

Freya's shadow rose as she went up the flight of concrete steps. But what was the point of worrying? Mitch thought. If I get fired, I get fired. I ought to be used to it by now.

Radio Brum was housed on part of the second floor of the broadcasting centre. The building was a squared Q. During the hot weather the central courtyard had been turned into a television studio for some of the regional programmes and as she went in she

11

could hear music in the distance. She passed rows of caged props and then climbed the back stairs. Radio Brum's engineers' rooms and production offices were in the tail of the Q.

No one looked up when she went in. At the far end of the production office Quentin Plunkett, chinagraph in pudgy hand, was sitting over a tape-editing machine. The pouch at the front of his fisherman's smock dribbled tape. Leland Church, slim, black, dreadlocked, sat on top of his desk in the lotus position. With his car keys he was tapping out a rhythm on his teeth, turning them into a much better instrument than most people's pianos. 'Hello,' she said.

No one answered.

She shrugged and went into the stock room. She took her tape recorder off its battery charger, threaded it with fresh tape, then tested it. Hefting the strap over her shoulder, she went back into the office.

'Did Digger Rooney manage to reach you?' the secretary asked. Twenty-year-old Trish was using the sole of her track shoe to shut the door behind her. Her arms were piled with the morning's post.

'He caught me just as I was leaving.'

'I wasn't sure of the time. I'm not going to change. I mean, I went to my gran's funeral in jeans, didn't I? I suppose you've heard the news?'

'What news?'

'They're holding the interviews for the manager's job in a couple of weeks.'

'Oh Lord . . .'

'I don't know what you're worrying about. I shouldn't think they'd give the job to Freya. I mean, not after Jon Stanton's suicide. She's not shown much talent in the way of man management. My God, we're going to fry.' Trish dropped the post on her desk and went over to the windows. After opening them, she began shutting the venetian blinds. 'Nothing feels right, does it?'

'What do you mean?' Mitch was rooting round her desk for a pen.

'Well, it's a perfect day. They say it'll be in the eighties by lunchtime. It's not at all the day for a funeral.'

'Hey. Are you all right?'

Trish brushed away the beginnings of tears. 'It just hits me now and then. Most of the time I don't believe it and then . . . I mean, he wasn't much older than me.'

'It was an awful shock.' *What would I do if it were my daughter? How could he do it?* Goosepimples prickled on Mitch's arms.

'Do you think what they're saying is true?

13

That he killed himself because Freya fired him?'

'No one finishes it all because they got the bullet from local radio. Anyway, I'd heard he'd another job lined up. Telly researcher.'

'It'll only be the second funeral I've ever been to.' Trish's mouth opened into a half-wail and then clamped shut.

'You needn't go, you know. No one will think the worse of you, Trish.'

'Don't you think people have to pay their respects?'

'Yes. Yes, I suppose you're right. He was such a nice lad. Normally I hate the products of our public schools. They seem to turn out the male equivalent of 'proper little madams'. Look, I've got to go. You are going to be all right?'

Trish nodded.

'Sure?'

'Sure.'

Eddie Murton, the footballer Mitch was to interview, lived in Burton-on-Trent, about twenty-five miles to the north of Birmingham. From Monday to Friday Mitch presented an early evening programme called 'City Talk'. Among the items she shoe-horned into her show were two sporting memories a week. Eddie was due to be included in Monday's edition.

14

He lived near Burton District Hospital, just off Snobell Road. A kilted gnome guarded the front door of his semi. Mitch soon realised that trying to interview Eddie was hopeless, but not for the reasons Digger had given her.

Mitch   You won thirty caps, didn't you, Eddie?

Eddie   Did I? There you are then, ducks.

Mitch   Your first cap was against France in 1951.

Eddie   France? France, you say?

Mitch   According to the record books. I checked.

Eddie   All right. All right. Will I get paid?

Mitch   I'm afraid not.

Eddie   Gazza gets paid.

Mitch   Gazza?

Eddie   I've only got my pension.

Mitch   Local radio never pays, I'm afraid. Now, you won five nil.

Eddie   Was that against Leeds?

Mitch   France. Against France.

Eddie   Teddy Briggs. Now 'e were a good player. By rights you should be seeing him.

Mitch   Your first international match was against France.

Eddie   Never been.

Over an hour later Mitch staggered through Eddie's front door with yards and yards of useless tape in her Uher and a notebook full of exclamation marks. Cursing the old footballer, cursing Shaun who had set up the interview, cursing all Friday the thirteenths, she climbed back into her TVR. Somehow or other she'd prise a five-minute item out of all that garbage. She was damned if she was going to spend her weekend finding another sporting memory. She glanced at her watch. It was already gone eleven. If she weren't careful she'd be late for Jon's funeral. She wound the window down and threaded her way back through the brewing town. The air was impregnated by a yeasty smell. In the heat haze distant buildings seemed to weave as if made legless by the promise of all that beer fermenting in stainless steel vats.

When she got back on to the A38 she put her foot down. Though she was fast, a macho male in a Mercedes, car phone to his ear, showed her how much quicker he was. He must have been doing a ton when he overtook her. But it was Mitch who was cut out and herded over to the hard shoulder by a cop car. If she'd been stopped by the police ten years ago she might have — figuratively speaking — opened the top button of her blouse. At fifty you had to come to terms with the fact that some stratagems no longer worked. But what could replace them?

The two policemen ambled towards her. 'Are you aware of the speed you were doing, madam?' One stayed by her while the other strolled round the car, touching wheel trim, looking thoughtfully at lights which weren't on.

'Actually, officer, I was overtaken. You must have seen that silver-blue car overtake me.'

'The Mercedes.'

'Well then . . . ' Mitch smiled. 'Well, I mean . . . if the Mercedes overtook me . . . '

'We were following you.' The policeman took out his notebook.

The other policeman had joined him. 'Yes. Definitely. We were following you.'

'This is awful. I'm on my way to a funeral.'

'Very few people touch ninety on their way to a funeral. It's more usual for the hearse to set the pace.'

'But . . . I mean it looks so fearfully bad. If one were to be late.'

'Licence, madam. Insurance.'

'I don't carry them with me.'

'You ladies. All the same.' The first policeman wagged his finger. 'We'll have to give you a chitty, won't we?'

'Then you can produce your documents at the police station,' said the second officer.

'But that Mercedes did overtake me, officer. You saw it.'

'We've explained all that. Miss? Mrs?'

'Em-ess!' Mitch found herself hissing.

'A lot of it about these days.'

'It's a good job I've not got my gauge on me,' said the second police officer. 'Those tyres, madam. No tread at all. Take my tip. Get them replaced. A load of mischief can come from bald tyres.'

'He's quite right. And I'd wash that number plate of yours, too. An offence, that.'

'You're making that up!'

'No need to, madam. It's in the book.'

'If it's not in the book it's all right,' said the second policeman. 'Then it doesn't happen.'

'In my experience very little doesn't happen,' the other one observed.

'If I'd have been driving that Mercedes this wouldn't have happened!'

'You're not entirely out of luck, ducks. After all, it's not your funeral.'

'You're quite all right. Some other poor bugger's got it in the neck.'

'Why follow me? After all, the Mercedes *did* overtake me.'

One of the officers squinted at the sun.

'Hot today,' the other said. He was getting out his biro. 'Not many people knock themselves out on a day like this. Super day.'

'You mean that while I was going too fast I wasn't going fast enough?'

'I didn't say that. You were speeding, madam.'

'You certainly were,' said the other officer.

'You shouldn't be in such a hurry. Not to get to a funeral.'

Mitch, chitty in her handbag, set off again at a very sedate pace. The policemen, shading their eyes, watched her go.

'Shit!' She ground her teeth. And then she thought of the clown with the car phone doing a ton. 'Shit. Shit. Shit!'

She was ten minutes late for Jon Stanton's funeral.

On her way through bright blue wrought-iron gates she saw a rook strutting under a stand of young birch trees. The crematorium's double pine doors were closed. She parked the car and changed into the black peep-toe shoes she'd brought with her, then tucked rebellious curls under the black straw hat.

Getting out of the car she looked up at the short pinky beige snout which reared above the copper roof of the crematorium. Beyond, the skies were cloudless and full of bird-song.

Mitch sighed and made her way up the rising tarmac drive. A vivid image of Jon Stanton sprang into her mind. He was wearing Oxfam gear, his lithe body turned belly up as he crab-walked on hands and feet across the production office floor. 'Let me do it to you baby . . . ' he was crooning. 'Do it. Do it. Do it . . . '

'Shut that little prick up!' Quentin Plunkett had bellowed. He had been on the phone.

'Let me do it to you, baby. Do it. Do it. Do it . . . '

That had been less than a month ago.

Mitch stopped outside the closed doors. They were studded with bronze elongated crosses and her hand went to finger one tentatively. Very cautiously she opened the door.

The vicar, arms raised, surplice frilling high above his cassock, looked down the central aisle at her. 'We brought nothing into this world and we take nothing out,' he said. 'The Lord gives, the Lord takes away; blessed be the name of the Lord.'

She crept in. The heavy door escaped her fingers and banged shut.

'We'll now sing 'The Lord Is My Shepherd'. Page forty-three. The green books.' All the seats were taken. She joined Digger Rooney who was standing at the back.

'Quite an entrance, blossom,' he whispered

20

as he took a hymn book from Trish who was in a pew in front of them. 'And that hat. *Très chic.*'

'Oh do shut up. I've just got stopped for speeding.'

'Everyone's here . . . ' His voice lilted upwards with the tune. When the congregation sat down again, Freya Adcock turned to look at her.

'I'd say Mummy's not pleased with you,' murmured Digger.

Mitch, pretending not to hear, looked at the catafalque which lay on the right of the chapel. The unadorned coffin rested side-on to the congregation. To the left, behind a small altar, were the purple and grey striped curtains which would soon enfold it. Mitch felt a tug of pity.

'Do not let your hearts be troubled. Trust in God still and trust in me. There are many rooms in my Father's house . . . '

Somewhere in the congregation there was a gulped sob. Silence. A bluebottle began buzzing.

The vicar began speaking again. 'Jon, in the fine flowering of his youth . . . '

How could a lad bursting at the seams with vitality kill himself? How could he be so cruel, she found herself thinking. 'Let me do it to you baby. Do it. Do it. Do it . . . ' His voice crooned on in her head. Her shoulders bowed.

'Merciful Father and Lord of all life, we praise you that we are made in your image and reflect your truth and light. We thank you for the life of your son, for the love and mercy he received from you and showed amongst us . . . '

Mitch, finding herself gazing again at that unadorned coffin, turned her head up to look at the ceiling. The chequerwork pine and blue ceiling began to blur in her vision. Oh dear, this is awful, she thought. I mustn't cry. I hardly knew the poor lad. She was relieved when the congregation rose to sing another hymn.

It was only when the mourners began to sit that she noticed Freya Adcock's feet. Was the woman wearing her shoes? Mitch looked down at her own feet just to check and then back at Freya's peeping toes. 'I do like those shoes.' She remembered Freya Adcock stopping her on the way to the canteen at the broadcasting centre. 'In fact you've some jolly nice clothes. I do admire the way you dress.'

'I heard a voice from heaven saying, 'Write this. Happy are the dead who die in the faith of Christ! Henceforth, says the spirit, they may rest from their labours; for they take with them the record of their deeds'.'

There was a silence and then a hum as the vicar began the words of committal; the curtains closed.

'He was just too bloody young, if you ask me,' Digger said. She turned and saw his tears. 'What a physique. Double-jointed, I bet. God. Just think of the mischief you could get up to with a body like that, blossom. What a waste.'

The congregation was shuffling to its feet. The vicar did not come back down the aisle but led the way out through a door to the left by the altar. He was followed by a very tall old lady wearing a wide-brimmed black hat. 'Old Mrs Stanton,' Digger told her. 'Apparently Jon's mother and father died when he was little. That's the grandmother who brought him up.'

'Freya Adcock's wearing my shoes,' Mitch told him. 'Look.'

Digger looked. 'Rather you than me, blossom. I wouldn't like that wolf in my sheep's clothing.'

'Why did Jon go and do such a terrible thing?'

'God knows.' Digger had wiped away his tears. 'Want my hankie?'

'Thanks.'

'All that money too.' He reached out and wrapped his hand round hers. 'Nothing you

23

can do about it, darling. I expect he was nuts.'

She followed his rotund shape down the aisle, forced into the slow shuffle dictated by the body of mourners. Digger and she were the last to emerge from the chapel, blinking in bright sunlight, nostrils suddenly filling with the dizzying scents from wreaths massed on each side of a pathway threading a U formation of crematorium walls.

'Oh dear. I do so hope I'm not going to cry again. One does so *hate* these kinds of occasion.'

'Here's the hankie,' said Mitch.

'Dreadful. Dreadful,' Digger said, shoulders heaving slightly as he vigorously blew his nose. 'And it's so fucking hot.'

The mourners were reassembling in groups on a wide lawn. Digger was looking back at the wreaths. 'One somehow doesn't expect the flowers at a middle-class funeral to be vulgar too. Quite neon.'

'I like a bit of vulgarity. Livens things up a bit.'

'Oh well. You're pretty much past redemption.' Digger put his handkerchief back in his pocket and unbuttoned his jacket to reveal expanses of white shirt and broad red braces. 'Good heavens. Old Mrs Stanton's coming our way. You shouldn't have come late, Mitch. Such bad form. Look at that back. Ramrod, my dear. And that chin. My God, one can positively feel one's willie shrivelling.'

'It is Miss Mitchell? I'm not mistaken, am I?' The old woman's hat shadowed all but one side of her chin.

'I really must apologise for being late.' Mitch found she was beginning to blush. 'Quite unforgivable of me. Absolutely awful — '

'No. No. I'm very glad you were. Otherwise, I might not have realised you were here. Such a lot of people . . . Good heavens, I haven't introduced myself. Madeleine Stanton, my dear. Jon's grandmother.'

'I'm so very sorry — I mean, about Jon. I — '

'You haven't changed a lot, you know.' The old woman cut across her condolences.

'I . . . ?'

'I remember you from that consumer programme you did on television. 'Fair Play.' I always watched.'

'That was ten years ago. Over ten years . . . Let me introduce you to Digger Rooney. He presents Radio Brum's teatime show.'

'I was one of your grandson's admirers, Mrs Stanton,' said Digger. 'In my opinion he had a great deal of talent.'

'Yes. Yes. Quite,' said Mrs Stanton. 'Do you mind if I talk to Miss Mitchell for a moment Mr, er, Mr . . . '

'Everyone calls me Digger.'

'Quite. Well, Mr er . . . It's been nice meeting you,' she said, turning her back on him. She told Mitch, 'I used to listen to you on the wireless, too. 'More Fair Play'. A very good programme, I thought. Investigative journalism at its best.'

'That's very kind of you, Mrs Stanton.'

'I can't think why you ever gave it up. I was most surprised when Jon told me you were now working for this whatsit local radio thing . . . Radio Brum.'

'It gave me up, Mrs Stanton. I'm afraid I was fired.'

'Really? How absurd. Everyone seems to get fired these days. Very unsettling. Now, you must be wondering what all this is about. I've a favour to ask, Miss Mitchell. Oh dear. More in the way of a business proposition. But we really can't discuss it here. I don't suppose you could come and see me — perhaps tomorrow?'

'I'm afraid it would have to be in the afternoon.'

'You're beginning to look quite worried. Please don't be. If you take me up I assure you that you'll be very well paid. When I saw you there at the door of the church I knew. 'That's your answer, Madeleine. She's the one'.' Suddenly she was aware of Mrs Stanton's eyes. They were translucent; they reminded her of shadowed rain on window panes.

When Mitch finally got home after presenting Friday's 'City Talk', she threw her peep-toe shoes in the dustbin, had a stiff gin and then phoned J. J. Woodward, a contact of hers who might be able to give her some information about the Stanton family. The answering machine said its piece, she said hers after the bleep and then she had another gin. Before she went to bed she fished the shoes back out of the bin, picking potato peelings out of the leather straps. She couldn't afford to buy another pair.

2

Mitch woke with a start. The room, not quite dark, was becoming lighter; shadows were forming into solid chunks of furniture. She'd been dreaming of Jon Stanton. His face was no longer freckled but strawberry red and so were his eyes. He'd opened his mouth to tell her something but all it revealed was a black hole. The hole had grown larger and larger until it had swallowed him.

She moved, pushing herself up on the pillows, trying to shake the images off.

It had been Trish, coming into the production office in much the same way as she'd done yesterday, who'd broken the news to them. 'Jon's killed himself.'

Even Quentin Plunkett had looked up from his tape machine. Something in her manner had made him reach for his earphones and take them off. 'Say again?'

'Jon's plugged a length of garden hose over the exhaust of that tacky old Beetle of his . . . He got into the driver's seat and . . . What do you do? Just sit there?' There had been a tinny knot of hysteria in her voice.

'Girlie, you're not serious?'

'Of course I'm bloody serious.'

'What a stupid little prick.' Quentin Plunkett had put the cans back on, holding his hands over them.

Mitch pulled herself higher up, plumping a pillow. She switched on the bedside lamp. The soft glow warmed the cruel dawn light.

Of course, Jon's corpse would have been flushed, she thought. As an eighteen-year-old cub reporter she'd covered the coroner's court once a week for her local paper — she'd been sent out to inquests later in her career, too, when she'd done freelance shifts in radio and television newsrooms. Carbon monoxide poisoning, a very popular way of ending it all, coloured blood a Technicolor shade of red, leaving very healthy-looking corpses.

Oh God. It's no use, she thought. I'll never get back to sleep now. She swung her legs out of bed, toes feeling for her flip-flops. She shook a kaftan down over her head.

Mitch had decided long ago that the only mean-spirited part of her house was the stairwell. It was jammed between the rear walls of the dining-room and the large kitchen. As she padded down the stairs she noticed again how much the landing needed decorating. Of course, the house was far too big for one person. Much too much to maintain. For ten years she'd been thinking of moving, ever since her husband Max had died. But, deep down, she loved having a lot of space about her and how could she part with any of the furniture she and Max had collected through the years? Most of all, selling the house would be like saying goodbye to Max all over again. He always seemed about the place, a friendly, shabby household spirit.

But it's not just the expense of decorating. How am I ever going to save enough to get the place rewired? Then there's the . . . But she wouldn't start a new day with all the and-then-there's . . . At fifty, if you really worked on it, you could achieve a little wisdom.

She made herself some coffee and took it through to the lounge. The grandfather clock was making its grumbling tick. It was always a heart-stopping affair if you listened; would it ever actually make its next t-t-tick? As she flopped on the black leather studded couch she noticed that the bowl of oriental poppies, cut only forty-eight hours ago, were dying even though she'd carefully burned the ends of all the stems. She drew her legs up, sniffed at the coffee, and began to wonder what sort of a problem Mrs Stanton was going to be. She's bound to ask me to do something I don't want to do, Mitch thought.

But what? She sighed. Finishing her coffee, she stretched her legs out. Her eyes began to close.

The phone woke her. It was much later; sunlight was filtering through the conservatory which had been built on to the end of the lounge at the turn of the century. The rooms were full of greenish light. Putting her flip-flops on as she went, she hopped and skipped to the kitchen.

'Mumsy . . . ' The word was punctuated by the ping of the satellite.

'Cassie? What's the matter?'

'Matter? Why should anything be the matter?'

'You called me Mumsy,' Mitch said. 'Besides, it must be in the middle of the night in Washington.'

'Almost three, if you really must know. We've been partying. You might say you're pleased to hear from me.'

'I am. Honestly. You know I am.'

'Well, you don't sound it. If I didn't ring you now I'd never get you. You're always out. You know you are. Anyway, you'll never guess what's happened. I mean really it's an opportunity I'll never have again. But the thing is . . . have you booked your flight yet?'

'Well, no. I was doing that this morning. Freya's been a real pain. I wasn't absolutely

31

sure I'd be able to come over until last
Monday . . . and then suddenly she was all
smiles and practically begging me to go. I'm
not sure what's at the bottom of all that yet.'

'Well, I've suddenly got this chance to go to
Japan for a month. It's come right out of the
blue —'

'Japan?'

'Someone else has had to drop out. It's a
university field trip thing. We're due to leave
in a couple of days. I was thrilled to be asked
. . . But of course . . . Though you know it's
far too hot in Washington at this time of
the year. Everyone's absolutely gasping.
Autumn's much better. September. But if you
really want to make the trip now . . . '

'No. You go off. I'll see if I can rearrange
things this end.'

'Love you. Love you. Love you. I always
knew you'd come up trumps. Ace. I told them
what a honey you are. I could hug you.'

Mitch suppressed what she was going to
say, that she hadn't seen Cassie for nine
months and wanted to check her over in the
flesh, make sure America was treating her
only child right, for God knew it was reputed
to be a dangerous place. She wanted to have a
gossip, look over the boyfriends, buy her
some clothes but not too many and grumble
about the price when she paid up. Generally

32

be a mum again for a while.

'Oh shit,' she said eventually when she put the receiver down. She grabbed her hair on both sides of her ears and pulled. 'Shitero-o-o-ooo!'

Cassie always made her aware of her shortcomings as a human being; her daughter had just depleted all her stocks of benevolent forbearance for some time to come. And yet other women had two, three and more kids. The world is full of saints, Mitch thought, and I haven't a hope of ever being one of them.

She managed to calm herself down enough to go and make her breakfast. There was no doubt in her mind that Freya Adcock, who had been extremely difficult about granting her leave, would be equally awkward about cancelling it. In fact she found the pro-gramme organiser almost impossible to deal with. Freya, she'd observed, was not like this with most of the other broadcasters at Radio Brum. Mitch supposed it was the prelude to her contract not being renewed when it ran out in three months' time. But she couldn't be absolutely sure of this. What, for instance, had the woman meant by not only admiring her clothes but by going out and buying a copy-cat pair of shoes?

She did wear them to a broadcaster's

funeral, Mitch reminded herself glumly.

Mitch knew she ought to have given up broadcasting ten years ago when she'd reached the top of her particular ladder. But her husband Max had died and she'd had a kid to bring up. Since that time, though, she'd worked her way through bad to worse programmes in lesser and lesser capacities until she'd found herself out of national broadcasting altogether and in local radio. Down, down the slithery snake until here she was looking at the bottomless pit which was her future. What do has-beens do, she wondered. Work the tills at Tesco? Clean offices? Panic set in. The coffee cup quivered so much she had to set it down. She wouldn't think about it. And she didn't.

She whistled up some spirits in the shower, pulled on jeans and a T-shirt and went down to the supermarket to stock up. She retrieved dry cleaning, called at the bank and then took the TVR's documentation down to the local police station.

After eating a sandwich out on the lawn, legs idly swinging from a deck chair, she was tempted to ring up Mrs Stanton and say she couldn't make it. But she couldn't quite tip herself over into doing it. My trouble is I'm not a big enough bastard. That's why I'm where I am today.

She went upstairs and opened her wardrobe door. What do you wear to visit a hare-brained old lady who is sick with grief? She shivered and rubbed her arms. She chose a straight beige linen skirt and a cotton poplin blouse. No one can quarrel with that, she decided as she tried to reduce her wiry curls into some form of order. She was growing her hair. At the turn of each decade Mitch felt she had to renew herself in some way. With the coming of the fearsome fifties she'd decided she must use less make-up — how she'd loved to slap it on — and to compensate she'd have fun with her hair.

Mitch would have liked to have been one of those tall elegant women who carried themselves as if they had a pile of books on their heads. She was short, inclined to be plump, with a peasant's broad pair of hands and too much sturdy calf muscle. But she had a good waist and slender ankles and a pair of very lively monkey-bright eyes. Because of her lack of height, she chose her clothes with great care; they must show off her waist and collars must properly frame her rather pretty heart-shaped face. In the right clothes Mitch felt girded for life's battles; but she had to admit, in darker moments, that wearing decent armour had not made her any more bullet-proof. And then there was her latest boss, Freya Adcock. When the management chose your gear for funerals surely it was time to stop and think. But think what?

She finished putting up her hair, applied a very decorous amount of make-up and adjusted a pair of her less cheerful, more expensive ear-rings. 'Right, Mrs Stanton,' she told the multiple image in the triple dressing-table mirror. 'Here we come.'

Jon's grandmother lived in Lichfield, a small cathedral city twenty miles to the north of Birmingham. The afternoon sun was hot, the tarmac on Spaghetti Junction shimmered in the haze; to the left of her were the towers of Aston Hall, to the right the chimney of the HP sauce factory. The road looped elegantly and dropped her off on the Tyburn road. This time when she picked up the A38 her eyes were constantly on the look-out for cop cars, the touch of her sandal on the accelerator of the TVR as light as a feather. Even a clapped-out bread van overtook her.

Lichfield slumbered under the protection of its three great spires. Housing estates congealed about its perimeters in raw red lumps. Roads funnelled as she approached the medieval core. Madeleine Stanton lived in Beacon Street, near a house once occupied by Erasmus Darwin, scientific investigator and grandfather of Charles.

The driveway to Ashmole House was at the side of the building. Mitch parked the car and examined her face in the driver's mirror. She dabbed her brow with a tissue, stretched her lips into an elongated O and dabbed them too. Mindful of her fearsome fifties resolutions she reapplied only a little make-up before climbing out of the TVR. She heard a bone in her knee click. No. She was not becoming arthritic, she told herself.

The elegant three-storey Georgian house was rendered in dove grey stucco with woodwork picked out in white. It was built far too close to the road for twentieth-century comfort; the shallow front garden growled with the sound of cars and lorries changing gear as they climbed towards the Stafford road. The portico entrance was set between two pairs of long sash windows. The brass bell sparkled in the sunlight.

The door was opened by a woman of Mitch's age. Hefty freckled arms protruded from a sleeveless Courtelle dress which bumped over breasts and belly. 'Maddy's out back,' the woman said, leading the way down a wide parquet-floored hall. 'Us'll get you tea? Coffee? There's lemonade. She likes us's lemonade.' The contents of the house had an almost unnatural shine, like pieces of army kit laid out for inspection. 'Or something stronger, ducks?'

'I'd love some lemonade.'

'I'm Cathy, by the way. Oh, that's where that dratted cat got to. Always where it's not supposed to be.' The tabby quickly removed its tail from the vicinity of the drawing-room door as a stout arm slammed it shut. Tail now upright, it preceded them into the kitchen. 'She's got company. Helen Brierley's staying with her for the weekend. Quite right, too. If you've got to put up with the woes of this world best have a friend along, eh? Through here, ducks.'

Madeleine Stanton was in the middle of the lawn, her back towards them. She was dressed in a black T-shirt, jeans cut off above the knee and a pair of trainers. A stout old lady, primrose with Liberty print, her thick grey hair swept up and knotted on the top of her head, was half turned towards her. She was scratching her ear with the tip of a pair of scissors. In her other hand was a bunch of white lilac. Cathy was still talking. 'When I think of our Jon . . . well, ducks, if you asks me I'd be forced to it. I'd have to come out with it. God can be plain wicked at times and that's no lie. And if he thinks us'll be on our hands and knees again he has another think coming. Rather pray to yon dustbin.' But she suddenly darted a look up to the sky as if she expected thunderbolts to appear. Cloudless blue stretched to horizons. Larks planed and plunged, blackbirds sang. The cat sat and watched.

Hearing Cathy's voice, the two women turned. 'Miss Mitchell! So very good of you to come.' Mrs Stanton called and they began to walk towards her. It wasn't until they were a yard or two away that Mitch realised Helen Brierley was no older than she was. It's the hair, Mitch thought, and her figure. Yellow doesn't help ageing skin. And she walks as though all the elastic's snapped. Oh God. Perhaps at a distance I look like an old trout, too.

'May I introduce Jon's godmother, Helen Brierley? We're keeping each other company this weekend.'

'But I must arrange this lilac, darling. You go and have your little chat.' She turned to Mitch. 'Such wonderful weather, my dear. We're quite Mediterranean, aren't we? You can sit under the apple tree. Dappled shade. One dreams of it in winter, doesn't one?'

'So good of Helen to come,' Mrs Stanton said as she led the way across a wide York stone terrace to a couple of cane chairs deep with cushions. 'I'm not much fun and people usually have enough troubles of their own.'

As they settled Cathy appeared with a large

finely wrought Georgian silver tray. On it were a jug and glasses which looked as if they had been bought at a discount store. As she set the tray down she turned and winked at Mitch. 'There you are, then,' she said before waddling away.

'Did you know my grandson well?' Mrs Stanton poured with a steady hand.

'No. Not really. He worked for one of the morning programmes while he was at Radio Brum — mine's an evening show.'

'Were people surprised when he was fired?'

'No. Broadcasting's a very insecure trade. Being fired . . . well, you could say it's almost part of the job. A programme organiser wants a different voice or management are introducing new programme schedules. Perhaps they're over budget. Then there are the management types who build a career simply out of the number of people they fire. I'm a ruthless macho man, or woman . . . blood on the walls, that kind of thing. It's not often people get the bullet because they aren't up to it. Jon certainly was. But you must know that. As I understand it, he got another job almost immediately with a television company.'

She nodded. 'Researcher. He was cock-a-hoop. Cock-a-hoop.' She began running the tip of a bony finger round the rim of her glass of lemonade. Leaves whispered overhead; Mitch could see apples no bigger than gooseberries forming at the end of baby stems. From the playing field came the distant sound of clunking as a cricket ball hit the bat.

Madeleine Stanton took off her sunglasses and looked at Mitch. 'I think Jon was murdered.'

Alarmed, Mitch banged her glass down on the table.

'Of course, the police believe I'm a foolish old woman. I've been told that the relatives of someone who commits suicide often find it impossible to come to terms with what's happened. I've been told . . . but what can I say? I really know he didn't kill himself.'

Mitch tried to choose her words with care. 'As a journalist I've covered many inquests. During most of them a reason comes to light . . . we know why someone thought . . . well, they must do it . . . But that's not always so. I remember being told by a psychiatrist that the first sign of acute depression can be a dead body.'

'You're a professional woman, Miss Mitchell — I think you could leave your own thoughts and beliefs about the matter aside while you dug out the facts. I remember you well from the days you did those investigative consumer programmes. You always got to the bottom of things. Always. More than one villain went to prison because of your work. Naturally I wouldn't want you to put yourself in any personal danger. Should any new evidence come to light we'll get in touch with the police and let them get on with it.'

'I'm not quite sure what you're suggesting, Mrs Stanton . . . '

'I want you to investigate my grandson's death. If you'll take the case I'll immediately pay you five thousand pounds. An advance which you will keep whatever happens. On completion of the investigation I suggest another five thousand pounds. I realise that the result . . . I mean, that the suicide verdict could be the correct one.'

'But I already have a job, Mrs Stanton. I can't just lay down tools — '

'Of course not. But can't you run 'em in tandem?' She sat back in the cane chair; shifting shadows of leaves played over her face. 'I see my little business proposition has astounded you, Miss Mitchell.'

'Mitch.'

'Have you never thought what a good private investigator you would make? I realised that as soon as I saw you coming through the church door. 'She's what one needs.' I knew immediately. 'She's the one

42

you're looking for.' I'd already interviewed two representatives from inquiry agencies. I was not impressed. Now, I'm sure you regard me as a silly old woman, too — but that won't stop you turning over every stone. That's what I want. That's what I'm after.'

'I'll have to think about this, Mrs Stanton.' She ought to say no, she knew that, but she found she couldn't so easily say goodbye to rewiring the house, decorating the stairs and landing . . . oh, that endless list. Also there was a small stirring of excitement, an idiotic feeling of wanting to lift her head, sniff the air. The joys of the hunt. She knew it from the old days.

'Quite. Natural enough.' Mrs Stanton was suddenly leaning forward. 'One's tried to be professional about this. Cathy's helped me clip all the cuttings about my . . . about . . . well, you know. The case. Perhaps you'll read them before you get back in touch?'

Half an hour later, a bright yellow file under her arm, Mitch was shown back to her car by Mrs Stanton. As she put the file on the passenger seat and began to climb in, Mrs Stanton clutched her arm: 'You'll be my avenging angel.'

Mitch's scalp prickled as the roots of her hair stiffened. 'I . . . Well . . . I don't promise.'

'No. Of course not. Please . . . ' The old

lady had embarrassed herself.

They both turned as Cathy hurried out to them. 'Stuck it in a Perrier bottle,' she said, making Mitch an offering of her home-made lemonade. When Mitch turned to wave she saw the pair of them on the driveway holding hands. They broke apart as Helen Brierley slowly walked along the gravel towards them. Before edging the TVR on to the road, Mitch looked again. She suddenly became convinced she'd seen Helen Brierley before. She shook her head. The memory escaped her.

3

The air was oily with the smell of softening tarmac. Ahead of her Mitch could see a jungle of concrete stilts. Soon she was swinging the TVR up on to Spaghetti Junction, down through the curving tunnel which was Queensway, nosing back into dead heat, then plunging towards the Bristol road. Though it was not yet five o'clock on a Saturday afternoon the carriageways were eerily deserted; perhaps the whole city, as sometimes happened on sunny weekends, had taken to the Welsh hills.

When she got home she threw off her clothes, showered, pulled on floppy print pants and a T-shirt and then went downstairs to make a pot of tea. She took the tray outside, wriggled her feet out of her flip-flops and sank on to the lounger.

Shutting her eyes as she lay back, she turned her face to the sun. She listened to the distant thrum of the city, never quiet even when it appeared deserted; in the garden birds were squabbling. The honeyed smells of alyssum and phlox drifted over her. Sighing, she wagged her toes.

Murder is always so unlikely, she found herself thinking. People have a better chance of a big pools win. And then when it does happen most of the time it is a family affair, dads killing mums, uncles killing nieces, boyfriends slicing up their girls. Most of the rest of the mayhem was accounted for by men with sexual kinks.

Jon Stanton's death didn't seem to fit any of these patterns. Mitch found herself shaking her head. It has to be suicide, she thought.

Why am I even thinking about it? Surely I don't actually intend to investigate Jon's death? It's quite absurd even to suppose I could. I've no access to things like the pathologist's report. I didn't even go to the inquest. I don't know who the witnesses were. Be my avenging angel. That's got to be a line out of one of those old black and white B movies they show on daytime television.

She suddenly had a vision of Mrs Stanton and Cathy holding hands on the driveway, a pair of twentieth-century Hansel and Gretels. Who else could they go to?

Oh no, she told herself. Be sensible. You're far too old for fairy stories. Jon Stanton did himself in and that's that. Quite a few do. If I remember correctly, eight of us in every hundred thousand. Oh, forget it . . . lie back and enjoy what remains of the sunshine.

Listen to that blackbird, she instructed herself.

She immediately fell asleep.

Waking half an hour later, she found herself being swallowed by rapidly advancing shadow. Rubbing chilled arms, she swung off the lounger, yawning. Her drink had gone cold.

While waiting for the kettle to boil again, she took the messages off her answering machine. Charlie Collins had called her three times. Eventually he said, 'Hang all this. I'm taking unilateral action. I'm coming round tonight with a box of goodies. I'll give you grilled turbot and a green salad. Wine. Peaches. Cheese and biscuits. How's that? Eight o'clock. If you aren't there I'll stand by your front door and I'll huff and I'll puff and I'll blow your house down. OK?'

Well, thought Mitch, you know how that'll land up. Is it what I want? She'd only had one serious affair since her husband Max had died, with Josh Hadley who had one of the city's biggest antique businesses. She'd even thought the arrangement might evolve into a permanent one, but six months ago he had ditched her. A little later she had seen him at a CBSO concert with a blonde young enough to be his daughter. She'd had breasts like nuclear warheads and there was enough

47

pumping going on below to blast them off.

Among all the other things Mitch had thought was: what the hell can a bimbo like that know about classical music? And it had come to her, with an awful certainty, that Josh's new love would have something like a Ph.D. in early Elizabethan notation. All spectacular bimbos these days seemed to have even more spectacular brains.

It took the heart out of her. She'd even thought of giving men up entirely. Why not get fat? Why not buy a felt hat, support stockings and a shopping trolley?

What hope was there?

She'd met Charlie Collins a couple of weeks ago at the opening of the summer show at the Seer Gallery. Since then he'd taken her out twice, once to a play about Colette and once to a travelling exhibition at Birmingham Art Gallery. Up to now things had been very chaste. Mitch didn't know a lot about him. He'd told her that he'd started work that Easter as a supply art teacher at Irongate, a highly academic private school in the city. She'd been surprised to discover they'd had an art department. Before that he'd been in Bolivia. He was a well-muscled burly man with lots of dark curly hair, charming, attentive, and he made her laugh a lot. Her main reservation about him was his age.

Charlie Collins was thirty-five years old. If she were honest she'd have to say that frightened her. She'd never been out with a man that much younger than herself.

She picked up the phone and began to dial his number, intending to put him off. She dropped the receiver back.

Why not? she asked herself. What's wrong with having some fun? Look at your day so far. One cancelled trip to America and an afternoon with a grief-crazed old woman.

But I've nothing to wear. That was always her first response when a social situation challenged her. She immediately thought of ear-rings. Her long dangly ones. Ear-rings — for reasons she could not fathom — always gave her a feeling of sexual confidence. And that black silk sleeveless blouse? With her mustard culottes?

I'd better forget the tea and have a gin, she thought. I need some Dutch courage.

Later she set a small marble-topped table in the conservatory — the dining-room table was too large for intimacy — broke open a box of candles and put a new bulb in the standard lamp.

She organised a coffee tray, ground some beans and was in the middle of lining her oven with silver foil — trying to disguise the disgusting state it was in — when the phone rang. It was her contact, J.J. Woodward. Woody had spent fifty years as a journalist on the *Birmingham Sentinel* before retiring earlier that year. He filled the gaps in her knowledge about newsworthy Birmingham folk and she gave him snippets to recycle and sell to the trade press. Ducks skateboarding past barns were sent to farming journals, priests who ran pubs went to the *Morning Advertiser* and naughty social workers found themselves in *Private Eye*.

'Hi, poppet. What can I do for you?' he asked.

'Oh yes, I rang, didn't I? I just wondered if you had anything on the Stantons.'

'The twelve-volume novel? A reader's digest? Or a four-par single-column last-edition job?'

'I didn't know the family carried that sort of weight. I mean, I knew they were rich and had something to do with tractors — '

'One of the great Quaker industrial families. Though I sure as hell wouldn't have liked to have been born a Stanton.'

'Why on earth not?'

'Very few of them died full of years in their own beds. It's all Italian opera with knobs on. Take this century, for instance. Two Stanton brothers. One dropped dead at eighteen on the rugger pitch. The other did marry and

50

there was a son but then he and his wife were killed in a car crash. The infant on the back seat — Jon Stanton — survived and Grandad and Grannie Stanton took him under their wing. Is this the sort of stuff you want to know?'

'It certainly is.'

'The grandparents got a nanny for young Jon and the next thing old Mr Stanton and the nanny — AWOL? — were in some sort of boating accident. They both drowned. That just left Jon and his grandmother.'

'So now there is only old Mrs Stanton? And their tractor business — I heard it was sold to the Japanese?'

'That was about five years ago. I suppose it became plain by then that Jon Stanton didn't fancy a career in tractors — '

'So it is probable that Jon was a very rich young lad. Would his share of the loot go to Mrs Stanton, I wonder?'

'I'm afraid I can't help you there.'

'Who ran the business after old Mr Stanton died?'

'If I remember correctly it was Henry Wellesley — a cousin of the Stantons. There are all sorts of junior lines in that family.'

'And when Madeleine Stanton dies the money would go to them?'

'I suppose so, poppet. Even I don't know

everything. What's your interest in all this, if I may be so bold?'

'I've received a business proposition to do with the Stantons. I'm sort of testing out the ground.'

'May I inquire further?'

'You may not. At least, not at this point.'

'Point in time, poppet. If you're going to play the politician with me get the lingo right.'

'Don't get testy.'

'Testy? You're talking to Mr Heart-of-Honey. And to prove it I'll give you more. I met young Mr Stanton the night before his death. I was at a do to celebrate the centenary of Boultons Theatre. Jon was there to represent his family — discreetly, of course.'

'Why discreetly?'

He sighed. 'It really is ABC with you, isn't it? Part of the Stanton creed is to give secretly to charities and the arts — '

'Then how do you know?'

'Everyone knows except you, apparently. You can't keep these things quiet in a nod-is-as-good-as-a-wink city like this. Anyway, one of the beneficiaries is Boultons.'

'Just how rich are the family?

'Think of stinking and then double it.'

'Madeleine Stanton lives in a nice place but not the kind you'd associate with that sort of money.' She paused. 'Jon Stanton drove a manky old orange Beetle. A real clapped-out heap.'

'Old man Stanton went to work on a motor bike. The family car used to be a baby Austin, if I remember correctly. I suppose it's the Quaker legacy. I shouldn't think even God Almighty would be allowed a company Rover. But don't get me wrong. The Stantons were never a stingy family. They just used their money differently.'

'Sounds good.'

'You certainly don't find much of it about nowadays.'

'Did Jon seem odd? I mean, the night you saw him? The night before he killed himself.'

'Not a bit of it. That's the *odd* thing. Talk about the human soul being unfathomable . . . He was already gathering ideas for this television magazine programme he was joining. He was pumping me for this and that.'

'Anything in particular?'

'Not that I recall. Oh, it came out one way and another that he was seeing some Chinese chap the next day.'

'The day he died?'

'Yes.'

'Do you know why?'

'Not sure. Some programme idea, I

imagine. He said this Chinese chap talked like the Duke of Edinburgh. Even walked with a clenched fist resting on his bum.'

'What was he called?'

'No idea. I didn't pick up on it. There aren't any Chinese trade mags, poppet. What could I do with it?'

'Whichever way you look at it, Woody, this kid doesn't sound as though he's got suicide in mind, does he? And yet, not twenty-four hours later, he's killed himself.'

'A lot can happen in that time. He could have found out he'd got Aids or his girlfriend had run off with another chap or perhaps he was putting on a big act. Now what have you got for me, poppet?'

Mitch traded some information and then said, 'I'll pop into the Scales one lunchtime next week and buy you a round or two.'

'Promises,' said Woody. 'It feels like that's all I ever get.'

'Oh, while I'm on . . . Have you ever heard of a woman called Helen Brierley, Woody? She was at the Stanton house when I went. I just have this feeling I've seen her before somewhere. But I can't place her.'

'Brierley. Brierley . . . ' and a toe-curling scratching sound came down the phone.

'Woody! Will you stop sliding your bloody biro over your teeth!'

'I was thinking. Brierley ... Brierley ... No, it's gone. Sorry, poppet. If it comes back to me I'll give you a bell. No. I'll save it up until you buy me that drink. Ta ta a bit.'

Mitch went back to finish lining her cooker. She also put bleach down the sink, got out two clean tea towels and sprayed the room with air freshener.

Later, standing naked in her bedroom, she carefully examined her body before the long mirror. Not bad for a fifty-year-old, she decided. But she'd not put the overhead light on. No point in pushing your luck, she thought.

She was ready by seven thirty. She began to have second thoughts. A thirty-five-year-old, for God's sake, she grumbled to herself. What do I think I'm up to? She took another look at herself in the mirror and pulled down her mouth. Time for another gin. She mixed a drink and then looked at her watch again. Seven thirty-five.

Oh, this is ridiculous, she thought, and went to pick up the bright yellow folder Madeleine Stanton had given her. She sat on the couch, pulling her feet up under her, and opened it.

Newspaper reports of the inquest were clipped together and lay on top. Underneath there was an envelope containing the address of Jon's flat, together with the keys, and a head and shoulders photograph of him which had been taken recently. He was smiling that lazy smile of his. Mitch's heart yawed. Oh, the pity of it.

She glanced through the longest of the inquest reports, clipped from the Lichfield slip edition of the *Birmingham Sentinel*. The pathologist had told the court that Jon had been drinking heavily before he died. Stomach contents contained both beer and whisky and there were traces of the Chinese meal he had eaten about three hours before his death. There was no evidence of any disease processes. The body was that of a healthy twenty-five-year-old.

The corpse was discovered by the postman. He saw exhaust fumes seeping out from beneath the closed wooden doors of the garage which adjoined the converted Victorian house in which Jon had a flat.

Jon was in the driver's seat. A piece of white rockery stone had been placed against the accelerator, not pressing the pedal down too far, but enough to prevent the engine from cutting out. A near-empty whisky bottle, some of the contents of which had spilled on to the seat, was next to the body. No note had been found. None of the witnesses called knew of any reason why Jon

Stanton had taken his life.

Mitch read through the report again. She didn't find it too surprising that Jon had eaten a Chinese meal before killing himself. She'd covered an inquest where a man had hanged himself directly after demolishing a double portion of fish and chips. Her own theory was that some suicides dissociate; they literally do not believe what they are doing even when they are doing it.

But no note. That was odd.

The coroner recorded a verdict that he took his own life while the balance of his mind was disturbed. The convention was that all the suicidal were mad. There was certainly no evidence of that in Jon's case.

The door bell rang. She closed the file with a sigh and got up.

'Thank Christ you stayed in,' said Charlie Collins. He carried a cardboard Tate and Lyle box full of groceries. 'I wasn't sure if you'd be wicked enough to leave a chap on your front door step clutching his spring onions.'

'As you see, I'm not,' she said, smiling at him. She led the way down to the kitchen.

There was a slight uneasiness between the two of them as she showed him round the cupboards. Neither knew where each other's corners were; they were afraid of skinning their knees and knuckles.

'I'll tell you what,' said Charlie, 'let's start with a glass of wine and move on from there. Good idea?' He got a bottle of Pouilly — Fumé out of the box and unhesitatingly went to the right cupboard and reached down two glasses. 'Corkscrew — ah, in here,' and he opened the right drawer.

'You certainly don't need showing twice. The artist's eye?'

'I'm not an artist. An art teacher.' He grinned. 'Doing games to improve my concentration is a fad of mine — weight-lifting of the mind, you might say. Just in case I don't get a second chance one day.'

'Second chance for what?'

'Getting it right. I also run. And I'm not a bad cook. What about you?'

'I'm low on virtues. You'll discover my vices soon enough.'

He grinned. 'Other people's virtues are always a pain. Whereas their vices . . . ' He poured out the drinks and gave her a glass. 'But I can safely leave making the salad to you?'

'I'm afraid I like my lettuce leaves in the buff.'

He was emptying the contents of the Tate and Lyle box. 'No French dressing? OK. Do it your way . . . ' and then, without asking her, he made a quick tour of the ground

58

floor of the house.

One hand holding down a head of lettuce, another chopping, she inclined her head towards the kitchen door, listening to his footsteps, to objects being picked up and put down. What do I know about him? He could be nicking things, she thought.

He reappeared. 'Lovely, and not at all how I imagined you'd live,' he said and then took down a pan. 'We're having new potatoes. God love you for the dishwasher.'

'What did you think my home would be like?'

'Modern or maybe 1930s art deco. Perhaps ivory carpets and Odeon-style wall lights. And here it is, large and shabby and elegant, too. And bizarre. What in Christ's name are those choppers doing on the telly?'

'They are Georgian false teeth. About one hundred and eighty years old. It's sort of an association of ideas. Always someone longer in the tooth than me in the house. Bucks me up on bad days.'

He laughed. 'I can see you'd need to be a crossword puzzle enthusiast to understand your mind.'

The meal made, they took it on trays into the conservatory. After another glass of wine, Mitch felt comfortable enough to examine him more carefully. He certainly hadn't dressed up. He was wearing a bright green T-shirt with a collar and crossed cricket bat motif on the breast pocket, beige cotton pants and old white tennis pumps.

He watched her watching him.

She said, 'No wife, then? No children?'

'I'm a rolling stone.' He had the sort of Captain Birdseye blue eyes that only the right sort of Celtic ancestry produces. 'I stay long enough in England to build up a bank balance and then I'm off again. Europe, Africa, America . . . '

'Bolivia . . . Painting expeditions?'

'I like looking and seeing . . . and hearing, of course. It interests me. I hear, for instance, that you are a widow. Your husband was an electronics boffin and you've a daughter who is currently in America.' He laughed at the expression on her face. 'Almost every school report I ever had said I was much too much of a smart-arse for my own good. Usually in more circumspect language than that.'

'Do you think you'll settle down in the end?'

He drained his third glass of wine. 'Nope. Let's open another bottle.'

'And you?' he asked when he came back in from the kitchen. He poured the wine and as he sat down their feet collided.

This is ludicrous, she was thinking, but she

60

left her foot where it was, touching his. 'I always seem to find myself at life's receiving end.'

'You're a victim? I can't believe that.'

'I often feel I am when a boss gives me the bullet! The older I get, the oftener that seems to happen. And, of course, being a parent . . . ' and she recounted the phone call she'd had from her daughter. 'Really, though, I'm just like most women. Made of indiarubber. Keep on bouncing back. And odd things happen to me, too. Fate sticks its oar in when I least expect it.' She found she was telling him about Madeleine Stanton's offer.

'Don't touch it with a barge pole.'

She stiffened.

'Sorry . . . really. Sorry. None of my business.'

'No, it isn't.' Her foot was no longer touching his. Both were firmly beneath her chair.

'I'll make the coffee,' he offered.

'I'll side the table,' she said.

'Side?'

'It's a Lancashire expression. That's where I was born.' This is really too uncomfortable, she was thinking. Fifteen years younger and telling me what to do! This really isn't going to work out. What a terrible mistake.

She picked up her glass of wine and emptied it. Things did then appear a little rosier but still nowhere near rosy enough.

He made very good coffee.

She opened the brandy.

He was now telling her tales about Chicago. She was aware he'd set out to charm her and that she really ought to call it a night now and show this self-confessed smart-arse to the door.

But when he ran his forefinger from the top of her breast to her nipple she knew she'd do no such thing.

4

Mitch's bedroom curtains were only partly drawn, filtering strong sunlight; the sash windows had been pulled up four or five inches and the blue and white fabric stirred and occasionally flapped. The furniture was an idiosyncratic mixture of old mahogany pieces and early twentieth-century Chinese lacquer which rioted with oriental figures in improbable settings. The shapes cast complicated moving shadows on expanses of ceiling. The room was full of bird-song and, though it was at the back of the house, the air hummed with distant traffic noises. On the bedside cabinet was a tray of coffee and toasted marmalade fingers. The Sunday newspapers and some weekly magazines were laid out on the artificial silk cover like a giant hand of cards. Mitch sat cross-legged in the middle, read at random and occasionally marked stories which might produce a good local angle for her show.

This Sunday morning, as sometimes happened, she missed her cigarettes, though she'd stopped smoking six years ago. She'd loved using her long, black cigarette holder;

she'd enjoyed the theatre. What fun to swagger now and then. Why was it that anything which added a bit of colour to life was bad for you?

Which brought her back to Charlie Collins, and she wasn't going to tease herself by thinking of him.

Listen to this. Drinking coffee helps you with your love life. Mark this one. Older people who have at least one cup a day are nearly twice as likely to be sexually active as those who shun it.

No, no. Nothing about sex on her show. Definitely not.

What about this bit of research which proves men are better drivers? That'll get a few listeners' backs up. A phone-in? Goody. The psychologist who did the research works at a local university.

And then Charlie Collins slithered back into her mind and she began to smile. She'd loved only two men, her husband and Josh Hadley, the Birmingham antique dealer who had torpedoed her for Miss Rocket Launcher. Sex with them had been like the English climate; soft and sweet, gentle and good. Sex with Charlie reminded her of the first time she'd been to the Mediterranean. She'd opened her eyes in Menton and thought she'd been cured of colour blindness.

Had Josh had such an experience? Was that why he'd dropped her for that blonde bimbo?

I'm too old for this kind of thing, she thought. Lust at fifty is one of my life's more ridiculous jokes. Do I even like him much? I was always in two minds about Menton, too. That's where my camera was stolen. Right out of my hand.

My God, though, he changed the colour of my litmus paper. Practically vaporised it. She began to blush, remembering the very undignified noises she'd made. That was one of the troubles of being a broadcaster. When you articulated anything it always came out fully orchestrated. Shit, shit, shit, she thought and was embarrassed all over again. And yet, though her flesh leapt eagerly off her bones when she conjured him up, she felt she couldn't be in love with him. She was nervous for much of the time she was with him, afraid either he or she would fall arse over tit. Conversations between them sometimes ground to an embarrassing halt. They were not, she felt, like-minded. Or did he appeal to some part of herself she'd assiduously failed to acknowledge? A devil within she even feared might destroy her?

Rubbish. No art supply teacher still half damp behind the ears was going to finish her off. Screw that.

Well, she would, she thought, if he called again. She began to laugh to herself.

She'd be hurt, though, she predicted. There would be pain.

Oh hell.

She made herself turn her attention back to the newspapers. And all the while her flesh glowed smugly, toes curled and uncurled, stray fingers brushed a thigh and, quite unknown to her, her nipples rose lark-high. Pensions, she was thinking. What about a package on the meaning of the European Court of Justice ruling? Article 119 and all that. Perhaps there was quite a lot to be said for retirement. Bath chairs in general. Unruly flesh tied down.

Oh dear, she thought, not pensions.

A snippet about the Chancellor caught her eye. The fifty-eight-year-old politician was pictured with his young blonde wife. *There's some wonderful news on the Home Front for Revell Ullman,* Mitch read. *His wife, Maya, 31, has announced she's pregnant. It will be the Chancellor's first child and he told the Diary: 'We're over the moon. Yes, I perhaps have left fatherhood a little late — now I can't wait. We don't care if it is a boy or girl.' The Rev, who has held the Birmingham East seat for twenty-four years, divorced his first wife Helen three years ago. He and Maya, an airline stewardess before their marriage, have kept on the family home in the Birmingham East constituency. Helen, who reverted to her maiden name of Brierley after the divorce, now has a cottage in Hamstall Ridware, a village on the north of Birmingham.*

So that's who she is, Mitch thought. My God. No wonder I had trouble recognising her. And she remembered the last time she'd seen her, five or six years ago. Then she'd looked young for her age, slim, a boyish cap of dark hair framing her face. Plenty of ping in her elastic in those days.

Mitch put a wondering finger up to her own face and then touched her hair. She began to panic. Perhaps I ought to have this damned wig cut? Highlights. A style with plenty of oomph.

What you need is a shower and some breakfast, she told herself firmly. For God's sake, pull yourself together. If you were past it, honeypot, Charlie Collins wouldn't come a-calling.

When she wondered what to wear she decided on the bottle green and crimson print top and skirt. It would be cooler than her usual Sunday garb of T-shirt and jeans. Of course, she knew the reason was quite other than this. She was going to wear the outfit because — who knew — he might drop round. She also took to going into the kitchen and looking at the phone. It began to hypnotise her. She was like a dog viewing a pork chop which was just out of reach.

She became disgusted with herself. I could be a silly seventeen-year-old. This has got to stop. Now.

It was in an effort to distract herself that she opened the yellow file again. The tagged keys fell out.

Am I going to work for Mrs Stanton or not?

The very fact that Charlie had counselled her against it made her favour the idea. Anyway, there could be no harm in looking round Jon's place. She reached for the A to Z. Templar's Rise was in Moseley, a district which had once been described to her as Birmingham's Left Bank: ' . . . you might say it has all the right attitudes — pity about the atmosphere.'

The easiest way to get there was to go down the Edgbaston road but Warwickshire's county ground was there and if a match was on she'd get caught in heavy traffic. She planned a circuitous route, dropped the A to Z and a notebook in her bag and made quite sure she didn't look at the phone on her way out.

The day was full of fleecy clouds and

rustling leaves. A pair of worms were mating on the gravel near the door of her TVR. Lots of people were probably doing it on the banks of the river Avon too. But she wasn't going to let her mind dwell on such matters.

Fifty years separated the houses which faced each other across the tarmac on Templar's Rise. To the left, above the road, were 1930s semis; opposite, partly obscured by lime and beech trees, were substantial Victorian piles. And Dracula has probably slept in every one of them, Mitch thought, as she parked her car opposite number 42.

The converted house Jon had lived in was smaller than the neighbouring ones; the walls were banded by lines of Staffordshire blue brick and the attic floor was topped by steep Gothic gabling. As she walked down the drive she saw the garage, a wooden structure with a corrugated iron roof. More corrugated iron panels acted as fencing, shielding the back door from the view of anyone walking down the driveway of the next house. They petered out into a hawthorn hedge.

Mitch ignored the mustard-coloured front door and walked down to the garage. A piece of white rockery stone had been used to keep the doors shut. She pushed it aside with her canvas shoe and the doors swung open. There was no car in the garage but a thin line of things were piled high against the walls. There was a mower and some gardening tools, but no garden hose pipe. She went in, stabbing at bundles of old newspapers with her toe. As she moved back a heap of them, bright sunlight glinted on an object. She picked it up and turned it over. It was shield-shaped, one side chrome, the other enamelled with a design of blue and white waves with a green circle in the centre. A fob for a car key-ring? Pocketing it, she toured the rest of the garage. Paint cans, empty cardboard boxes which had contained hi-fi equipment, a broken chair, an old pan, a plastic bottle of motor oil. The concrete floor was cracked and stained, leaves from a Russian vine were invading through the roof, plugging gaps, and looking quite healthy too; either the leaves were resistant to carbon monoxide poisoning or this was fresh growth.

She went back outside into the sunlight, rolling the piece of rockery back with her foot as she shut the door. What a crummy place to die in, she thought.

There was still no sign of anyone, so she opened dustbin lids and, with a twig, stirred the contents around. Beer cans, chicken carcasses, wine bottles, frozen dinner wrappers, poll tax demands. Too long after Jon's death to yield anything useful, she decided, and put the lids back.

She took a look round the back of the house. The garden was a big one and the grass was neatly cut; old flower beds now had more the appearance of lawn than herbaceous borders. A row of washing hung between two trees. So someone was still here then, someone young, judging by the stretch Lycra leggings, minuscule briefs and rock band world tour T-shirts. Most of the socks, she couldn't help noticing, were hung in mis-matched pairs and were full of holes.

She went back round to the front door and tried the keys until she found the one that fitted the lock. The gloomy hall was blocked off at one end by a bright orange hardboard-panelled door. An airline luggage label had been taped on. A green felt-tipped pen had been used to write: Ms Bettina Mayo.

She went up the stairs. A door was open on the first-floor landing. The rooms were empty and judging from the dampish, musty smell had been vacant for a few months.

Jon's flat was on the top floor. She paused after unlocking the door, nervous, finding in herself a reluctance to invade his privacy. But he is dead, she told herself. He has no more rights. If he really was murdered, justice belongs to those who loved him.

The attic flat was surprisingly roomy; under the sloping eaves a lounge, bedroom, kitchen and bathroom had been carved out. The Stanton money showed itself; expensive grey wool fitted carpeting in what was cheap rented accommodation, top of the range hi-fi equipment, a personal tape-editing machine, lamps from Christopher Wray, an Italian black leather couch. A set of beer and coke cans wearing sun-glasses were ranged on the mantelpiece above a small cast iron fireplace. She turned them on and began to whistle. Slowly all the cans except one broken one went about their ghostly dance. Tears came into her eyes. She blinked them back and picked up an axe. When she hit her wrist with it the axe blade gave a frightful groan. He was just a big kid, she thought.

A desk was in one of the recessed walls which flanked the fire-place. Above it was a pinboard with various names and telephone numbers tacked up, one or two official invitations to opening nights and theatre events and some concert programmes.

What am I looking for? she wondered. How can I hope to find answers if I haven't formed the questions?

But she pulled off one of the slips of paper from the board. Tommy Hung. The Chinese man Jon was due to see the day he died?

There was a Birmingham telephone number. She jotted the information down and re-pinned the paper to the board.

Bookshelves had been built into the other recess, P. G. Wodehouse, E. F. Benson, Tom Sharpe. A brightly painted papier mâché clown somersaulted from a trapeze hung from one of the shelves. There were two photographs in perspex frames, one of Madeleine Stanton taken about ten years ago and another of a youth in Bermuda shorts windsurfing. He was waving to someone, perhaps Jon?

She explored the kitchen. The washing up had been done, the trash cleared away. She realised then that she'd seen no dead plants or old newspapers. It would seem that someone — Mrs Stanton's housekeeper, Cathy? — had cleaned the flat after Jon's death. And where was the Beetle? As she went through the cupboards she also realised that something else was missing: alcohol. She recalled the empty bottles in the bins, but surely they must have been thrown out recently. Miss Bettina Mayo?

Jon's bedroom overlooked the back garden. The first thing to arrest her attention were two small oils above the sleigh-shaped bed. They were both pictures of tropical plants. She recognised *Ipomoea alba*, called the moon-flower because its richly fragrant blooms only opened at night, but the other plant, which had petals like lobsters' claws, defeated her. Mitch had presented two series of six progammes called 'The Glories of the Greenhouse' for ITV about seven years ago and though the show had never really taken off she had learned a lot about tropical plants. She could see why Jon had put these oils above his bed. They exuded sexuality; the dense softnesses of petals and leaves were full of velvet crevices which shaded to midnight hues. She had to restrain her fingers from stretching out and stroking the surfaces.

She continued to turn. Scarlet curtains framed a surprisingly large attic window. On the window sill were a pair of Nike baseball boots together with an empty cassette and a felt-tipped pen. Had they perhaps been picked up off the floor before hoovering?

Still turning, she looked into the sightless eyes of a skull. It wore earphones.

Her heels rose from the rubber soles of her canvas shoes.

It's a lamp, she realised almost immediately. She'd bought a similar one for a young nephew of hers last Christmas, though that, unlike this one, hadn't been life-sized. As she went closer she recognised the cans. They were the ones Jon had used when he'd

74

worked at Radio Brum. They were similar to those many presenters wore, but Mitch never made a mistake about whose equipment was whose. Most broadcasters were as careful with their gear as fiddlers with their violins.

She went back into the lounge. It suddenly occurred to her that she'd not come across any mail; but that would be in the hall. It also occurred to her that the only glasses she'd seen had been tumblers; no wine glasses, none for spirits or brandy.

She heard a car — cars? — pull up on the gravel driveway and doors being slammed. Going back into the lounge, she sidled behind curtains but could see nothing. The cars must be parked side by side beyond the gable end of the house.

Should she make herself known? There were certainly some questions she'd like to ask Bettina Mayo.

She found she was disinclined to do so. Not yet. I want to think about things a bit more first. I'm not even sure that I want to be involved. Below, there was a banging of doors and noises in the back garden. She went into Jon's bedroom, and, partly shielded by the curtains, looked out.

The garden faced east, a broad stripe of sun dividing two areas of deep shade. A girl carrying folded canvas chairs emerged out of the shadow near the house and began to set them up on the lawn. She was a leggy youngster, a man's T-shirt completely covering her shorts when she straightened up. Her blonde hair was cropped closely about her head but behind each ear a half-inch thick plait spouted like a jet of water. When the girl looked upwards and Mitch saw her face she was put in mind of a deviant Heidi doll. It's the plaits, she thought, framing that pale punk face.

Three chairs were set up when a man holding a plastic kitchen table over his head appeared. There was a bull-like strength about his neck and shoulders; a lot of thickly muscled thigh showed beneath his sliced-off jeans. They'd dropped far enough to show the crease in his bottom.

The girl was now shouting — but Mitch realised it was to someone beyond the man. Freya Adcock emerged. She was bearing a tray of drinks, her head cocked and skittishly to one side. She was wearing what looked like ancient gym kit. A scarf, which was acting as a belt, was very similar to one Mitch owned and sometimes used with shorts or trousers. Mitch slowly realised it wasn't similar; it was exactly the same. Radio Brum's programme organiser put down the tray and as she did so the girl came up to her and whispered something in her ear and squeezed her arm. They both turned to look at the man who was now checking the chairs to see if they had been erected properly. From behind Freya the girl winked at him. He began to grin.

Mitch stole out of the room, locked up the flat and went downstairs. She found Jon's post stacked in a pile on an old-fashioned hall stand. She took it and let herself out of the front door.

Getting into the TVR, she found herself almost weak with relief that she'd not been noticed. She rationalised it by telling herself she would have found it very embarrassing to explain to Freya why she was there.

She checked her answering machine when she got home. Madeleine Stanton had asked her to ring back. Hayden Murrey from the Mid Arts Association left a message about sound sculptures. Venus de Milo made out of noise? Mitch wondered as she jotted down a note.

Charlie Collins hadn't rung.

5

'Look, Mrs Stanton, I'd hate to mislead you
. . . the probability must be that your
grandson killed himself.' Mitch was clutching
the phone with her right hand, putting on a
red high-heeled shoe with her left and
screwing her head round so she could see the
kitchen clock.

'You'll take our case! That's the ticket. Atta
girl!'

'I can't do a lot this week because I've a
show to get out every night. I'm on holiday
for a couple of weeks after that. I should have
been going to America but my daughter's had
to cry off.'

'I'm so pleased. Oh dear. Not about your
daughter, of course.'

'Mrs Stanton — '

'I know, I know . . . But there's jolly well
something wrong. That's what I feel. And I've
every confidence you'll find out what it is. You
don't let go, Miss Mitchell. That's what used
to impress me about those consumer
investigations you did. You were tiptop.
Absolutely tiptop.'

'I'll get over to see you later this week but

78

there are one or two things I'd like to ask now. I went to Jon's flat yesterday and though I found tumblers there were no glasses for spirits or wine. Nor was there any alcohol. But the flat did look as if it had been recently cleaned up. Oh, and the Beetle. What happened to that?'

'The car's in the coach house here for the time being. We didn't feel we could leave it over there after what happened. There's a young girl living in the bottom flat.'

'Bettina Mayo.'

'I have a feeling Jon talked about her once — she used to work at some southern local radio station. Not a girlfriend, though, I gathered at the time. Cathy went over to clean the flat out after Jon's death. We were thinking of milk going sour and of course he would eat bananas in the bed and leave the skins about. We didn't want the place to get too frightful. One has to think of who might live there next, though the lease doesn't actually run out until December. There would be no alcohol in the flat because Jon wasn't much of a drinker. The occasional beer. No wine and certainly not spirits.'

'Though he had drunk heavily on the night he died. Beer and, I gathered from the reports of the inquest, a great deal of whisky.'

'Yes, I know. But he never drank spirits,

never — it completely disagreed with him. It made his heart palpitate. Naturally I told the police.'

'And what did they say?'

'They seemed to believe that on this occasion he acted out of character. They told me that most suicidal people drink before they do it — gets up the courage for the final act. But I still don't believe Jon would have drunk whisky. He really hated having palpitations. He absolutely loathed that happening.'

'Is this the reason you don't believe Jon killed himself?'

'It's not as cut and dried as that. I simply have this over-whelming gut feeling that he didn't. But the police weren't prepared to listen. I suppose many relatives feel that someone they love deeply could never have done such a thing. But I *know* something is wrong. I can't explain it.'

Mitch glanced at the kitchen clock again. 'Look, I'll have to go in a minute. Just one more quick thing. I take it that Jon was a wealthy young man. Who does his money go to?'

'His will is made out in favour of his cousin. I say cousin but actually the relationship is a bit more tenuous than that. One or two times removed. I'm afraid the main Stanton line has practically died out. His money goes to Ann Wellesley. She's local. She's a lecturer at one of the polytechnics.'

'What's she like?'

'I remember her best from ten years ago. I went to the twenty-first party her parents gave for her. She turned up with her head shaved and wearing army boots and quite literally a tramp's jacket. The pong was awful. Her mother was in floods of tears.'

'My own daughter went through a similar period two years ago. Ann must have grown out of it.'

'She did. But I never could quite bring myself to forgive the wretched girl. Her mother was dying of cancer at the time. No doubt psychologists could explain it all quite beautifully but I felt like biffing her one. Since then my relationship with her has been . . . well, I suppose you'd say prickly. But Jon got on well with her. They were both very interested in Green issues.'

'You don't happen to have her address?'

'Yes. I can dig that out for you.'

'You do realise, Mrs Stanton, that I have never tackled an investigation like this?'

'You'll manage splendidly. Oh . . . now that went completely out of my mind. Oh dear . . . '

'What is it?'

'Jon's money . . . the bulk of it goes to his cousin, of course. But I'd quite forgotten that friend of his. Robin Pemberton. He gets the house in Gozo and a little legacy too.'

'Who is he?'

'Robin? Jon was at school with him and they went on to university together. Robin became something in the Civil Service in London but he really didn't fit in. No, it wasn't his kind of life at all.'

Mitch almost interrupted but decided that, after all, it didn't matter too much if she arrived at the broadcasting centre later than usual.

'Jon was left the house in Gozo — a holiday house, you know — when his parents died. Do you know Gozo? It's an island off Malta. Robin decided he wanted to be a painter and Jon let him use the house. Just a base. Robin's often away. Though he uses the Gozo house, Robin has a flat in Birmingham too. In the Hockley area, I believe. Actually, he's on a painting trip to France at the moment and we've been unable to contact him. He doesn't yet know Jon's died.'

'They were good friends?'

'Best friends. They were very close. But Jon wouldn't have seen him for a good three months before he died.'

'Well, thank you, Mrs Stanton. I've plenty

to be going on with and I'll give you a ring and let you know when I can get over to Lichfield.'

'I'm so glad you've decided to do this for us. Anything you need. Anything.'

'Oh, I picked up Jon's post at his flat. Can I open it?'

'My dear girl. Jolly well get cracking.'

It had rained in the night. When Mitch eventually banged the front door behind her she found a lawn seeded with diamonds, an azalea laced with cobwebs of emeralds and light spinning off the chrome trimmings of her car in a chandelier blaze.

She knew what that meant. Oh God, I'm in love, she thought. She hadn't seen the world like this since the early days with Max and then with Josh Hadley.

Oh shit. Who the hell is Charlie Collins, anyway?

The man who hasn't rung, she thought gloomily as she climbed into her TVR. But such is the power of love that the world didn't cease to glitter.

It was so late that by the time she reached the broadcasting centre the car-park was full and she had to leave the TVR in a back street a quarter of a mile away. As she lugged the carrier bag stuffed with her gear out of the back she reflected that it would have been easier to walk to work.

And yet she found she was smiling as she locked the car door and began the tramp along tarmac pavements. 'To open up my legs any wider,' she'd told Charlie, 'I'd have to be double-jointed.' His finger had trickled down her nose. 'Then tilt your bum up . . . Let's cram a bit more in.' She'd thought he had all the right ideas. She was still smiling when she went in the front entrance of the broadcasting centre; the security guard who checked her pass thought she was smiling at him. Josie, Radio Brum's receptionist, was chatting to the girl who manned television reception. She smiled back.

It was week twenty-five, a fact printed in all the organisation's diaries which people took out and consulted even if they sat opposite each other. 'Let's see . . . make it ten o'clock Thursday. We'll meet to talk about it then,' one would tell the other and if both didn't disappear again behind their newspapers they would perhaps synchronise watches by glancing at a big clock.

There was always a big clock. Clocks sought you out from over single doors, double doors, studio doors and lift doors; no one could move in or out, up or down, without knowing they had five minutes less to do it in than they'd had five minutes before.

Mitch had nothing to do with any of this. At her age all her time in this place was borrowed and there seemed no sense in drawing attention to the fact.

She passed television's foyer studio and walked down the corridor and up the stairs. Radio Brum's output, pumped into the corridor between the management's offices and the studios, was being drowned by a curious noise coming from the gram library. A ladies' choir was singing 'Jerusalem' through tinfoil gullets. What will people get up to next? Mitch hurried by.

'Kiddo!'

It was Freya Adcock calling. Mitch almost cringed as she turned but today the programme organiser hadn't stolen a stitch of her clothing. Anyone but Freya wouldn't have been seen dead in that broderie anglaise blouse, nor the gingham skirt which seemed to have been created for a retread square dancer.

'Have you a mo?'

Mitch warily entered the gram library.

'What do you think? What can one think? After all, he's always telling everyone he's been a broadcaster for over twenty years. Perhaps it's the mid-life crisis,' she said. 'Naturally you heard his show.'

Freya thought that the station's presenters

should listen to every second of the output. All declined on the grounds of retaining their sanity but none thought it politic to inform her of their decision. 'Jerusalem'-sort music, Mitch was thinking. It must surely be out of Quentin Plunkett's 'More Maestro Please' Sunday show. Who else on this station would choose it?

'I mean, one can't stand by while someone castrates the whole of a Welsh male voice choir, kiddo,' Freya said. 'And usually he's so reliable.'

'Quentin, you mean?'

'And she's such a wonderful woman. His wife. Surely he can't be having nestie-westie probs?'

Mitch vaguely remembered a puce lady. She couldn't recall now whether Quentin's wife had been wearing puce or if it was the colour of her face. 'They always seemed a well-matched couple to me.'

Freya adjusted the speed of the turntable. As it dropped a rich baritone sound emanated from the machine. 'He's a very touchy man but one will have to have a little word, I'm afraid. One can — at a stretch — understand starting a record at the wrong speed. But then to play it all the way through! Do you think he's having a nervous breakdown, kiddo?'

'Perhaps he just slipped out of the studio for a pee?'

'Broadcasters visit the lavatory before they go on air. One isn't running a kindergarten.' She lowered the volume. 'Of course, this business about Jon Stanton has upset us all.'

'Quentin didn't even go to his funeral.'

'So painful for him, d'you see? It was Quentin who introduced Jon to the station.'

'Really?'

'The Plunketts work with Ann Wellesley. You must know that marvellous Green for Good woman? Jon was Ann's cousin.'

'The Plunketts are Greens too?' Mitch was astonished.

'Quentin's wife is the major Green. She and Ann run the Green for Good campaign. Marjorie does the organising and Ann's the . . . well, she's the driving spirit of the thing. A very interesting woman.'

'I've never met her.'

'Oh, if only you and me could be like her, kiddo. So very few forces for good in this world. One does so envy these visionary types.'

As often happened in conversations with Freya, Mitch was left looking not just for the right word but any word at all.

'By the way, when I was out on Sunday I saw a car just like yours . . .'

'You did?' Mitch's heartbeats fell over each other.

'If only you'd take the trouble to keep yours as clean. Really, it's just as smart as this one was. All it needs is a good wash and brush up.'

Mitch hurried to make her escape. Freya, replaying the record, moved the speed up. 'Perhaps Quentin just mistook it for a ladies' choir? When you get used to the sound it sort of grows on you . . . ' and she started to hum along with the tune.

Mitch was half-way through the door when Freya yelled, 'Those culottes look good on you, kiddo!'

Shaun O'Neill, Mitch's assistant, was back at work and hanging loose in the production office. His legs were hooked over each side of his armchair and both arms supported a head which looked towards the ceiling. In this cradle a phone was wedged between ear and chin. From the movements flickering about his face it was clear that while he was holding on he was watching a 3D feelie in his head. Shaun was of an age when lust caused even his pores to leak. Like a plumbing system under too much pressure, seepage was everywhere.

The secretary, Trish, legs locked together, was operating her word processor. Quentin

Plunkett, blissfully unaware of the talk he was shortly going to have with Freya Adcock, was hunched over his editing machine and nodding vigorously. He'd obviously said something on tape he agreed with. Sizemore Jackson, the early afternoon presenter, had gone blond overnight and was surreptitiously viewing the results in a pocket mirror. On output the mid-morning presenter was telling a listener from Yardley that she had some very interesting views on artificial insemination and now back to the professor.

Mitch dropped her bags, viewed her pile of post and then went round to stand over Shaun.

'Eddie Merton,' she hissed. She was a very good hisser.

'What?' Shaun scrambled into a sitting position.

'That footballer you fixed up for the sporting memories spot. I'm not going to forgive you, Shaun. I've never in my life been landed with so many yards of gibberish.'

'Oh fuck.'

'It's too late to get anyone else. I'm going to have to spend a couple of hours slaving over an editing machine. That tape is going to have more joints than the Eiffel Tower.'

'Listen, duckie — ' and then he put an

index finger up. His connection had come on the line.

Mitch went back to her desk and began to open her post.

'Reception on the line,' Trish called to her. 'It's your big day. A bouquet has just been brought in for you.'

'Me?' Mitch was filled with intimations of Charlie Collins; many of them were startlingly rude.

'You're bright red,' laughed Trish.

'Rubbish,' she said, already on her feet. Downstairs Josie, the receptionist, pointed to a huge bunch of roses.

Oh! He really shouldn't have, Mitch was thinking as she pulled out the card from under the florist's ribbon.

For a mum in a million. Cassie.

Tears of disappointment mixed with tears of guilt for being disappointed. Memories, too, of her child's gifts of dandelions and bluebells and flag irises nicked from a neighbour's garden. Carefully tucking her arm round the flowers, she made her way back up to the production office.

Both Shaun's fists were in the air and he was wagging them triumphantly. 'You're going to love me. You're going to kiss my bum for this one. You're going to buy me lunch and cuddle me to death! The MP for

Birmingham East — '

'The Chancellor's agreed!'

'Ninety per cent certain.' Shaun was looking at the calendar stuck on the wall. 'Week twenty-eight. He's in his constituency for a whole week. Coming down on Wednesday — '

'How ninety per cent is ninety per cent really?'

'The PA can confirm it early next week.'

'Let's keep it under wraps for the moment, then. In particular we don't want anyone else sneaking behind our backs and putting in bids for him. We'll say nothing until we've got him in the bag.'

'OK, chief.' Shaun rubbed his hands. 'Well smart, eh? Who's a pretty boy, then? Eddie Merton forgotten and forgiven? You'll be back from your hols, too. Will you turn the whole show over to him? Phone-in too, perhaps?'

'Let me think about it.'

'Who sent the roses?'

She told him about the cancellation of her trip to America. 'I suppose you'll be presenting 'City Talk' while I'm on holiday?'

'I've pinned Freya down twice but the old cow won't confirm it,' he said.

'That probably means she wants to try out a new voice. Which also probably means she's thinking of not renewing my contract.'

'When's it up?'

'In three months.'

'We'll have a new station manager by then. He'll make the decisions, not her.'

'*He'll?*'

'Surely you don't want *her* to get the job?'

'There are other women in the world.'

'The other seven candidates are men. Digger Rooney heard it from the E-i-C who had it from Personnel in London.'

'They might think it their duty to promote Freya.' The appalling thought struck Mitch for the first time. 'Boost the number of women at that management level.'

'Cheer up, duckie. You're not dead yet. If we can get a few more Chancellors on the show . . . '

'There's only one,' Mitch pointed out and then laughed. 'No point in worrying, honeypot. Let's get on. I want you to get hold of a chap about sound sculptures and then I want you to round up a woman psychologist who says men are better drivers . . . '

She went off to package Eddie. It was early afternoon before she'd cleared sufficient work to think about ringing Tommy Hung. Really she knew she shouldn't have agreed to take on the investigation. Among the worst of the problems it posed was the fact that she felt she couldn't go about it in a straightforward way. It would not go down at all well at Radio Brum if it were discovered she was investigating Jon's death. He hadn't even died in suspicious circumstances. At the least they would think her absurd for trying to question a coroner's verdict in such an open and shut case; some of them, she knew, would accuse her of gulling a grief-stricken old woman out of money for spurious work. It could very well lead to her losing her job at the station, but this didn't weigh too heavily because she felt the chances of her contract being renewed were pretty remote. One got Brownie points for firing fifty-year-olds, not hiring them.

But when it came to Tommy Hung she simply couldn't think of a reasonable cover story for asking him the questions she wanted an answer to. Jon Stanton wouldn't have got in touch with him solely because he talked like the Duke of Edinburgh. There must be some other story attached, one she didn't know of. In the end, because he wasn't in any way connected with the radio station, she decided to be honest with him. In her experience honesty was not the best policy; it was like bowling a ball underarm to a West Indian batsman. She quite expected Mr Tommy Hung to knock her for six.

He used his astoundingly upper-class accent not to wither away her extremities but to warm her with his enthusiasm for the project. She was astonished. She felt perhaps he'd misunderstood her.

'No, no, my dear girl. But it would help one if you could come today. If you could make it pronto even better.'

'Well, actually I think I can,' she said. 'Let's say half an hour?'

She went to the cloakroom to tidy herself up and then found Shaun. 'Can you cover?' she asked him. 'I've to go out for half an hour.'

'What for?'

'Women's troubles.' She'd always found this answer completely killed male curiosity.

Shaun was making a paper aeroplane. 'I've chalked in the driving piece for Wednesday,' he told her.

'What does this psychologist sound like?' She dropped a notebook in her bag and watching him watching her added, 'Might have time to pop in the reference library on the way back. The Chancellor, you know.'

'He's not in the bag yet.'

'Is she a good parrot?' Mitch ignored his observation. 'The psychologist?'

'A what-ho knicker-dropper I'd say.'

'You would?'

'Oh yes.' He shut his eyes. 'I see a good bit of knicker on a nice broad beam. Ripe and juicy. Runny even.'

'You're disgusting, Shaun O'Neill. Do you ever come off the boil?'

He shook his head. 'It's quite worrying.'

'Well, for God's sake don't chase her around the studio. However broad her beam turns out to be.'

The overnight rain had brought a change in the weather. Though it was sunny there were many more clouds in the sky and the temperature still seemed to be dropping. As she walked down the road to the street she'd parked in, Mitch buttoned up her jacket. The TVR was still there, wheels on, windscreen wipers unbroken.

Tommy Hung lived in a small three-storey block of flats off Sir Harry's Road in Edgbaston, a district full of the sterling worth of leaf-shaded pavements, curling drives and the gentle twittering of birds tempted into gardens by gourmet morsels hung from trees or served on trays. Tommy's flat was on the ground floor at the end of the block, wide windows overlooking well-trimmed lawn. She found herself in not so much a lounge as the reading room at a men's club. She'd never actually been in such a club, only seen their interiors in spy films. Perhaps this was also the extent of Mr Hung's knowledge, for Mitch would bet money that in reality such rooms would be full of institutional grime and gloom. Most obviously missing was the male servant who needed oil in his joints and probably in his can as well.

Mr Hung was a delight, a small, slim, dapper man who, though well into his seventies, obviously had no need of oil anywhere. Behind glasses, eyes which were as openly curious as any two-year-old's studied her.

'Tea?'

'Thank you.'

'Won't be a jiffy.'

He disappeared into the kitchen and she strolled across to look at his bookshelves. Sherlock Holmes adventures, Dorothy L. Sayers, Agatha Christie, a shelf of Simenon, less well-known authors such as Ethel Lina White and A. E. W. Mason; hardly a jacket was without a gun, a corpse, or a knife dripping blood. American writers had a series of shelves to themselves, every book by not only Chandler but, as far as she could tell, John D. MacDonald. No living author seemed represented in the collection.

The tea service was silver, the tea Indian and the cups plain white china. 'Darjeeling,' Mr Hung informed her. 'For me an acquired taste. Though I liked Christmas pudding straight away. One didn't have to try at all.

No sugar? Now . . . Mr Stanton. What can I tell you about him?' Little finger nicely adjusted, he handed her a cup; her fingers waving around uncertainly, she placed it on the saucer. 'He was with me about an hour, I suppose, on the afternoon before his death. I was most surprised to read about his suicide. He certainly didn't give me cause to think he planned to kill himself. Not at all.'

'So you thought it odd?'

'I find much that is odd about the occidental mind. Bizarre even.'

'What did he come to see you about, Mr Hung?'

'If you feel you can bring yourself to call me Tommy . . . He was interested in the Unofficials. I was one for twenty years before I came ashore and went into other enterprises. We were Chinese laundrymen to the Royal Navy, my dear. I was recruited in Hong Kong as were so many of the others. Ten of us manned an aircraft carrier, two a destroyer and I think it was two to a frigate as well. I believe the navy has a couple of Chinese shoemakers, too, and some tailors. But I was one of the laundrymen. Mr Stanton was researching the possibility of doing a feature for a television programme. I couldn't help much but I gave him the names of two of the contractors.'

'I'd no idea Her Majesty's sailors had Chinese laundrymen!'

'I believe two were killed in the Falklands. The practice goes back to the China Station in the last century.' He smiled. 'Mr Stanton seemed quite enthusiastic. About his feature, I mean.'

'Did he mention other plans?'

'As a matter of fact he did say he was going to the Jade Dragon that night. Taking a young lady out, I believe.'

'And he certainly went,' said Mitch. 'That meal was mentioned at the inquest. But there was nothing about a girl.'

Mr Hung was silent for a moment and then he said, 'Could I perhaps be permitted to help? I know Sung Shun Chin, the owner of the restaurant. If you had a photograph perhaps I could go along and show it to the waiters. Investigate?'

Mitch was taken aback. 'Well . . . I . . .'

'You know one's always dreamed of emulating Lord Peter Wimsey. More tea?'

Mitch held out her cup. She began to smile. 'I don't see that it can do any harm.'

'And, of course, there was the woman he was taking the potted palm to. She might be worth a visit?'

'The who?'

'I accompanied Mr Stanton out to his car.

98

I'd a letter to post and there's a box across the road. This palm practically filled the back seat of his Beetle. He told me it was for his godmother. He planned to deliver it after seeing me because it was her birthday the next day.'

'Helen? Would that be Helen Brierley?'

'He didn't mention a name.'

'I'll find out her address and see her as soon as I can. Thank you, Mr Hung.'

'Tommy.'

'Tommy.'

When Mitch got back to the broadcasting centre she was relieved to find the car-park was no longer full. 'Why can't they extend the damned thing? There's a whole field behind it going to waste,' she grumbled to the security guard.

'What would the football team do?'

'What football team?'

'Well, there are goalposts.'

'That was for the production of 'Injury Time Blues'.'

'I might have known these shits wouldn't play football. Hockey more like. Big girls' blouses.'

Mitch shook her head. 'Media people never play team games.'

After parking the TVR, she went into the ops room on her way back to the production office to find out which studio she would be in that evening.

'Your usual. The engineers have finished,' the station assistant told her.

'What were they doing?'

He shrugged and picked up the phone. 'Mavis? Well, Mavis, have you got the answer? What is the mystery object?'

'There you are, kiddo.' The ops room, at the centre of a suite of two studios, was a long room with two doors and Freya had appeared through the top one. There was someone behind her. Mitch slowly recognised the girl she'd seen on the lawn at 42 Templar's Rise. Today the rat-tail plaits were looped and tied with red bows. She was wearing a man's T-shirt, Lycra leggings and a pair of black monkey boots. 'This is Bettina Mayo,' Freya introduced her. 'She was with Radio Wessex.'

'Hi,' said Bettina.

'She'll be presenting your show while you're on holiday, Mitch.'

'I listened on Friday night,' said Bettina. 'I pictured someone different.'

'How different?' Mitch suddenly saw herself through those Heidi doll eyes, a candidate for a bus pass and free prescriptions.

'You know . . . ' Bettina shrugged her shoulders.

'What did you think of the show?'

Bettina looked at Freya and then at her. She picked her words carefully. 'I'd say a lot of pretty solid work went into it.' And then she added, 'Freya gave me the figures. But audiences are always down in summer.'

'I'm sure you two will get on splendidly,' said Freya. She was beaming.

6

Mitch had arranged to see J. J. Woodward, the retired newsman, in the Scales at lunchtime on Wednesday. She was trying to decide which was the best way to approach Jon's heir Ann Wellesley and wanted to gather more background information. The only thing in Jon Stanton's post to catch her eye had been a Green for Good leaflet advertising a lecture to be given by Ann and a brief personal note from her at the bottom of it. *Jon-Jon . . . you know the Minister for the Environment is coming to Birmingham at the end of July? We want to tackle him about that dreadful proposal for open-cast coal mining in the Shakeshaft Nature Reserve south of the city. Ideas? See you Thursday.* It had a PS. *B.M. proving very useful.*

Bettina Mayo?

There had already been bids by all the presenters of shows at Radio Brum for a crack at the Environment Minister, Spencer Sackville Thumper. Digger Rooney had managed to bag him simply because of the timing — Freya wanted the minister to broadcast live.

'If we pre-record and he drops a brick we'll get leant on by some pip arse in Whitehall. They'll want to try and make us edit it out,' Freya had said. 'If Spencer shits live on air there's no way it won't hit the fan, kiddos.'

And no one could disagree with that, thought Mitch, feeding her small change into the Pay-and-Display unit in the car-park at Masshouse. Much of Thumper's political fame came from the judicious use of the injudicious remark.

It was a fifteen-minute walk to the Scales from Masshouse, a centre-city car-park forested with concrete trunks which held aloft the giant spread of the Moor Street — Queensway interchange. As she crossed to the exit tunnel, she noticed many empty parking spaces between the ranks of cars baking in the noisy, oily heat of a fine day in late spring. The city, beached and leached by recession, was far less busy than it had been just a couple of months ago. Even the closing down sale at one of Birmingham's biggest department stores had failed to bring out the shoppers. Heading over High Street, she tossed a coin down to a pavement artist whose box was practically empty.

There was more bustle on Corporation Street but the crowds thinned out as she cut through to the cathedral. The Georgian building stood modestly in its neat square of lawns, fine wire mesh guarding the Edward Burne-Jones stained glass windows. The clock on the Italianate domed tower struck one. She was a little early.

The Scales was in Waterloo Passage, an alley at the back of a street dense with the stone facades of building societies, banks and lawyers' offices. Why it had become the haunt of journalists was something of a mystery. 'Except that you always find us at the arse end of respectability,' Woody Woodward had said.

At the bottom of the passageway were wheeled grey skips piled so high with rubbish that their blue lids wouldn't shut. Wind had blown paper into gutters and gratings. But at the top end a well-swept concrete apron, its perimeter marked out with tubs of geraniums and lobelia, announced the railed stairway which led down to the Scales basement bar. Today the doors stood open and alcohol fumes rose in a column, like smoke from a fire.

With no regard to its locale at the centre of one of England's great industrial cities, nor even to its name, the Scales was draped in fishermen's nets and a large ship's bell stood on a bar made of fake rum barrels. Equally insouciant were the clientele, most of whom

104

felt they couldn't write another story about a thirty per cent drop in car sales or detail factory closures without shelling out more money for extra grog. A mass heaved about the bar though there were empty tables around the walls. Mitch ordered a shandy and headed for a corner. As Woody hadn't yet arrived she unfolded a lunchtime edition of the *Birmingham Sentinel* she'd filched from the newsroom.

'Mitch, my angel!' Her former lover Josh Hadley loomed over the top edge of her paper, a rangy man in his mid-fifties. He had a pint of bitter in one hand and a Park Drive in the other; his unruly grey hair was pulled back and tied in a pony tail. She found he still had the power to do nasty things to her heart; she listened to the knocking noises which often warn a driver his engine's about to pack up.

'I've not seen you for ages,' she said. 'Actually, I'm waiting for Woody. How's business? Oh dear. Perhaps I shouldn't have asked.'

'We're surviving. I'm doing more with pictures than I did.'

'You always told me that market was quicksand!'

'It's Amanda's doing, really. She's hot on *fin de siècle* stuff.'

Hadn't she known Josh's blonde bimbo would have brains? 'What's her job?'

'At the moment she's doing postgraduate research into the Arts and Crafts movement.'

'Cradle snatcher!' The words were out before she could stop them.

He suddenly seemed a little shy. 'Oh well . . . ' He fingered the tortoiseshell rim of his glasses, then shrugged. 'I'm just a station on her way. She'll probably switch lines completely at Crewe. And you?'

'Oh, you know me. The Barbara Cartland female.' She put her fingers in the air. 'V for virtue.'

'Not the way I hear it. What about this pushy young artist kid? Sorry. Scrub that. None of my business. Listen, I've got some nice early twentieth-century black lacquer pieces down at the warehouse. Want to take a peek before I start knocking them out?'

'I very well might,' said Mitch. 'It looks as if I've got some extra funds coming my way.'

'Woody's signalling you. I tell you what, give me a ring. And have a round on me . . . '

By the time Woody had eased himself into a chair, loosened his tie, searched in each pocket and finally located a half-smoked cigar, Josh had sent their drinks over.

'He's still with the blonde,' Woody told her

as they smiled and raised their glasses in his direction.

'I know.'

'I always hoped to be best man at your wedding. Why didn't you nail him while the going was good?'

Mitch shrugged. 'You know how it is . . .'

'Mind you, she's a real looker.'

'Whose side are you on?'

'My wife gets her dander up every time she sees them together. Funny that. Isobel was a real goer when she was young. One of the Bluebell Girls. But now she's had her sixtieth birthday she only has to see a flash pair of knockers to give me a sermon. As if it's my fault the world's still full of tasty tarts!' He shook his round bald head. 'When women change they never change for the better. They're always a bloody sight worse.'

'Come on, Woody. Your wife's a little darling.'

'A chap sees a lot more when he's home all the time, Mitch. Doesn't do. Can't live in sight of someone twenty-four hours a day and like 'em. Not humanly possible. Talk about Tom and Jerry. And that's on a good day. Anyway. Enough of that. Cheers.' And then: 'Now, what can you do me for?'

'I'm still trying to get a few lines on the Stanton family. Or what's left of it. Do you know anything about Ann Wellesley?'

'Ann?' His knuckle sank into his chin and he fingered his jaw-bone. 'A real punk kid at one time. A bundle of trouble. But she straightened out. She came into Daddy's money about four years ago and financed this women's press in the city. The reviewers did her in as much as anybody. They praised the stuff to the skies. Bis-function. *Aperçu*. All those words which make you want to puke. The whole enterprise went kaput about nine months ago. She lost a packet.'

'Wiped out, would you say?'

'Well, I don't think a broke Stanton is in the nature of things. But I've been told she was pretty well left on her uppers. She's now got a job teaching at some poly.'

'I hear she's also into Green politics.'

'She's a founder member of Green for Good. The movement started in Birmingham about six years ago. She's always been a driving force.'

'Have they got a militant wing? Like the anti-vivisectionists?'

'Pussy cats. As far as I know the nearest they've come to violence is invading the pitch at an Old Trafford test match and kissing Ian Botham. I think it was Ian. Six girls in nothing more than a coat of green paint grabbed him and then strung out in a line

108

kicking up their legs while words popped up on their head-dresses. Green for God. One of the Os went AWOL. We ran the picture across four on page one. What else do you do with such a fine display of bouncing bums and knockers?'

'Have you ever met her? Ann, I mean?'

'Funnily enough, I ran into her at the *Sentinel* offices a couple of weeks ago. I'd gone in to flog a couple of features. She was lobbying for some editorial comment. She wanted the *Sentinel* to come out against the plan for an open-cast coal mine in the Shakeshaft Nature Reserve — a campaign to tie in with the Environment Minister's visit to Birmingham. What's he called?'

'Sackville Thumper. What's Ann . . . Well, how would you describe her?'

'Very wimmin. But quite a nice kid. To tell the truth, I always feel sorry for 'em.'

'Wimmin?'

'Idealists.'

'Why?'

'Well, it's not an ideal world is it?'

'Some people's idea of fun is a bed of nails,' said Mitch. 'Drink up and I'll send another across. I'm afraid I'll have to make tracks, honeypot. I've some more bits for you but they're at the office. I'll shove the stuff into an envelope and put it in tonight's post.'

'Aren't you going to ask me about Helen Brierley?'

'I already know. The Chancellor's ex.'

'Nice woman. Used to be a real looker when she was younger.'

'Must have been a very dirty divorce.'

'Why do you say that?'

'Well, she went back to her maiden name, didn't she?'

'Should have thought she'd have been glad to see the back of the pompous prick.'

'Wash your mouth out. You're talking about a Minister of the Crown I've got my eye on . . .'

'You?'

Mitch winked. 'For my show, honeypot.' She stood up. 'Anything else you get on the Stantons . . .'

'I'll give you a bell.'

She stooped and kissed his cheek. 'Love you.'

Walking back down to Masshouse, Mitch reviewed the information Woody had given her. Not all of it added up. On the one hand there was the women's libber, on the other a row of bouncing bums and knockers. Could it be that Ann Wellesley now had little authority in a movement which was rapidly growing into an international organisation? Or was it just another example of practice

110

subverting principle?

But, with her business bust, Ann Wellesley did have a strong motive for killing her cousin. Am I really prepared to consider it? She found she still couldn't believe Jon Stanton had been murdered. But was that not a normal reaction to what was, after all, a very rare crime? Was she just discovering that it was not only the police who wanted an apparent suicide to actually be just that?

She met Digger Rooney as she went through the back entrance of the broadcasting centre.

'I'm off to the Hilton to see some frightful American woman,' he informed her, shifting his tape recorder to his other shoulder. 'You know the type. Even if you ask them something totally innocent . . . 'Do you like cheese?' . . . They answer, 'Do *you* like cheese?' One's tape begins to sound like some ghastly avant-garde play.'

'Why go?'

'She's a celeb. God. How one hates the little wankers. By the way, your holiday stand-in has already decanted herself into your chair.'

'Bettina Mayo?'

'Young Shaun O'Neill's getting well stuck in. But if the crunch came would he be up to it? When one thinks of a girlie like that emerging from her Lycra leggings . . . ' He thought about it. 'One is so put in mind of the time one was an actor. You know, those bog-awful crits. 'His costume appears to have been donated by Brentford Nylons. His performance failed to match up to it.' '

Mitch laughed. 'Shaun's only got his manhood to lose. My job's on the line.'

'You're not really worried about your contract being renewed? Jesus. How ridiculous can you get.'

'I'm serious, Digger.'

'Freya's very fond of you, blossom.'

'Fond?' Mitch felt her jaw loosening.

'Sweetie, you've no idea when it comes to what makes people tick. None at all.'

Before she could reposition her jaw he had chugged past her.

'There's a call for you on my line!' Trish called, as she went into the production office. Mitch turned and saw that Bettina Mayo was using hers. She was swinging a rat-plait with one hand and her left monkey boot was resting on the edge of the desk.

Trish looked at Bettina and sketched a shrug as she handed Mitch the phone.

'Do you think you could manage Saturday night? I've just got tickets for the CBSO concert. If you don't say yes I'm going to

112

grab hold of a couple of boulders and jump in the canal.'

'Charlie?'

'Yes.'

'Yes,' she said.

'I'll collect you at your place some time after six. That OK?'

'Fine,' she said. Beaming, she handed the receiver back to Trish. She even beamed at Bettina Mayo who had looked up.

'You haven't won the pools?' Trish asked her.

'Better than that, honeypot,' and she retired to Digger Rooney's desk with the post she'd not yet opened.

She slit the top jiffy bag and pulled out a book and a press release. *JOLLY ROGERS — homosexuality among pirates on the Barbary Coast,* she read. The review copy of the book had been sent by a well-known university press. *A detailed investigation of homosexual practices in hierarchical group-ings of gay sailing communes, the variations of synchrony and diachrony in buccaneering life with parochial impacting on men engaged in almost constant . . .*

Long John Silver, she thought, will never seem the same, and she turned her attention to the more orthodox pursuits of needle-makers in Redditch. She then began typing her cues.

'Call!' Trish was waving the phone. 'Do you want it on that line?'

'Please!'

'Am I speaking to Miss Mitchell?' She identified the voice immediately as that of Mr Hung. Somewhere under that crystal-cracking English lurked sampans and chop-sticks. Or was it simply that she knew they should be there?

'You've got some news for me? You are quick.'

'One shook a leg,' he said. 'I was very well aware of following a long and honourable tradition.'

As the pause lengthened Mitch became aware he was following another long and honourable tradition — that of creating suspense. 'And?' she prodded.

'The photo you gave me is obviously a good one of him. He was recognised immediately. He had dinner that evening with a young lady. I was told they laughed a lot.'

'Were you able to get a description of the girl?'

'Very striking, apparently. Short blonde hair but two long very thin plaits sticking out from behind her ears. Do you know such a person?'

'I do.' Mitch glanced in the direction of her

desk but Bettina was no longer in her chair.

'They had one of the dinners for two. She had two glasses of the house wine. He drank a lager.'

'No whisky?'

'No. No spirits of any kind. They left about ten thirty. My informant guesses they were friends. He thinks they were having too much fun for lovers.'

'I suppose love is a dreadfully serious business,' said Mitch.

'They were still laughing and joking when they left the Jade Dragon.'

'And yet barely four or five hours later he'd committed suicide . . .'

'One's life can change in the space of a word or two,' he reminded her.

'If that happened to Jon, what changed it? There's the whisky, too. He never drank spirits, according to his grandmother.'

'The trouble is that you can't rely on people being what they're supposed to be,' said Mr Hung.

And that, coming from Mr Hung, rather illustrates the point, Mitch thought.

'The girl hasn't visited the restaurant since but my chap will keep an eye on things for us.'

Mitch, though she noted the 'for us' with some alarm, thanked him profusely.

'My dear girl, it's a pleasure. Bye bye for now.'

When she put the phone down she looked round the room. Bettina was no longer there. There had been no mention of the girl in any of the newspaper reports of the inquest. But then, no one had known about Mr Hung either. Still, it was odd about the girl. She lived in the same house. She must have been questioned by the police.

Would she have laughed and joked with Jon while planning his murder? Even though Mitch disliked the girl, she found that hard to believe. And what possible motive could she have had?

At the inquest Mrs Edna Cowley, a neighbour living across the way, was said to have been the last person to see Jon alive. She had noticed the orange Beetle pull into the drive at five o'clock that evening. He must, Mitch thought, have been returning from Helen Brierley's.

Even if she hadn't been questioned by the police, why hadn't Bettina Mayo come forward? Perhaps it was simply that she didn't want to get involved. Perhaps . . . Why not ask her? thought Mitch, irritated with herself, and she got up.

But though she tried both the management offices and the studios she couldn't find

Bettina Mayo. She did see Quentin Plunkett looking out of the window in the engineers' room and was reminded of Charlie Collins's invitation.

'Do you happen to know what the CBSO are doing on Saturday?'

'*Daphnis et Chloé*.'

'Stravinsky?'

'Ravel.'

'Ravel?'

'How can it matter to you? My dear girl, when have you even been able to tell the difference between a fart and a flugelhorn?'

'I'm pretty hot on tempo though.'

'That retread Shirley Temple's been yattering, eh?' Quentin's cheeks began to flush. 'I have never in my life played a record at the wrong speed. The trouble with our kiddo is she's mutt and jeff. Mutt and jeff.'

'Look. All I asked about was the CBSO concert. I'm not going to row with you — '

'Rather not. Hardly up to my weight, dear.'

Mitch clamped her teeth together and wheeled out.

'Stravinsky. Stravinsky indeed. Jesus. What a moron.' His jibe burned in her ears but still she did not turn.

She found Bettina in the Ladies. She was hauling up her leggings with such force that her heels left the ground. 'Nothing looks worse than wrinkles,' she said. 'Know what I mean?'

Mitch, catching a glimpse of both Bettina's posterior and her own face above it in the mirror, said, 'I don't think any amount of hauling is going to help me much.'

Bettina, satisfied that she was now wrinkle-free, took a lipstick out of her brass-studded carpet bag. 'It's not a bad little station at all. I really think I'm going to like it here. The last place was so naff. Jesus. Was it naff.'

'You're fixed up here then?'

'Could be. You never know.'

Mitch began to fiddle with her hair. 'It's a small world. I've just been talking to a friend of mine. I mentioned to him that you were doing my show while I was away. He said he saw you at the Jade Dragon. You were eating dinner with Jon Stanton just before Jon died.'

'What? Christ! He told you what? What did you say?' Her skin was sucked towards her lips which were pushing further and further from parting teeth.

Mitch felt herself stiffen. 'I said that you were seen dining with Jon Stanton on the night he died.'

'Lying bitch!' The carpet bag rose above Bettina's head.

Mitch dodged away but a brass-studded

118

edge caught her on the chin.

'Jesus. What are you trying to do to me!' Bettina shouted.

Mitch reeled as another blow caught her on the side of the head. Her spine hit the tiled wall. She sank to the floor, one leg under her, the other jammed against rows of piping.

'Turd!' Bettina threw herself by Freya who was coming in through the door.

'She hit me.' Mitch's astonished voice almost rose off the register.

'Christ, kiddo, you've really upset her,' Freya said. 'What the hell's going on? Jesus. Sometimes I think I'm running a play group . . . ' and she held out a well-muscled arm which sported three pink plastic bracelets.

'I can manage.' Mitch, sorting out her legs, was mustering as much dignity as she could. She tottered slightly as she got up.

'One has to nurture the young,' said Freya. 'Light the way. There weren't really any fisticuffs, I hope? I take it this was actually an accident? It's a very nasty cut. Shall I call Sister?

'No.' Mitch cautiously moved a finger up her chin.

'Beginning to swell,' said Freya. 'Looks like there's going to be some bruising. Still, it won't affect the voice.'

7

Mitch decided that you couldn't say it was raining. This drizzle so lacked conviction it didn't even slide down the panes of the conservatory. It fogged them slightly.

She was holed up in a cane armchair nibbling at marmalade soldiers. Her coffee cup was on the Moorish patterned floor tiles, not quite within comfortable reach, but she couldn't be bothered to pull up the occasional table.

She wasn't going in to the madhouse that morning. 'The thing is, I'm going to suss out a story in Walsall,' she'd told Shaun when she'd rung the office.

When Shaun found it all unbearable he sussed out stories in Smethwick. 'You've not packaged your needle-makers' tape,' he warned her.

'I'll do that later. I'll be in about one. Has this Bettina thing turned up?'

'No. But Freya's not starting to pay her until Monday. What do you think? Tasty, eh? Legs practically up to her fucking skull.'

'I think if you actually thought, you'd see that tasty piece has gobbled up your chance

120

to get presenter experience. She's standing in for me. You're not. Gene machines really reached the state of the art in you.'

'Oh Christ. You're really having one of your mornings, aren't you?'

'No, I'm not,' she'd told him and she'd slammed the receiver down.

But, of course, she was. Though she'd had occasional mornings like this all her life she now put them down to the menopause. She'd not yet arrived at that great divide but no doubt she was trembling on the brink. You were bound to feel awful as you revved down; Christ knew what happened when you stopped.

When she tumbled into these small black holes she usually went to the shops. She'd not the confidence to buy anything, but it comforted her to see rows of bright orange bikinis, plastic outdoor furniture manufactured for sunny days, day-glo sandals decorated with daisies, T-shirts blinking with blue birds made of sequins. They held out the tiny — almost impossibly remote — hope that somewhere beyond her horizons were rays of light. These small black holes of hers usually lasted no more than two or three hours, but when she was down one they were for ever.

Today, though, she was thinking of doing

without her fix of day-glo. She'd half a mind to see Edna Cowley, the woman the police said was the last person to see Jon Stanton alive. That she could even contemplate going while in such a mood made her realise just how much of the hunter was in her. It seemed that Madeleine Stanton, in choosing her, had understood this fundamental element in her nature better than she did herself.

She reached down for her coffee and began to review the information she was gathering. She found she could now sketch in most of Jon Stanton's last hours. None of it added up to a picture of a young man who was about to commit suicide. But Edna Cowley or Helen Brierley — another name on the growing list of people to see — might change all that. She felt it would be prudent to bypass Bettina Mayo for the moment, perhaps coming back to her after seeing Jon's heir Ann Wellesley. She had already decided to attend the lecture Ann was giving on Saturday afternoon with a view to tackling her afterwards. Let's hope she doesn't tote a carpet bag, she thought grimly.

Then there was Freya Adcock. She couldn't ignore the fact that she'd seen her at Jon's place with Bettina and that — as yet unknown — man. Just contemplating Radio Brum's programme organiser disordered her thought processes so much that she counted herself lucky to emerge clutching one positive point. The woman hadn't worn one item of her clothing when last seen.

'Sweetie, you've absolutely no idea when it comes to what makes people tick,' Digger had told her. She had to acknowledge that when it came to Freya he was quite right.

But of all of them there was only one person who obviously benefited from Jon Stanton's death and that was Ann Wellesley. No, two, she reminded herself. I mustn't forget the wandering painter. What was his name? Robin Pemberton. At some stage I'm going to have to write all this down. Try and bring a bit of method into the investigation. All I seem to be doing at the moment is lurching about between them. This morning the very thought of doing any such thing made her shrink deeper into the burrow of her chair. I will go and see Edna Cowley though, she told herself.

But another minute or two passed before she could gather the energy to get up and crawl into her rain gear. Wet weather clothing did not feature much in her wardrobe; it depressed her so much that when she went to buy it she always came out of the shop with something more cheerful. She put on a twenty-year-old riding mac — she and horses had soon parted company for good — and found a ten-year-old fedora for her head.

After rechecking the address of Edna Cowley, she adjusted the angle of the hat in the hall mirror. Turning, she saw a pair of Georgian false teeth grinning at her through the open lounge door. She must have skewed them round as she passed the television set. They reminded her that she must make an appointment with the dentist. If I don't go soon the sheer weight of muck will make my teeth drop out, she thought gloomily. I need a breast scan, too. And a smear. And I haven't emptied the hoover.

She got out of the house before any more sticks appeared to beat her.

Oh, how she hated mornings like these. When she put on the wipers in the TVR they squealed against the windscreen because there wasn't enough wet; when she turned them off her nose was practically up against the glass as she peered through something not quite definite enough to be called mist.

The flag at Warwickshire's county cricket ground was as pissed off as she was. It was so wrung out it couldn't even piddle down its pole. She decided that the root cause of her trouble was that she was too old for him. When he was forty-five she'd be sixty. When he was as old as Josh Hadley she'd be seventy.

Charlie. Charlie. What I'd give to be a few years younger. Wax isn't trickling down my candle. There's an avalanche.

And what can I do about that?

She parked her car five minutes' walk away from Templar's Rise, Freya Adcock's remarks having taught her a lesson. If I'm going to take this investigation lark seriously I'm going to have to trade in the TVR for an invisible hatchback, she thought. Some crap-wheeled Japanese job. She remained in the driver's seat. Just what did she think she was up to? Troubling inquest witnesses. Taking ten thousand pounds off a poor old lady who'd gone quite mad with grief. Demon doubt almost made her turn the key in the ignition.

But she hauled herself out of the depths of the TVR's racing driver's seat. Poseur, she mocked herself. Aren't you too old to fly about with your bum twelve inches off the tarmac? What you need is a high-backed Parker Knoll job. You're not a kid any more.

I'm too old for him.

And wrapped in a rain so inconclusive that the atmosphere it produced wasn't positive enough to merit the words wishy-washy, she trudged up to Templar's Rise.

Shaun had said that Bettina Mayo wasn't in the office so that meant she could bump into her. The thought got her brain moving again. She felt her chin. A two-inch graze ran along its length.

If I see the little monster I'll tell her Madeleine Stanton's sent me along to pick up some of Jon's things, she decided. And the car? It overheated so I left it in Queensbridge Road.

Do real detectives have to spin such yarns to justify being where they are?

She reminded herself grimly that ten thousand pounds said she was a real detective.

Just why had that monkey-booted kid lashed out? It's the truth that usually gets people hopping mad, she thought. The truth is a highly explosive commodity.

Mrs Edna Cowley lived in one of the 1930s semis perched on a bank overlooking the Victorian houses across the way. By the side of the steeply rising concrete driveway were cushions of London pride and alyssum. Saxifrage and lobelia cascaded over white rockery stones. Mitch found herself wondering if one of these stones had been used to wedge the accelerator of the Beetle. The front door had recently been given a coat of baby pink paint. There was a small round stained glass window above the letter box; a galleon sailed the seven seas. Mitch rang the bell.

Edna Cowley was a big silver-haired

woman who wore purple winged glasses which she now adjusted with floury fingers. 'What is it, dear?' A strong, sweetish waft of Devon violets enveloped Mitch.

'My name is Measham.' She thought it better to use a name very like her own; if the sin came to light later she could always claim she'd been misheard. 'The fact is, I'm due to sign a lease on the house opposite. Only I've just heard . . . they say the last tenant committed suicide. I didn't . . . one is always thinking . . . did he do it in the bedroom . . . or . . . Oh dear. I suppose I must sound so very silly.'

'Bound to play on your mind, a thing like that,' Edna Cowley said. 'But you needn't worry. He did it in the garage. Pots of money and no more than just turned twenty-five. Makes you wonder, doesn't it? You'll have to come in, dear. I must get my pie in. I'm behind myself good and proper. Put the wood in the 'ole, there's a lamb.'

As Mitch followed Mrs Cowley down the hall she thought she saw the lounge door open a crack but it sighed back into the wood again. The kitchen, opposite the front door, was no wider than the hall. A folded Formica-topped breakfast bar and a couple of stools stood against one wall. There wasn't enough space for Mitch to sit behind her as she worked, so with a velvet mule Edna Cowley pushed a stool in front of the back door. 'There you are, ducks. Not room to swing a cat. But there's only him and me.' She turned dough on to a floured board. 'I'm not kidding you. There was a real to-do. The postman found him. Glad it were 'im and not me. When my mother passed on 'er went so slack 'er false teeth popped out. The fact is, you don't want to be seeing a body. Pictures keep popping back in your head when you least expect it. Most people have enough on their plate without that. So you're thinking of taking the flat, eh?' and her look, though friendly, priced and placed her and Mitch had the impression the sum added up to only half the value she put on herself.

'Well . . . to tell you the truth, I'm having second thoughts. It's not just — though what happened is terrible, terrible — but I understand the only other tenant there is a young girl. I'm not against the young, believe me. But I've my work to go to every morning. One worries about all night parties . . . '

'Very quiet,' Mrs Cowley assured her. 'A bit odd, really. She's not there for nights on end. Fred — that's my hubby — says 'er is probably a traveller from one of these firms. That's what his reckoning is.'

'That sounds encouraging,' but Mitch still

contrived to look dubious. 'She's been living there for a year or two, has she?'

'No more than two or three months and, to tell the truth, Fred and I don't think she'll be there much longer.'

'Why's that?'

'Well, 'er and that young man who topped himself. They went out together more than once. Us seen 'em and we're not the only ones. Not by a long chalk. You take my word for it. He was sweet on her. That's at the bottom of it all. Why would 'e be taking them photos otherwise? You tell me that.'

'What photos?'

'It were no more than a few days before it happened, dear. There's this girl — what do they think they look like prancing around in them legging affairs? I ask you — well, she's out on the pavement in front of the house talking to a fellow who has rolled along in a van. I'm upstairs see, about to give the goatskin a shake out of the window, and then I see that poor chap in the top flat. He's got a camera with one of them big sausage-shaped things clamped on which make a pin as big as a pikestaff . . . Clicking away, he is.'

'Taking pictures of the girl and the man?'

'That's what I'm telling you. Click, click, ruddy well click. And it's not cheap, you know. Film.'

'Well, they couldn't have been up to much. Not on the pavement in broad daylight.'

'But it were plain to see that 'er could hardly keep 'er hands off this chap. Not that I blame her. 'E 'ad the looks and knew it, if you ask me.'

Mitch pictured the man she'd seen with Bettina and Freya in the back garden of the house. 'I like a man to have plenty of muscle,' she said. 'Plenty of beef in his shoulders. Give me a he-man any day.'

Mrs Cowley, pie aloft as she turned in a waft of Devon violets, was astonished. Mitch realised she'd been presenting herself as something of a joyless middle-aged spinster and now she was talking like a nymphomaniac. 'When I was younger,' she added hastily. 'In my heyday.'

'You can't say this one were Cary Grant,' said Mrs Cowley, trimming the edges of the pie with the bread knife. 'Didn't have much in the way of muscles, neither. But as they breed 'em now he did well enough.'

'Why did the chap in the top flat take pictures of them?'

'Spying on 'em, that's Fred's and my reckoning. Surprising what the little green-eyed monster drives a body to. In the end it were the death of the poor chap. Takes some like that. Love.'

'What did the police think?'

'To tell the truth me and Fred . . . Well, we didn't have the right of it straight away, see. Too much of a shock to add two and two. And later — what good would it do? Dead's dead and leave 'em to it. That's Fred's philosophy. 'Just tell what you saw at the inquest. Stick to that,' Fred said. And I couldn't quarrel with that.'

'You went to the inquest?'

She swelled a little. 'I were the last to see him, see. Before he did it. Saw that Beetle thing draw up in the drive just after five. 'Im gets out as sprightly as you please. I'll never forget it. You don't expect it, do you? Not in a chap about to top himself. You expect a bit of misery. I'll not go as far as tears. But not springing about like a bloody new-born lamb. Fred reckoned 'e were a throwback to the old type of Englishman. A grin and a joke and plenty of stiff upper lip. But have you seen one around like that lately? Bottoms hanging out of jeans more like. That's your Englishman these days. Anyway, we reckon Miss Tricky Knickers will be leaving as soon as maybe what with her old boyfriend finishing himself off a few yard from 'er back door. She won't want the reminder, will she? Not if she's made of flesh and blood like the rest of us.'

131

'Where was she the night it happened? Was she there?'

'Fred and I reckon she must have been away. I mean, she weren't called as a witness nor nothing. We reckon she was doing that travelling or whatever it is.'

Not travelling, thought Mitch, so what can she be up to? A boyfriend? She wanted to ask for a description of the van but at first couldn't think of a way without blowing her cover story. She came up with: 'Funnily enough there was a van outside when I first came to see the flat. Such a handsome chap in the driving seat. Probably the current boyfriend? A white van with some lettering on . . . '

Edna Cowley was taking a critical look at the edging on the pie. 'This were green, dear. But not a posh green like Harrods or the BBC.' She bent to put her pie in the oven. 'You'll have to shift your carcass. Us needs to get at the sink.'

'I must be going. I'll take one more look at the flat but . . . '

'Wouldn't do for me neither.' The two women's buttocks clashed as they moved.

They untangled and when Mrs Cowley escorted her back down the hall she told her, 'You do put me in mind of someone. First I thought it were the wife of our vicar but it's that woman who used to be on the telly. The one who got after the time-share cheats and I don't know what all. Now that's going back a fair bit. That's when our Fred was still working at Longbridge. She were taller, of course. Younger. But she had ever such a nice voice too.' She opened the front door and looked at the house across the way. 'Won't suit, you know. Not for someone like you and me. Suicide's never nice.'

'I might as well take another look, seeing I'm here,' said Mitch. 'But I'm afraid you're right . . . ' moving nimbly to one side to avoid clashing with Mrs Cowley again.

She'd almost reached the other side of the road when, hypnotised by eyes she couldn't see, she turned round. She expected Mrs Cowley to be standing in her front door but saw instead an old man looking down on her from the lounge window. His skull seemed to have shrunk; a flared skirt of flesh tumbled round it.

Of course, Mrs Cowley had talked about Fred but she'd supposed he'd been off out somewhere. And then she remembered the door sighing towards the wood.

Watched, the watcher remained unmoving. Feeling disconcerted, Mitch turned and walked down to the front door. She was glad to see no car in the drive. She didn't feel up

133

to confronting Bettina Mayo. She tried not to dwell on the thought of a monkey-booted foot sinking into her stomach. When it came to physical pain she had a yellow streak where her spine should be.

Behind the front door she found a litter of post. Most of it was for Bettina. It looks as though she's not been here since Sunday, Mitch thought. She stood still, listening; the quiet was broken by the noise of birds and, somewhere in the house, a fridge motor turned itself on. She had to consciously stop herself from creeping up to Jon's top-floor flat.

She searched it more thoroughly this time. She did find some expensive Japanese camera equipment but there was no trace of the photographs Mrs Cowley said she'd seen Jon take. She did find a more recent picture of Jon, wearing the cords she'd often seen him in, bright red laces tying up brown suede shoes. With him was a smoothly handsome young thruster, straight hair sleeked down, in a boxy Italian jacket cut to hang so loose it practically fell off. She took the photograph of the windsurfer off the bookshelf and compared it. Jon's companion probably was the surfer, but he was too far from the camera for her to be absolutely sure.

Could this be the fellow Mrs Cowley had

seen with Bettina? He is certainly very handsome, thought Mitch. But that still left the question — why had Jon taken the photographs?

She shook her head and dropped the picture in her bag. It did cross her mind that while she was here she could try a bit of breaking and entering and snoop round Bettina's flat. She liked to think it was the time factor which deterred her and not the kid's undoubted muscular superiority.

When she got back in her car she realised, relieved, that her gloom had lifted. Each time it happened she felt like a jinni who had escaped from an exceedingly murky bottle.

She noticed that Shaun was all weather eye when she walked back into the production office. He began to relax back into his chair. 'Firing on all cylinders again?'

Mitch was airily dismissive. 'As you get older you naturally hear the gentle flap of tempus fugiting. Sometimes the flap becomes such a roar it blows your bloody ears off.'

'All right now, though.'

'All right now.'

'OK, chief. Here's the score. I've packaged the post office piece, done the cues, typed a menu. This goodie good boy is the best. And — pin your ears back — I no longer give a fuck for girls with legs up to their eyebrows.

I'm into little ladies with enough crackling on their pork to pop your braces.'

'What chief could ask for more?'

'Is it true? Quentin Plunkett's just told me Bettina whacked you with her handbag?'

'Can you think of any good reason why Ms Mayo would want to do that?'

8

The red transmission light was on.

'And coming up next week . . . One child in seven leaves school functionally illiterate. Are we happy with that figure? What if that child looks like being *your* child? What can we, as parents, do? In the studios will be teachers, school inspectors, councillors, parents . . . and at the end of a phone we hope you'll be there with your comments. Plus the EC ban on crisps, the man who'll spend the next three months up an oak tree and cricketer Chris Coombs — our sporting memory . . .'

Mitch faded up the music. 'Presenting this and much, much more for the next two weeks will be Radio Brum newcomer Bettina Mayo. I know you'll give her a warm Midlands welcome. I'll be back in July for more 'City Talk' . . . '

After a five-second pause, Mitch banged in the trail for the rest of Friday night's programmes, broke for the signature tune and then played the trail Bettina had made to introduce herself. More signature tune filled the five seconds left to the seven o'clock news bulletin. The transmission light went out.

Shaun stopped chatting to the station assistant in the ops room long enough to put his thumb up. Mitch, stretching, observed him through a broad pane of studio glass. Does that kid ever stop hustling skirt? she wondered. Already her adrenalin high was seeping away. Her back ached a little. That man from the canal society had turned out to be a waste of time, she was thinking. The weight loss feature worked out well, though. She yawned, clasped her hands behind her head and leaned back.

'I must be off my head,' she told Shaun, who had come into the studio to round up tapes and records.

He was saying, 'The diet phone-in was magic . . . ' He paused. 'Off your head?'

'Why did I arrange to go out to Lichfield? I'm whacked. Cream crackered.' She yawned again.

'You're always zonked after a show. Bound to be when you think about it. Coming out of the air and landing back in reality. You'll be all right, kiddo. Give it five minutes.'

'Don't you start calling me kiddo, for God's sake. Freya's more than bad enough.'

Shaun had now dropped the debris of the show into a wire shopping basket which had started out life in a supermarket. 'That's the trouble with working on a radio station. Your English goes to pot.'

Mitch yawned again. 'Right on, honeypot. Are my bones creaking?' she asked, concerned, as she got up.

'Only a bit.'

She chucked an empty polystyrene coffee cup at him.

Ten minutes later, heading down the A38 towards Lichfield, she began to think about the coming meeting with Madeleine Stanton. She'd already received and banked Mrs Stanton's five thousand pounds so all her thoughts were serious.

She reached Lichfield just before eight and parked in the drive at Ashmole House. As she locked the car, wind suddenly tumbled hair into her eyes. She looked up. Cloud was building behind the chill easterly which had sprung up. A shivering azalea salted the narrow strip of lawn with falling blossom.

The front door opened before she reached it. Canned laughter and a faint smell of fried onions blew around Cathy's stolid figure. 'I'll take you now,' she told Mitch. 'No need for her to be there. She's not half so blinking brave as she thinks she is. I'm real glad I've caught you.'

'Take me where?'

'You'll want to see the car, won't you? It's

in the coach house. Can hardly bear to look at it myself. Mind that rose. Real vicious bugger, that one.'

An almost new VW Polo stood a few feet away from the scarred sliding doors of the two-storey coach house. 'Guttering's kaput,' Cathy said. 'And it's not as though she hasn't got the money. The old can't be bothered, you know. They don't want the hassle.' She rolled back one door over the other and switched on the light. The beam motored down the drive, illuminating the side of the house and the shrubbery on the other side of the gravel. The noise of wind in branches grew. A small piece of broken twig, born on the wings of two new leaves, sailed over their heads and through the doorway. 'Well, there you are then, ducks. I'll leave you to it, if you don't mind. When you've done just shut the door and come in by the kitchen. It'll save my legs.'

Mitch nodded and went into the coach house. Jon's Beetle was parked in the front half of the building, which rose to distant rafters and was quite capable of housing a fair-sized carriage. The rear had a second storey which appeared to have been a hay loft with stabling beneath. She didn't expect to find anything, but she opened the driver's door and fumbled for the boot release knob.

She looked into the boot. It contained a jack, an old pair of track shoes, a large oily rag, a Tesco bag with a T-shirt in it, a tin of baked beans and the telephoto lens of a camera. No camera, no film, nothing else.

Mitch stepped back so she could get a better view of the collection. It's all so woolly, she found herself thinking. She was aware of a growing sense of frustration. I can't seem to focus down. Well, it's hardly to be wondered at. I've been getting a show out every day this week. I've had no time to concentrate on anything else.

But it wasn't that. Not really. It wasn't even that she didn't know what pieces of evidence she was looking for, as she had in the consumer investigations she'd carried out. It's something much more fundamental, she realised. I can't believe someone killed Jon Stanton. I can't believe there is any evidence to find. That's why it all feels so hopelessly woolly. I've embarked on a wild-goose chase, that's what I've done.

Why on earth did I decide to get involved? Money, she thought. But not just that. It's the picture of those two women standing on the gravel drive holding hands and looking so . . . so . . . lost.

What am I going to do?

She groaned.

I'll give it one week, she decided. One week of concentrated work and if I come up with nothing I'll return Mrs Stanton's cash to her and get the hell out from under.

She banged the boot shut and quickly went through the interior of the car. There were toffee papers, parking tickets and an old railway timetable. She saw the stain on the passenger seat. Her heart skipped out of rhythm. The whisky bottle, she thought. It must have tipped over. For a moment she saw Jon's fingers begin to relax in death, the bottle starting to slide.

Why did he do it?

Perhaps if she found that out she would at least have accomplished something.

It was still light when she shut the coach house door though looming banks of cloud were darkening the garden. Apple tree branches squealed as growing wood rubbed together. In the distance a dog howled. Mitch hurried across the gravel to the kitchen door. A hail of canned laughter hit her as she closed it behind her. Cathy was sitting knitting and watching the television on the big dresser.

'Oh, doesn't she look good,' the games host was saying. 'Face me. Face me if you will. It's time to go for the twenty stars and five bars. Take your time. Take your time, dear . . . Are you married at all?' 'She's after a microwave,' said Cathy. 'Can't care for them myself. Seen all you want, ducks? Maddy's in the drawing-room. First left down the hall.' Her eyes had strayed back to the television. Stitches were whirring off her short cable pin.

Mrs Stanton was sitting by a log fire, a glass of whisky in one hand and a tipped cigarette in the other. The brindled cat was in her lap, snorting a little in its sleep. 'Do have something. Whisky. Gin. Sherry . . . '

'It had better be a very thin gin,' said Mitch. 'I'm driving.'

'Do you mind mixing it yourself? Puss will be so annoyed if I disturb him.'

'Sure.'

'Well. How are things going?'

As she mixed her drink Mitch began to tell the old lady what she had found out so far. She felt a twinge of guilt when Mrs Stanton said, 'I knew you were right for the job.'

'Look, please don't expect . . . Well, I mean . . . '

'Tush. Come nearer the fire, my dear. Warm your toots. The temperature must have dropped ten degrees this evening.'

Mitch settled down in a shabby chintz-covered armchair. She refused a cigarette. 'I don't suppose you've come across the photographs Jon took of Bettina and this man?'

'I'm afraid not.'

'I suppose it's just possible they are at a printer's waiting to be collected.' Mitch took a photograph out of her bag. 'I found this at the flat. And this chap with Jon is certainly good-looking. Who is it?'

'Can you get my specs for me? On the mantelpiece. And you'd better switch the lamp on.'

Mitch gave the old woman her spectacles. In the firelight Madeleine Stanton's skin appeared almost translucent, as though the flesh beneath was melting away. 'It's Robin Pemberton. You know. He's the lad I told you about, Jon's artist friend. The one who sometimes uses Jon's house on Gozo. The picture was taken while he was over here. Let's see . . . ' She took off her glasses and sucked the end. 'That would be about Easter time. Yes. That's right. Jon brought him to tea. Robin was off the next day, intending to spend a few weeks in France before going back to Gozo. Or was he coming straight back to England? I don't think he'd decided.'

'And as far as you know Robin is still in France and doesn't yet know of Jon's death?'

'That's right. Absolutely. And even if Robin wasn't in France — even if the chap were in Birmingham seeing this Bettina — why should Jon take pictures of them together?'

'It has been suggested to me that Jon was a jealous lover.'

'What? My dear girl. That's laughable. Really. Even if Bettina was his girlfriend — and I'm pretty sure he didn't have a girlfriend at the time he died — Jon was a lovely, easygoing chap. Ask anyone. Well, you knew him, didn't you?'

'Only slightly. But I have to say I found nothing intense or obsessive about him. He struck me, too, as a happy-go-lucky type.'

'Jon's last girl was called Karen and that finished just after Christmas. We can be pretty sure of that. If he took pictures of this Bettina it certainly wasn't because he was jealous. And even if he were, why should he do that?'

'Yes. I agree. It may make sense to the Cowleys but it doesn't seem plausible to me. And then there's the fact that he apparently went out with the girl on the night he died.'

'Do you think she had a hand in whatever happened?'

'But why would she want Jon dead? What motive could she have? I'm going to see Ann Wellesley tomorrow. At least there's a motive there. Is there anything more you can tell me about her?'

'As I told you, I'm afraid we never hit it off. It isn't that she's a feminist or involved in this Green for Good movement. I find her so

. . . so . . . self-righteous. Oh dear. I shouldn't say that. The fact is that when that women's press of hers started to get into financial difficulties I resented the fact that she had the nerve to expect me to get her out of them. Why should I? I know she approached Jon too but at that time his money was still in trust. He couldn't help her and I packed her off with a flea in her ear. If you want the truth, she really got my back up. One simply can't preach to someone as old as I am. In the first place one has heard it all before. And in the second place one isn't foolish enough to believe a word of it.'

'What happened after that?'

'She and Jon kept in touch but she kept her distance as far as I was concerned.'

'When did Jon come into his money?'

'April this year.'

'Did he supply her with any funds?'

'I've no idea. It was then very much *not* my business.'

'She would know she was the major heir?'

'Oh yes. But really my dear . . . I mean, I admit it, I don't like the girl. But that hardly makes her a murderer. I can't believe it.'

'Look, I have to weigh up all the possibilities. Do you have her address? And I'd like Helen Brierley's address too. She saw Jon just a few hours before he died.'

'Oh, but I'm sure Helen would have told me if — '

'Still, I must see her. Just in case . . . ' Then, looking at the old woman's face: 'You're not sorry you started all this?'

'No. It was you mentioning all possibilities . . . Do you remember me telling you that Robin Pemberton was a civil servant before he chucked it all in to become an artist? Well, I can't be sure — I certainly can't swear to it — but I was always under the impression he did something hush-hush. But, of course, Jon may have been pulling my leg. He loved a joke. He liked practical jokes, too. Cushions which burped, that sort of thing. He was a tease.'

'My God, surely we can't be involved in anything the security forces have an interest in.'

'I should think it highly unlikely. Jon was completely apolitical. But you did say — '

'I know . . . and I do think we have to look at all the possibilities.'

'Thank you for not saying it.'

'Saying what?'

'That the likeliest possibility — no, the probability — is that Jon killed himself. I really do assure you, Miss Mitchell, that I'm aware of that. You needn't be tactful with me.'

'All we can do is keep on asking questions

until we hopefully come up with some answers.'

'Precisely.'

But the next day she didn't immediately turn her attention to the investigation. It'll just have to wait, she told herself as she cleared her breakfast pots. I've got to get cracking. She'd gone to Lichfield straight after presenting her show 'City Talk' so she'd be free on Saturday morning to catch up with her housework and shopping. As she was now on holiday, she could have done it all later but she was going to invite Charlie Collins back to the house after the CBSO concert.

'Charlie is my darling, my darling . . . ' she found herself humming as she hoovered the lounge. 'Charlie. Charlie Collins.' She simply liked to conjure his name. But I can't have fallen in love with a smart-arsed chancer. Can I? No. I can't be serious about a man fifteen years younger than myself.

Don't be serious, siren voices sang. Enjoy yourself.

But what happens if he leaves me? Common sense, outraged, would be heard.

That's tomorrow. Not today.

'Charlie, Charlie Collins . . . '

She gave up on herself.

There was one thing about the advent of

Charlie. Without difficulty she limited herself to two crispbreads and cottage cheese for lunch. If she kept this up, by the time he ran out on her she'd be in pretty good shape.

It wasn't until she got into her car after lunch that she managed to haul her attention back to Ann Wellesley. Her lecture — 'S.O.S. — Save Our Shakeshaft' — was being held at the Mechanics Hall near Digbeth Coach Station.

Heavy overnight rain had cleared but intermittent showers spiked the edges of wind gusting across the city. Though it was Saturday afternoon, traffic wasn't heavy. She drove along Smallbrook Queensway into St Martin's Circus, skirting the Bull Ring and the church as she made her way downhill to Digbeth. The Mechanics Hall was at the back of High Street, a red-brick four-storey neo-Gothic building. It was squashed between a motor repair shop and a art deco cinema which had been turned into a Price Rite store.

She parked her car on a patch of wasteland a street away. A hoarding on the side of a bottling plant told her all about a bank which liked to say yes — though her own experience with the bank in question had not proved so positive. She skipped over a puddle and let the scudding wind push her over couch grass and cigarette packets to the scarred pavement. As she turned the street corner she saw a knot of people drifting up the steps of the institute. She glanced at her watch, saw she was a little late, and hurried after them into the august gloom the Victorians were so good at creating in their buildings. She spotted Woody lounging against a tea-coloured tiled dado near the doors to the hall.

'What on earth are you doing here?'

'I could say the same, poppet. Hardly your kind of afternoon, I'd have thought. Actually, I'm earning a bob or two. The news editor rang me this morning and asked if I'd cover the meeting for them. They've decided to link up with the Greenies and try to save the Shakeshaft Nature Reserve.'

'So Ann's lobbying paid off?'

'Looks like it.'

'Why isn't one of the staff men doing it?'

'Short-handed. My guess is they've made so many people redundant they've practically run out of bodies. The trouble is that firing people gets to be addictive. And people like to follow fashion, of course. There're plenty of Brownie points in rationalising — leaner, fitter . . . all the rest of the crap words. Still, if it puts the jam on my bread I'm not complaining.'

Mitch began to shiver. 'Christ. It's cold in here.'

'The Victorians wore more clothing than we did. And what are you doing here? Still on the Stanton trail?'

'Thought I might take a look-see — ' Suddenly she saw the man who had been in the back garden with Freya and Bettina. 'Who's that?'

'Oh, him. Lygo Pim. He does some of the press liaison work for Green for Good. You know the sort. A handshake like a steam shovel.'

'Doesn't at all sound like Freya's type,' Mitch murmured to herself.

'Are you talking about that woman who makes Medusa look like a big girl's blouse?' Woody had had one or two run-ins with Freya.

'She's in line for the manager's job.'

'Seriously?'

'Seriously.'

'I'd retire, poppet. Leave the buggers to it.'

'I need the money.'

People were now pushing their way into the hall. 'Oh Lord,' moaned Woody. 'Here comes our *mauvais quart d'heure*. At least I've got the Wellesley woman's speech. I don't have to sod about with shorthand.'

'Why stay, then?'

151

'When you don't stay the speaker gets shot, the hall burns down, the audience riots or Prince Charles drops in to say what naff buildings Birmingham has. That's been my experience. Besides, if I don't get out of the house for a while I'll garrotte the wife.'

'And you're advising me to retire!'

'You're not married.'

The hall made Mitch think she was inside a Nonconformist church. It was with some surprise that she realised the three stained glass windows at the west end depicted men wielding spanners, not crosses. The platform was under these windows. Chairs stood behind three deal tables which had been pushed together. In front of them stood a lectern pinned with a poster showing a round green earth apparently sailing in water. Mitch was immediately reminded of the key tab she'd found in the garage at Templar's Rise.

A stocky woman — Mitch saw her as a handy full back in a hockey team — came on the stage and began to arrange notes on the lectern. Her curly hair was disconcertingly like Jon Stanton's though she resembled him in no other way. When she turned to smile at the others filing on to the platform she was transformed into a mischievous school kid. A latecomer emerged from a side door to join them. Freya Adcock, in the sailor outfit she'd worn to Jon's funeral, a red, white and blue bow in her hair, was trotting across the boards in the kind of one-bar sandals mums buy for their tiny tots, only her feet must have been size seven. Very white cotton socks were folded over her ankles. She joined the others sitting at the extended table.

'Looks like Freya's joined the merry band of goodie Greenies,' murmured Woody.

'She's an admirer of Ann Wellesley,' said Mitch.

'Really?' Woody's eyebrows kept on rising.

'Don't even think it.'

'No. You're right. AC-DC is too simple. I shouldn't think even the Chinese alphabet would cover your programme organiser.'

The hum in the hall subsided. Ann Wellesley turned out to be a very able speaker. Good timing, Mitch noted, knew how to fill the telling silence with an even more telling gesture and — very unusual in a woman in Mitch's experience — lightened her speech with well-delivered jokes. She even silenced Woody's cynical *sotto voce* asides.

Mitch began to look surreptitiously around her for Lygo Pim. He was standing near the platform in a side aisle, hard and heavy, but built more like a sprinter than a weight-lifter. It was a moment before she realised he was looking at her. There was a cast in his left eye;

light caught the iris of one, but not the other. She gazed back at the platform.

All the Greenies sitting behind Ann, except Freya, were moving about a little; she, like an infant Voltaire, rested a chin on praying hands and absorbed.

Suddenly Mitch saw Bettina Mayo striding down the side aisle towards Lygo Pim. She was hefting a bag which appeared to be full of leaflets. Mitch had planned to tackle Ann Wellesley after the meeting, introducing herself as the presenter of 'City Talk' and discussing the possibility of an on-air interview about the group's campaign. From there she'd hoped to side-track into inquiries about Jon. She'd not expected either Freya or Bettina Mayo to turn up. With them present she saw too many difficulties and decided to abort. I'll just have to bowl along to the Wellesley woman's address, she decided as she got up.

'You going, poppet?'

'I'll probably ring you later,' she said. She became aware of one or two heads turning as she walked back along the central aisle. One was oriental. She felt sure of that. But when she looked again she saw only a dim sea of white faces.

It was raining when she reached the street. Shielding her head with her patent leather

154

handbag, she made a dash for her car.

When she got back home she ran a bath. The phone rang twice. She cursed herself for not having put on the answering machine, but she didn't get out of the water to answer it. When it rang again, just before teatime, she was at the bottom of the garden cutting delphiniums. By the time she got back to the house the phone was silent.

It was, after all, Stravinsky. Quentin Plunkett had been wrong. The CBSO were performing the complete ballet score for *The Firebird* of 1910. The evening surpassed her expectations. Wrapped in the designer liner atmosphere of Birmingham's Symphony Hall, she and Charlie watched Simon Rattle and his orchestra take their places. As the notes began to form, the acoustic strengths of the new hall began to make themselves felt. The explosive chords of the Infernal Dance propelled them both out of their seats. Later, by her log effect fire — to her chagrin it had made the top ten in the *Daily Mail's* Good Guide to Bad Taste — they ate gentlemen's relish off butter puffs and drank *vinho verde*.

They took their time about undressing because they were stuffing each other with morsels of Walker's crisps as they did so.

Towards dawn, alone again in her bed, she fell asleep with a smile as big as Australia on her face. Down under, the billy can still threw up an occasional bubble. The camp fire burned on in her dreams, only now flesh was hung from the tripod of sticks. She smacked her lips as she smelled the goose that was being cooked.

God. She was so hungry.

9

Hamstall Ridware, a hamlet west of the village of Yoxall, clustered near water meadows in the fertile farmlands of south Staffordshire. There was a church — a rosy brick manor house with a fine range of outbuildings — now a craft centre — a pub, cottages and strings of semi-detached houses. Mitch, driving into it through squalls of blustery rain, wondered why Helen Brierley had chosen to bury herself in such a place. Some women, she knew, found the process of divorce shaming. Had the former wife of Britain's Chancellor deliberately cut herself off from her metropolitan friends?

A big-eared ginger dog, a baby pheasant hanging from the side of its soft lips, trotted across the road just in front of her. Her body lurched into the steering wheel as she slammed on the brakes. 'Good God!' she yelled. The dog turned its head in her direction, gently wafted its prey to and fro, and then moved on. A rain-beaded ball of down danced over its tail. Trusses of budding hawthorn parted on the other side of the road and the dog disappeared.

I don't know why people go on about the country, Mitch thought. It's appalling. She drew up on the opposite side of the road to Badger Cottage. As she got out of the TVR she surveyed Helen Brierley's home with a jaundiced eye. It was a seventeenth-century cruck-framed building of soft magenta brick, set back about three feet from the tarmac pavement. On each side of the front porch massed bluebells and primroses were fading in their cramped beds. Foxgloves, not yet in flower, grew against the walls. They were almost as high as the front door. Mitch skipped over running puddles, one hand on her skirt, anchoring a rebellious hemline. A splatter of rain tingled against her cheeks.

'So you've found me.' Helen Brierley, in an Aran sweater and flowered cotton baggies, appeared on the doorstep, an empty milk bottle in her hand.

'It is off the beaten track.'

'Well, you'd better come in,' she said, bending to put the milk bottle on the step. 'It feels so jolly cold after all that sunshine earlier in the month. I've lit a fire. Hang it all, I thought. But one can never be sure about the weather. Spring can be so treacherous, my dear. I'll get us some coffee? Yes?'

'Thank you.'

The room Mitch was shown into was

oak-panelled, the atmosphere slightly hazed with wood smoke. A copper bowl of feverfew, the daisy-like flowers already beginning to wilt, sat on the window sill next to a pile of books. More books were heaped on a tripod table near the fire burning in the inglenook. A witch bowl, hanging from one of the beams, blazed with reflected light.

Mitch knelt on a hand-knotted rag rug and extended her hands towards the warmth. She turned as Helen Brierley came in with a tray. 'I'm sorry to disturb your Sunday morning.'

'I'm afraid you'll find you've had a wasted journey. It's as I told you on the phone. Just as I said, my dear, Jon turned up with this plant. A palm for my birthday. He was so very nice, you know.'

'I know. How did he seem to you that day? I mean — '

'I know what you mean. He was cheerful. When I heard he'd committed suicide that night — or was it early morning? — I simply couldn't believe it.'

'Do you believe it now?'

'Of course I do. One never quite knows what to make of people. They can be so jolly devious. You think you know everything about them and then . . . Or do I miss the signs? Those tiny clues?' She shook her head. 'But I certainly don't believe Jon was . . . you know

159

. . . Great heavens above! I don't believe that for a moment. Not that I think it wrong of Maddy to employ you, my dear. You mustn't run away with that idea. It could help her get through a very sticky period . . . something to turn her mind away from . . . well . . . and I can't help feeling it might ease things for her a little if you find out why he did such a dreadful thing. There must be a reason. I mean, the poor boy wasn't potty or anything so . . . Well, there's got to be an explanation, hasn't there?'

'I haven't yet come across a hint of what it might be.'

'I'm afraid I can't be of any help at all. I did tell you when you phoned.'

'What time did Jon get here that day?'

'He arrived about half-past three and left an hour later. He'd a packet to send off and wanted to get to a post office before closing time.'

'Did you see the packet? Did he say who it was for?'

'Robin. Robin Pemberton. He was laughing about it. But I didn't see the packet. He must have left it in his car. 'Robin's in for a real surprise.' That's what he said, And he laughed. I assumed it was some sort of practical joke. Jon was very fond of that sort of thing. Whoopee cushions. Bad smells. Axes whose blades groaned horribly. One has to admit that side of his nature could be very wearing.'

'Would he have sent a joke package to a friend shortly before killing himself?'

'I've jolly well got past being amazed by what people do, Miss Mitchell. One simply just plods on. Much the best thing. Don't you think?'

'Don't you have to try and understand?'

'To understand all is to forgive all? That's only a good philosophy for door mats. And, of course, the truth is that I don't know what was in the packet. I'm only telling you what I assumed at the time. You'll have to ask Robin Pemberton. I would judge he's your best bet anyway. If Jon had troubles that is who he would turn to. They were best friends.'

'No one seems to know quite where he is. The plant Jon gave you . . . '

'It's in the kitchen. Palms don't seem to go with beams and inglenooks. Come and take a look.'

'No, no. I must be going. I've taken up too much of your time already.'

'Might as well see it now you're here.' She put down her coffee cup. 'I've always hankered after living in a cottage, you know. Somewhere really nice and quiet. My husband's taste — my ex-husband, I should

161

say — his taste ran along much more grandiose lines. He'll tell you himself, 'I'm a bit of a showman.' Here we are.'

Mitch followed her into an L-shaped kitchen. The plant stood on a ceramic floor at the dining end, its fronds almost filling one half of a french window.

'Healthy-looking brute, isn't it?' Helen Brierley said. 'One really ought to repot it. There's not enough drainage. The crocks at the bottom of the pot must be too tightly packed. But one hardly likes to disturb it while it is doing so well.'

'It's a beauty,' said Mitch.

'Jon's friend Robin is very keen on plants. He taught Jon a thing or two. No. Through there, my dear . . . ' and she led Mitch back to the front door. A large marmalade cat sat beside the milk bottle on the top step. Mitch looked down into its sphinx-like eyes and saw, as she always did when she looked into the eyes of a cat, a chilling glimpse of the infinite. The cat got up, stretched itself, and then strolled past her into Badger Cottage.

As she drove back to Birmingham, Mitch reviewed her meeting with Helen Brierley. For Jon to have made a special trip out to her with a birthday gift surely meant that they were on very good terms. Could a would-be suicide conceal his intentions from a friend who presumably knew him well? Why had he apparently gone about his business as usual? Why hadn't he just sat at home and waited for the middle of the night, when he would know he would be able to carry out his plans without being interrupted?

Am I missing something obvious?

Mitch went back over all the information she'd received. How did it stack up? A cheerful young broadcaster, researching programme ideas, visits Tommy Hung, then takes a birthday gift to his godmother Helen Brierley, posts a packet to a friend and then goes out to a Chinese restaurant with another friend where they are seen laughing and joking. He then kills himself.

Likely?

Mitch shook her head.

But she found she still didn't believe she was looking at murder. She heard the telephone buzzing as she opened her front door. She dropped her bag and hurried into the kitchen.

'Mitch! At last. I was getting absolutely desperate. I simply couldn't get hold of you. Tried most of yesterday and this morning. My dear, yesterday lunchtime Jon's friend Robin Pemberton rang from Agay. That's a small coastal resort in the south of France. Hello. Are you there?'

'Yes. Just a little out of breath. I've only just come in.'

'When he's away on longish painting trips a woman friend of his in Gozo sees to his affairs. Opens his mail, pays the water and electricity bills. He called her when he touched base in Agay and she told him of Jon's death. He rang me immediately. He can't seem to believe it.' The word 'believe' detached itself from the others and shook. It was a moment before she went on. 'The girl told him that in his post were some photos. Quite big ones of a man and a woman.'

'So Jon sent the pictures to Robin. They must have been in the packet he was posting on the afternoon before his death . . .' and she told Mrs Stanton of her visit to Helen Brierley.

'She's never mentioned that to me.'

'Well, she probably didn't think it important.'

'Look, we want you to go out to Gozo. Robin's going straight back out there. He arrives on Monday. Can you manage the trip?'

'Of course,' said Mitch. 'We don't just need to see the pictures, do we? We need to talk to Robin as well.'

'I don't know how you're going to take this . . . but we've already booked you out on a flight to Malta from East Midlands.'

'That's fine. That's good. When do I go?'

'That's it . . . I mean, the flight leaves East Midlands at nine tonight. I've arranged for a taxi to meet you at Luqa Airport and take you down to the ferry point. A launch will take you to Gozo — to the resort of Xlendi. I've booked you in at the Ggantija. You've got Robin's Gharb address.'

'My God. We could do with your organisational skills when we set up our outside broadcasts.'

'One likes to get cracking. Ring before you set off, won't you?'

She promised. She'd had her lunch and half packed her case when she realised she'd no more than twenty pounds on her. For short periods Mitch had been the proud owner of PIN numbers, but the latest — noted in last year's diary — had been inadvertently binned when she'd had a clear-out and she'd not yet got the bank to give her the number again. That'll teach me, she told herself, thinking longingly of all those cash points filled with notes.

What am I going to do?

She ran through an inventory of broadcasters. But would any of them have a wad of ready money available? Mrs Stanton, then? She shook her head. Who in their right mind kept a large amount of cash at home these days? Josh Hadley. Like most dealers, he always kept a float. But what if the frightful Miss Boobs Bimbo answers the phone? Mitch, who was a reasonably fair-minded woman, scolded herself. How did she know the kid was frightful? She'd barely spoken to her. She did know she was more than just a rocket-launching pad. She had brains, too. Oh God. Life was so bloody unfair. What chance did a fifty-year-old have if girls in their twenties not only packed nuclear capabilities but were eggheads too? Call it a day, honeypot.

But Mitch knew she'd be in there still pitching when she was a ninety-year-old powered only by the electric motor in her wheelchair. And anyway, Charlie doesn't think I'm too old, she told herself. Charlie doesn't think that at all. Bless him. She felt herself going all dreamy and pulled herself up abruptly. No time for that. She rang Josh Hadley's number.

'Yes?' Josh barked.

'Have you got two or three hundred pounds in cash?'

'Mitch? What the hell have you been up to?'

She told him, organising the details of her story with all the skill of a woman who had done her duty as a bulletins editor in radio and television newsrooms.

'Private investigators get seventeen pounds an hour for serving court injunctions on little farts whose cover has been blown. They do not go gallivanting off to Malta on wild-goose chases. Let's bloody well hope it *is* a wild-goose chase. Otherwise you could get yourself into a very dangerous situation. You could land up in the Med with a rock round your ankle. Are you out of your mind?'

Mitch counted to five. It wasn't long enough. She upped it to ten. Then she said, 'Are you going to lend me the cash or not?'

'Oh Christ . . . ' and then he said, 'I suppose you'll go anyway. I'll be right round.'

She'd only just put the receiver down when the phone rang again. Charlie? Her heart rip-rapped into her skull.

'Hello, kiddo. I was very surprised to see you at our Green for Good rally on Saturday. I take it your American trip fell through?'

'Good heavens. Freya. Yes. I'm afraid it did.'

'People are so unreliable. That's what I find. Are you thinking of joining the cause? Becoming a Green for Good bod?'

'Well, I wouldn't go as far as — '

'Someone's got to do something about this planet, kiddo. Wouldn't you say? Might as well be me and you. Even if it means putting up with ego trippers like Quentin.'

'He's a member?'

'I thought I'd told you. I thought you knew. But, really, one hardly notices the little prick. Anyway, it's his wife, not him, who is the big Green. Marjorie's chairman.'

'What does Ann Wellesley do, then?'

'President, I think. It hardly matters what she's called. She's the guts of the organisation. Very committed. One does so admire women like that.'

'Yes. I remember you saying.'

'I mean, when one really thinks . . . Here we are bumbling along shitting on each other and there she is, kiddo. Eye on the greater good. Just striding over us pygmies. If only there were more like her.'

'I suppose so,' said Mitch, and then was silent, waiting for Freya to tell her why she'd rung.

'Actually, I wondered if you could make dinner on Friday night. At my place.'

'Dinner? I'm flying to Malta this evening . . . but I should be back in time . . . '

'Little hol?'

'I'm running an errand for Mrs Stanton. Jon's grandmother.'

'I saw you talking to her at the funeral. I didn't know until then you were acquainted.

168

You do get around, Mitch. Of course, that's what a broadcaster is. His contacts.'

Mitch, transformed into a quasi-male and only rendered effective by people she knew, wondered if she could possibly cope at any dinner party given by Freya. 'Who else will be there? I mean, on Friday?'

'Just you and me, kiddo. I'm going to have a crack at some fish.'

What is the woman up to, Mitch wondered as she put the phone down. Is she acting as recruitment officer for Green for Good? Has she somehow got infected by Ann Wellesley's enthusiasm for improving the lot of humanity? Are broadcasters now only going to be fired after she's fattened them up? The door bell put an end to her alarming speculations.

Josh Hadley, rain beading his hair and staining the shoulders of his leather jacket, towered above her although he was standing on the bottom step. She wondered, as she had often before, if her attitudes would be different if she had not spent the whole of her life looking up to almost every other human being. 'I'll put the coffee on,' she said, leading him down the hall.

'I don't suppose you'll change your mind about this crackpot expedition of yours?'

'No.'

'When you say no it has a brick wall quality

about it that no one else achieves.'

'Rubbish. You're just as good at it. Look at your hair : . .'

Josh's hair, tied back in a black rubber band, had caused more than one row between them. She'd wanted him to have it cut. 'It makes you look like a has-been fairground attendant,' she'd complained.

'I like it,' he'd told her. 'It's me.'

'You're not really an old reprobate.'

'Just watch me.'

Not three months later he'd sloped out of her bed and jumped into the sheets with the brainy bimbo.

Now he took the cash out of the inside pocket of his jacket and put it on the breakfast bar. She perked the coffee and then wrote him a cheque. He viewed it with such suspicion that she said, 'It won't bounce.'

His eyebrows rose.

'I've never written a cheque that's bounced.'

His eyebrows climbed higher.

'Hardly ever. Anyway, I'm in funds at the moment. Remember? You asked if I'd like to take a look at that black lacquer stuff you've got.'

He pocketed the cheque. 'But I never really expect you to pay me, Mitch. You must admit it. Your aptitude for finance is on a par with some of Britain's great entrepreneurs.'

'I'm not that bad.'

'You spend it and pray. Pray isn't pay . . . ' His attention had been distracted by the sight of the empty wine bottle in the waste bin. 'And how is . . . '

'Charlie. He's called Charlie.'

'I see you had a good evening.'

'And?'

'I told you. Amanda. It's Amanda.'

'Hot on *fin de siècle* pictures,' Mitch remembered. She poured their coffee. The tension between them eased when he began to describe an auction he'd just been to.

Later, on the door step, he stooped and kissed her ear. 'Look after yourself, idiot. Any trouble, ring.'

'I'm as tough as old boots.'

'I know that.' And, seeing her eyes narrow, quickly added, 'But looking younger by the day.'

'Flattery will get you to the parts other words never reach,' she said and watched him cross the gravel to his car. Josh had always yearned for a posh car. 'A real pose-mobile. Something that would knock your eyes out.' But, though there had been times when he could have afforded a Porsche or a Ferrari, he always drove the same kind of nondescript hatchback. 'When you get down to it this is a very small city,' he'd always maintained. 'If I started going round on fancy wheels my punters would know how much I was ripping them off for.'

At the moment though, she guessed, times would be pretty lean. Not much buying of Paul de Lamerie silver gilt in a recession.

She waved and went back in. After finishing packing her suitcase she looked round for her very dog-eared copy of Angela Thirkell's *The Brandons*. When it came to flying, Mitch was a coward. To her the plane's skin looked no thicker than a sardine tin. How could such flimsiness carry the tonnage of jet engines? Discovering her fear, Digger Rooney had revealed himself a fellow sufferer.

'But I'm pretty OK now. I always take *The Brandons* along. I just sink back into this pre-war world. My dear, Angela's such a giggle. And the food. Crab apple jelly and potted salmon. Gooseberry fool. Marsala. Parsnip wine. Of course, one couldn't really enjoy it if Hooper weren't in the background with the Rolls Royce and the rugs. Oh, if only Angela had had the sense to ask her characters' cooks for the recipes. Then — bliss!' He'd kissed his fingertips. 'Believe me, one wouldn't mind dying while Nurse was sewing on one's buttons. No wonder the British once had an empire.'

Mitch had tried Digger's remedy. To her amazement it had worked. Well, worked for most of the time. And during the process of her journeying she'd become a fanatical admirer of Mrs Brandon, a wealthy widow with two grown-up children. Mrs Brandon was so wonderfully pretty and lovable that not only did men of all ages fall for her, but legions of servants practically killed each other for the honour of bringing her a cushion, or tea, or a telephone message.

That's the life, thought Mitch. Christ. That's paradise.

Digger had decided that when the wings fell off the plane he would go out on the cook putting her soul into the beef tea, and Mitch fancied the bit where Aunt Sissie was described as an elderly Caligula disguised as Elizabeth Fry. 'It would be so wonderful to be saying goodbye to all the Aunt Sissies of my life. All my bosses. All the great and the good.'

Making sure that her version of a St Christopher was safely in her handbag, Mitch then put the file on Jon Stanton into an overnight bag she always used as hand luggage.

By teatime she was already a little queasy. She fed herself a banana and two chocolate biscuits — something heavy enough, she hoped, to keep her stomach in place. It was now five o'clock. She'd an hour to kill before driving to the East Midlands airport.

She wanted to phone Charlie. She'd a perfect excuse, after all. She was going away for a day or two.

Charlie, leaving at one o'clock in the morning, had not said when he'd see her again. Pride had stopped her from asking. Now she refused to let herself pick up the receiver. She and Charlie were in that initial state of flux when patterns for their relationship were about to be laid down. If she picked up the phone she felt it marked the beginning of her pursuit of him.

Her eyes might switch on to mega-wattage when she caught sight of him, her knees start to come unhinged, but there was no way in this world that she was going to chase after a temporary supply teacher not old enough to have ever owned a ration book. Period.

But the telephone began to hold such an attraction for her that her hands literally began to itch. In the end she rang Mrs Stanton and then made herself settle down and read through the newspaper cuttings the old lady had given her. Before leaving, she checked the house and then carried her bags to the car. It had begun raining heavily and as she edged the TVR's bonnet out on to the

Bristol road she switched on the side lights.

She travelled north on the A38, turning off at Willington. The rain began to ease as she drove more than ten miles across country, picking her way through junctions in deserted country villages. They were not the kind of places harassed city dwellers dreamt of, she thought. These were plain little working-class communities housed mostly in thin prim Victorian terraces. Even the fields contrived not to look as picturesque as those south of Birmingham. Near the race track at Castle Donington she got caught in a traffic snarl-up. Her heart began to beat faster as she checked her watch every two minutes. But she need not have worried. She reached the airport only to find there was a flight delay of thirty minutes.

She stood in the middle of the bustle, watching queues shuffling towards the baggage check-in. Suddenly she was panicking. Soon she'd be out on the tarmac walking towards the plane and the stewardess would tell her not to walk under the wings. Were they afraid those itsy-bitsy efforts would fall apart even before the aircraft took off?

She was absolutely sure of it. On this flight she'd open *The Brandons* and read her last words.

She really better ring up Charlie Collins

now. While the going was good. Oh, just to hear the voice of her love.

He wasn't too pleased. She'd got him out of the bath. There were so many things she wanted to say to him. Poets would not use words half so well. What she actually said was, 'I won't be away more than a day or two.'

She'd just picked up her bags and was joining the queue when she was paged.

'A telephone call for you,' the girl on the information desk said.

'There's been a most almighty mix-up,' Mrs Stanton said. 'That girl of Robin's in Gozo — the one I told you about — posted the photographs back to England, to Robin's flat in Hockley. Can you hear me? Mitch, are you there?'

'I'm here.'

'I'm most frightfully sorry about this. Robin's flying back to England. Really. I don't quite know what to say. It would have been so jolly dreadful if I'd not managed to catch you in time.'

'Don't apologise. It's not your fault.'

'Robin's going to ring you. You're to meet him at his place in Birmingham tomorrow. Really, I'm so sorry you have been messed about in this appalling way.'

'Honestly. It's all right.'

And for five minutes it was; she despised

176

herself for feeling so relieved. But before she reached home again a deadening sense of anticlimax had set in. 'Wherever else I get to this summer it seems it won't be abroad!' she thought. 'Oh, what a pig's ear.'

She arrived back in the house before the flight was due to take off. She dumped her bags in the lounge but she was too dispirited to unpack. She poured herself a stiff gin and tried to watch some television. Exasperated, she chucked a cushion at the set and poured herself another drink.

'I'm fed up with continually being pissed about!' she told the avuncular newscaster. He smiled out of the set and handed her over to their correspondent in Iraq. She turned the television off. She didn't want to know that there they really had problems.

She decided to go to bed. When she climbed between the sheets she began to think of Charlie, dressed in bath water and not much else. She groaned and turned over. 'I'll never get to sleep,' she thought. 'Charlie is my darl . . . i . . . n . . . g . . . '

She woke with a start and switched on the bedside lamp. The rosy glow fell on the figure of a bone-headed Chinaman. The bundle on the end of his stick was so heavy he was bent double. He was one of the decorations on a black lacquer cabinet in which she kept all her papers relating to money, or lack of it.

She was shifting her feet under the sheets, getting ready to haul herself out of bed to go for a pee. But no. That wasn't why she'd woken up. There it was again. What was it?

Someone was walking about downstairs.

She felt the roots of her hair beginning to stiffen. Her right hand reached out for the telephone on the bedside table. She stayed her fingers. Am I hearing things?

She leaned forward, left hand pushing back hair from her ear. There it was again. Footsteps. A charge of fear bolted down her spine; shock waves prickled over her flesh.

Should I shout out? Investigate?

Don't be a bloody idiot.

Her hand shuddered then tightened on the telephone receiver. She took a deep breath and punched 999. The noise of each click seemed to grow, to echo round the room. There was no connecting buzz. All she could hear was static. She knew immediately what had happened. The intruder had taken the phone off the hook in the kitchen. Sweat was now beginning to damp her shoulders, film the soles of her feet.

Jesus. What do I do?

Even though she now knew it was useless, she tried the emergency number again. Bile was rising, souring the back of her throat.

Carefully, making as little noise as possible, she dropped the receiver back.

Why don't I keep a guard dog? A nice big Alsatian? Or a Dobermann?

Because a dog like that would scare you stiff. Stop squawking and think. Think. Think.

Perhaps if I just stayed very quiet the thief would get what he wanted and go?

The bathroom has a lock on the door. Perhaps I could sneak down the landing and lock myself in there. That's the good thing about an old house. All the doors are stout.

Her eye had lit on the alabaster base of the bedside lamp. Oh shit. Oh no. No, you don't. You'll end up in hospital. Your face will look like a sewage treatment works. You'll end up in the crem. Smoke in the chimney.

Jesus. You idiot.

But Mitch's feet were already on the floor. Very quietly, she unplugged the light, wrapped the flex round the stem and turned the lamp upside down. The square base packed a good five pounds of marble. She had just started to steal across the carpet when she heard a door shut. Her heels rose slightly as her toes jarred to a standstill. Listening intently, all she could hear was the wild fluttering in her heart. Her ears began to pick up another sound.

179

Gravel?

That was it.

Gravel? Was someone now on the outside of the house? Perhaps there were more than one?

Or had the intruder left?

Taking a firmer grip on the lamp, she stole out of the bedroom and then on to the landing. She halted, listening again. The whirr of the freezer turning itself on, the geriatric tick of the grandfather clock in the lounge and . . . nothing.

Had he gone?

She suddenly made her decision. She snapped the light on and yelled, 'Is anyone there!' A faint rattling. Very slowly she realised it was the sound of rain on the glass roof of the conservatory. It always seemed to make a louder noise there than on the house's window panes.

Half-way down the stairs she realised she was naked. Well, it's a bit late now, she thought, and continued to the bottom. She switched on the hall light, crossed quickly to the lounge and put on more lights. She investigated the conservatory, then the kitchen and then went back upstairs and looked in bedrooms and the bathroom.

The intruder, whoever it was, had gone. She went into her bedroom and put a wrap on before checking the valuables in the house. Nothing, so far as she could discover, had been taken. Josh's money was still in her purse. The little bit of jewellery and silver she had was undisturbed. The television, video, tape recorders and her broadcasting equipment was untouched.

I ought to call the police.

The receiver on the kitchen phone was slightly askew in its cradle, disconnecting the line.

I could have done that last time I put down the phone. I've done it before.

All the same, I certainly heard someone. I'm sure of it.

But what good would calling the police do? Nothing had been taken. There wouldn't even be an insurance claim to fill in.

Oh, balls to it, she thought, replaced the receiver properly and went back to bed.

I could have been killed, a childish voice cried in her as she climbed between the sheets.

Oh shut up, she told it roughly. You don't want to spend the rest of the night being messed about by the police, do you? I'd have thought you'd been given enough of a run-around for one day.

All's well that ends well.

Now be quiet and let's get some sleep.

10

She had unwrapped the cellophane and plunged the flowers in a bucket. Coffee tray in her hands, she saw them again as she used her bum to push open the kitchen door. Tommy Hung's lilies were florist's orange; the colour squealed against the yellow plastic bucket. How on earth do I arrange those? she wondered as she crossed through the hall and lounge into the conservatory. That though, she thought, was the least of her worries.

Tommy Hung, slender, glossily groomed in beige slacks and matching cashmere sweater, was sitting in a much-painted Lloyd Loom chair, his head haloed by the sword-shaped leaves of Mitch's dragon tree. The edges of the leaves bled red in watery sunlight. Tommy's fingers were steepled over his stomach and his ankles were crossed, small toe tucked against heel in supple loafers. He leaned forward slightly as she came in. 'You were saying you didn't realise anything was missing until you unpacked your bags this morning?'

She shook her head, setting the tray on a brass-topped Indian occasional table.

'Black, please. No sugar,' he said, answering her inquiring look. She was feeling disconcerted, unable to match that fat plum of an English voice to an oriental face. A sage's face, she was thinking, or what a Westerner would expect an Eastern sage to look like. He was perfectly at ease. 'Tell me again what had been taken.'

'From my handbag? A novel I intended to read on the plane — Angela Thirkell's *The Brandons* — a comb and my lipstick. From my overnight bag a T-shirt had gone, and a kaftan I use as a nightdress when I go away. At home I always sleep in the buff but I wouldn't want to embarrass others. I mean, if one were caught in a fire.'

'And your money — your valuables?'

'Untouched. It's bizarre.'

'Have you rung the police?'

'No. I mean, the things are worthless. To anyone but me, I mean.'

'But Mitch! Someone broke into your house — '

'What good would it do? They're not going to nail anyone, are they? It's all going to be a waste of everyone's time. It's such minor league stuff it will be at the bottom of their list — if it's on at all.'

Tommy was silent for a moment. His head dipped towards his fingers. 'Let's assume that the break-in was connected with your investigation. Who knew that the house would be empty — that you were on your way to Malta?'

'Mrs Stanton and Cathy, her housekeeper. Josh, a friend of mine who lent me some ready cash. Freya Adcock from Radio Brum. Charlie, another friend. I rang him at the airport. But what had any of them to gain from breaking into my house?'

'To find out how far your investigation into Jon's death has got? To read your notes, for instance? Maybe you're worrying him.'

'There aren't any notes. All I've got is a small file of stuff made up by Mrs Stanton. Just newspaper clippings. Oh, and the keys to Jon's flat. But they are still in the zipped compartment of my handbag. Untouched.'

'But you would be expected to have notes. Most investigators — the police, for instance — write reports on their interviews. One supposes they study them later, looking for discrepancies, or to cross-reference evidence, that sort of thing . . . '

Mitch was stricken. 'I've not been applying much method, have I?'

'I remember that series you did on television. You must have worked out an excellent technique then. You were very successful.'

'As I am beginning to discover, those inquiries were very different. There I was told by the people who had been ripped off not only who had done it but how. All I had to do was prove it. In this case I'm trying to disprove what has apparently taken place. An added complication is that right from the beginning I've thought Jon committed suicide.'

'Why?'

'Put simply, it's odds on he did. Murder, after all, is still a very rare crime.'

'Hmm,' said Tommy. 'If, for a moment, you abandon your position and assume he was killed . . . what have you got?'

'There is his behaviour. He doesn't appear to have acted like a would-be suicide. But one can't place too much reliance on that. Unless you're in someone's head, how the hell do you know what is going on?'

'Quite,' said Tommy, studying Mitch's very Western profile.

'And it gets complicated by the fact that we often project our own feelings on others. We will have it, for instance, that they are awful rather than admit the fault lies with us. Trying to judge the behaviour of others is an absolute minefield. So often one finds one is judging the behaviour of oneself.'

'We are rather toddling towards metaphysics here.'

'And away from the point.' Mitch grinned. 'The other thing is these photographs Jon took.' She told him about the evidence of Edna Cowley. 'But I will be seeing Robin Pemberton today so that aspect can be cleared up.'

'Anything else?'

'Well, Mrs Stanton told me that Jon had said Robin did something hush-hush in the Government before he chucked it up for a painter's life. But there need not be any truth in that. Jon was a lad who enjoyed a joke. As well as playing practical jokes, he was always winding people up. Of course, Robin can answer that when I see him.'

'Then we come to the business last night,' said Tommy. 'I think there we actually do have to assume it has something to do with your investigation.'

'Why?'

'If it were an ordinary break-in, would the thief have left the money in your purse and taken a comb and a lipstick?'

Mitch shivered.

'Are you cold?'

'It isn't that. Someone walked over my grave.'

'What do you mean? I know the expression,

of course. I mean, what caused that feeling?'

'I . . . ' Mitch was going to shrug but she stopped and thought about it. The sun had gone in. Rain began to rattle on the conservatory roof. 'Well, if I were to suppose that Jon Stanton was murdered . . . it was done in such a calculated, cold-blooded manner, wasn't it?'

'Meticulously thought out and planned . . . '

'To imagine someone capable of that walking about your home in the dead of night . . . '

'One wouldn't feel too sanguine. Quite,' said Tommy. 'But he — or she — obviously intended you no harm because presumably whoever did it thought you were half-way to Malta.'

'My car was parked in the driveway . . . but then, I could have taken a taxi to the airport, couldn't I?'

'How did the intruder get in?'

'I did check the house before I left.' She began to look a little shamefaced. 'I'm afraid I didn't do it very well. I left the bathroom window open a crack. All you'd have to do is climb on the kitchen roof. The bathroom's just underneath. But you'd need to be fairly fit to do that and if he did get in that way, he left no traces. Of course, he could have had a flexible piece of plastic and some expertise. These old houses are a doddle. And, of course, there is no alarm system.'

'One must assume it wouldn't be until he saw your bags that he realised you hadn't gone.' Tommy's chin rested on the top of his steepled fingertips. 'What possessed the fellow to carry off a comb, a lipstick, a novel, a kaftan and . . . a . . . '

'T-shirt.'

'Are we looking at a fetish?' Tommy asked.

'If we are, it need have nothing to do with the case. It could be coincidence he broke in last night. To be honest, that sounds the likeliest explanation to me. After all, I am a broadcaster and one always picks up one or two weirdos . . . '

'But still presuming that it has something to do with your investigation . . . he breaks in to check up on you, to see how far you've got. He probably finds the newspaper clippings but discards them. They won't tell him anything the whole world doesn't know. Then there are the keys.'

'But would he know they were the keys to Jon's flat? They weren't tagged.'

'In any event, he leaves them and the clippings but takes away selected personal items.'

'You have to admit it doesn't make any sense.'

'If that reading of what happened is correct, it must do. We just can't see the sense in it at the moment. That's all. He sees the bags, perhaps has opened them, looked in . . . and one has to suppose an idea strikes him. What kind of idea?'

'You tell me,' said Mitch.

'Quite.'

'I hope this line of thought is taking us right up a gum tree.'

'Why?'

'Because we are creating some kind of monster. Someone capable of conceiving and carrying out a most cold-blooded murder — and who is now planning God knows what. It is not a comfortable thought. No wonder someone walked over my grave.'

'Well, yes. Exactly so.'

'Luckily it's far more probable we're turning a molehill into a mountain. Oh God. I must have been mad to get myself involved in all this. Truly bonkers. And you've been up to something, haven't you? Didn't I see you at that Green for Good lecture on Saturday?'

'You're scolding.' He smiled, a seventy-year-old mischievous schoolboy — prep schoolboy — not quite eleven. 'I thought you wouldn't mind my helping if I were very, very discreet. One spends a lifetime fashioning exactly the life one wants — one's paradise on earth — and one finds it's a hell of a bore.' He was still smiling at her. 'I did a little checking of my own and found out that Jon Stanton's heir is Ann Wellesley. That's why I went to the meeting and, of course, when I spotted you there I knew I was on the right track.'

Mitch was going to interrupt but he stopped her with his hand. 'Hear me out. Later I made the acquaintance of a Miss Jeanie Campbell, a member of the executive committee. I'm taking her out to a meal and a show later this week. One hopes to very discreetly learn a bit more.'

'Tommy!' Mitch exploded.

'Can't I help? Can't you take a gamble on a chap like me?'

'Like you?' Mitch stared at him.

'I assure you I'm a jolly good chap to have around. Though one tries not to boast. I know it's not quite the thing.'

But you're a complete fake! Mitch wanted to yell, outraged, and yet she was amused at the same time. 'Look, Tommy, Mrs Stanton is paying me a great deal of money to try to get to the bottom of this. I mean, this isn't . . . Her grandson is dead, for God's sake.'

'One is jolly well aware of that. Absolutely.

I came this morning to offer you my services. Free, of course. A trial period. If you find me useful and we progress to other things — '

'What other things?'

'Investigations, I meant,' he said, grinning.

'Really, Mr Hung . . . Tommy . . . I can't imagine — '

'But you don't mind my helping? Very discreetly? For now?'

'Oh, why not,' and she found she was smiling. 'In for a penny . . . I don't know why the hell I'm doing this anyway — '

'Tremendous!' Tommy, his face alight, was rising.

'Listen, I've given myself a week to come up with something. Then I'm calling a halt. I can't play silly beggars for ever.'

After he'd gone Mitch, feeling rather foolish, sat down on the Lloyd Loom chair he'd vacated. What have I done? And suddenly there came to her a vision of Mrs Stanton and Cathy holding hands on the drive, only now the figures had become Tommy and herself, a real pair of babes in the wood.

I'm absolutely crackers, she thought, but she was smiling again. Well, why not? When life stops being an adventure, she thought, what's left? All the same, she saw no virtue in amateurishness and put herself in detention for the next two hours while she recalled and recorded the evidence she'd gathered so far.

She cleared out a box file and put the papers in. She again began to think of Tommy. She balked, once more feeling outraged. He's pure *Boys' Own*. What the hell do I think I'm up to?

Oh, stop being so stuffy. What's the matter with you? Are you too old to swing out on a limb? Take a chance? Ride with it?

She rang Josh Hadley to explain what had happened and tell him she'd return his cash the next day.

'Grounded, eh?' He sounded smug. 'I'll be at the warehouse in the morning. Pop along before lunch, chickadee, and you can see that black lacquer stuff I told you about.'

She had a late lunch, made some coffee and then found herself padding restlessly about the house. Robin Pemberton still hadn't called. She tried sitting in the lotus position, a thing she hadn't done for ten years, and found she could no longer make it. That proves you need to loosen up, she told herself. Well, I can't just wait about for ever for that painter. It is, after all, Ann Wellesley who is the main heir. She rang the number Mrs Stanton had given her, not really expecting that Ann would agree to see her.

'I'm so glad you've called,' Ann Wellesley

told her. 'I was thinking of phoning you. What about eleven tomorrow? Can you come here? I'm working at home in the morning.'

Mitch, surprised that Ann was so keen to see her, knew she should have been pleased, but found she felt apprehensive. In her experience when you got what you wanted easily you found it wasn't what you wanted at all.

She sighed and settled down to read through the stuff she'd written that morning.

Shutting the file, a name flashed into her mind. Bernie Cornfield. Why didn't I think of him before? The Detective Inspector was an old contact from her newsroom days. When she eventually tracked him down, he could hardly keep the surprise out of his voice. 'I thought you'd stopped chasing fellows like me, Mitch.'

'Well, I certainly haven't had much to do with courts and villains lately,' and she told him about her show on Radio Brum. 'But it is all about as secure as a loose tooth. And when I fall out of Radio Brum my broadcasting days are over. So I've got one or two other irons in the fire.' Then she added — an inspiration of the moment — 'Projects of a rather fictional nature.'

She described the suicide of Jon Stanton. 'But say he didn't kill himself. Say it was murder. Given what I've told you, would the police suspect anything?'

'Let me get this straight. This character in your story was induced by some means to drink enough to make him unconscious. Then he is placed in his car, the hose pipe attached to the exhaust and fed in — and Bob's your uncle?'

'Got it, honeypot.'

'I'd say it's the perfect murder.'

'Why?'

'When the police go to a scene where there's a dead body what they don't want to find is a murder victim. No way. Murder is too expensive. Now my patch is south Staffordshire. A while back the IRA killed a soldier at the railway station in Lichfield. We drafted in four hundred and fifty detectives for three days. A reasonably average-sized town — say Tamworth — only has twelve detectives, three off duty at any one time, so you can see what's involved.'

'The logistics are horrendous.'

'Not the logistics. The overtime. Recently we had an attempted murder. We used twelve detectives on that. We can't afford murder. What we are looking for is suicide or natural causes. Much easier on the budget. What I am saying is that if it looks like suicide, that's what it is.'

194

'So if the forensics don't quite add up — '

'What forensics? A PM would be done, of course, and if that agreed with the circumstances in which the body was found no one is going to chuck aluminium powder about. Suicide or attempted suicide hasn't been an offence for over thirty years.'

'What if — say — this chap was known to drink very little and the pathologist found a high level of alcohol in the body?'

'Normal. Ninety per cent of suicides drink before they do it, often heavily.'

'So unless a second person was actually seen — '

'Even the victim wouldn't know he was being murdered — '

'He'd think he was having a jar with a friend. But if his drink was being stiffened — '

'Whisky and beer is a pretty lethal combination. Thieves sometimes use it. The businessman staying at a hotel has a drink or two at the bar, starts chatting with his neighbour. They go back to his room for a night-cap. Whisky is being slipped into the pints. The businessman thinks he's only on his fourth when — boom. Twelve hours later he wakes up to find his credit cards, wallet, keys, car, Christ knows what all gone.'

'Thanks, Bernie. You've been a great help.'

'Have you really thought this through, Mitch? The perfect murder is never solved. If you're trying your hand at . . . detective fiction? — the murder has got to be solved, hasn't it? Even Poirot would get his knickers in a twist over this one. You're not to cheat, you know.'

Mitch laughed. 'When did I ever go by the book?'

'I'll take a signed copy and I'll have you under the Trades Description Act if you try any funny business.'

'I'll try and be good, Bernie. Thanks.'

'If you want my advice,' said the policeman, 'I'd stick to that good old reliable — the blunt instrument. And there's the double-barrelled shot-gun if you want plenty of gore. If you use big game calibre shot the word 'burst' shows you just what it can do.'

'I never realised you were such a bloodthirsty devil.'

'I like a bit of gore myself,' Bernie confessed. 'I like my fictional killings to be true to life. Ring again if I can be of help.'

Mitch immediately dug the Stanton file out. She checked, even though she knew. Yes. Here it was. Beer and whisky had been found in the stomach contents.

Clearly no one had seen Jon Stanton dragged — perhaps carried, if the muscleman

Lygo Pim had been around — to his car.

Which is, of course, supposing Jon Stanton was murdered, and I still can't believe he was. She looked at the clock. It was teatime and Robin Pemberton still hadn't rung. Five minutes later he did.

'I'm at Euston,' he told her. 'I flew into Heathrow just over an hour ago. My train to Birmingham gets in at seven. I'll need half an hour to get back to Hockley . . . bath, shave, drink . . . Shall we say my place at around nine? You've got the address?'

'Peg Lane off Carver Street? I always thought Hockley was a business area?'

'It is. Carver Street was where Joseph Lucas started his lighting business in the 1830s. I live in a flat over my uncle's business. He's got a partitioning and suspended ceilings business. There's the works entrance in the middle then a door next to a scrapyard. That's my entrance. It's basically a stairway. I'm three floors up at the top of the building. It's well lit. I'll leave the bottom door open for you.'

'What's the business called?'

'More Walls.'

'I'll be there.'

'What the hell is this all about?'

'I'm hoping you might be able to help us a bit there — '

197

'Got to go. See you.'

Mitch — faced with a long wait — curled up on the couch and watched some television but all the same she was ready to leave the house before half-past eight. She dug out her A to Z. She could get there by going under the Hockley flyover and down Ickneild Street. The whole district, she thought, was too near the inner-city area of Handsworth for comfort. She remembered Josh Hadley's appalling joke. 'What do they call a cat with a tail in Handsworth?' She belted her old riding mac. 'A tourist,' she said aloud, grimacing. She could, of course, take along a sock with a brick in it but, in the event of trouble, it was more likely she'd get hit with it than the mugger. Why the hell couldn't Robin Pemberton give up and be the middle-class soul he undoubtedly was and have a flat in Edgbaston or — if he must be trendier than thou — Moseley?

But Hockley is a business area, she reassured herself. The place will be deserted by this time.

Unless Monday night is ram-raiding night.

But what little arse-hole would want to steal a suspended ceiling? You can't inject it or plug it in and dance to it.

Nevertheless, she pocketed the household

pepper pot. Much good may it do you, she thought.

She opened the front door. Rain fell, sloshing into the gully between lawn and gravel, swilling down the steep driveway. A continuing wall of spray rose over the boundary hedge, thrown up by the steady flow of traffic on the Bristol Road. She went back in, jammed the fedora on her head, turned up her collar and faced the night, head well bent. She reversed the TVR down the drive, turned the car on the pavement and eased into the northbound traffic. Lights were appearing everywhere; the city winked like newly cleaned brass.

She eased the car through Spaghetti Junction, not the quickest route to Hockley but the one she knew best. She took a left at Dartmouth Circus into New St John Street West and cruised down towards the Hockley flyover. Cliffs of inner-city tower blocks began to rise to her left, trees dwarfed by twenty-two storeys of wet grey concrete. Rain, caught in many lighted windows, cast a glittering halo about them.

Second left Hockley, third left Handsworth? she wondered as she hit another roundabout. She knew she'd taken the right road when she began to pass the cemetery. She slowed when she reached the mint.

Surely Carver Street was around here? She pulled off the road into a slipway running through a large triangle of pavement. She cut the engine. Across a side road was a boarded-up chemist's shop, paint hanging off pitted white walls. A pasted TO LET sign partly obscured the chemist's name. Next to it was a Chinese takeaway which shouted in red on yellow that it was also a FISH AND CHIPS SHOP. Grids of turquoise iron mesh protected windows and the doorway but glass in the upper storeys of both premises was shattered. Guttering was coming loose, one piece swung drunkenly. She could see no street names.

She looked round. Though there were plenty of cars on the main road, the side streets were deserted. She jammed the fedora more firmly on her head and got out to explore. She found the side street was called Warstone Lane. It forked almost immediately into Carver Street. She returned to the car and opened up her A to Z. From the map it appeared she crossed over from Carver Street into Peg Lane.

She started the car. She had no difficulty in finding More Walls. It was housed in a three-storey Georgian building, the kind of place that's so thin, she thought, it looks as though it's been extruded. It had been reroofed with corrugated iron sheeting; ten-foot-high double steel doors formed the main entrance. To the left, next to a scrapyard, was the door Robin Pemberton had told her about.

Mitch parked the car on the opposite side of the street and looked about her before getting out. She realised she was much nearer the city centre than she had supposed. Just beyond More Walls, to the right of a heap of scrap in the yard, she could just make out the lights at the top of the Post Office tower. Beyond the scrapyard were more workshops, housed in premises built at the beginning of the Industrial Revolution. Though she could see no one she could hear footsteps, and the noise was coming from that direction. It died.

She noticed a small pencil of light outlining the doorway Robin Pemberton said he'd leave open for her. The reflections refracted from puddles forming in the much-repaired sur-faces of the tarmac road. She got out and locked the car. A wind was getting up. The surfaces of the puddles began to shiver. She quickly hopped over them and pushed open the door. She found herself in a well, concrete steps immediately before her. The brick walls were a dingy yellow; they sweated slightly in the fluorescent light.

She climbed the stairs rapidly, two at a

time. There was a locked plated steel door on the first floor, presumably a second works entrance. She was breathing heavily by the time she reached the top floor. She turned on to the short concrete landing. The rain was drumming noisily on the corrugated iron roof. Dampness was leaching through on to a corner of the ceiling. She knocked on the newish pine door. There was no answer though she could hear music, low, liquid, some old Queen track, she thought. She knocked again. The rain drummed on. She pushed down the aluminium door lever, hesitated a moment longer, one foot swaying uncertainly in the air, and then she walked in. She found herself in a small hall, a door to her left, a window overlooking the street to her right. The light wasn't on but illumination from the street lamp cast a beam across the rush matting on the floor. 'Hello!' she called.

There was no answer.

'Hi there!'

She realised there was another door in front of her. She opened it. She found herself in a large room running from the front to the back of the building. On the left was a kitchen, a four-foot-high brick wall dividing it from the lounge area on the street side. Twin steel standard lamps with aluminium dishes cast light upwards to the ceiling. There was a huddle of chrome leather seating and huge unframed canvases were hung on raw brick walls. Baggage, topped by a white anorak, was on a moulded white plastic table. A half-drunk glass of whisky stood on a steel rack of hi-fi equipment.

'Hello!'

As she waited she found her apprehension growing. Her fingers began to curl, to knot. There was another door in the far wall. Crossing quickly, she stood for a moment before it. She flung it open.

Light from the other room flooded a large expanse of wall. A massive half-finished picture on board hung from an arrangement of horizontal girders and pulleys. Stepladders and a trestle table loaded with painting materials were ranged in front of it. She turned slowly. She saw the dark green duvet on the double bed. There was something crumpled on it which she very slowly began to recognise. Her kaftan. Shock jolted bone against cartilage. She stepped back and switched on the light.

Her T-shirt was draped across a bentwood chair. One sandal — from a pair she'd not noticed was missing — was sole-up on the floor.

'Jesus,' she breathed. She stared uncompre-hendingly. Her scalp was contracting; flesh rubbed softly against her skull.

'Hello!' she yelled. The shock of sound brought her heels off the floor. She fought down bile.

What the hell is going on?

She turned and half ran back across the lounge into the hall. She opened the door she'd first seen when she'd come into the flat. She realised it was the bathroom before she switched on the light.

Blood was on the ceiling, not a lot, a dash of elongated blobs. More was splattered on the tiling over the bath; it formed a distinct hook. Some had seeped into a wash of condensation, a glittering frosting of pink. There was a pool on the grey thermo-plastic tiles of the floor. The edges had dried but it was runny in the middle. Blood smeared the tiles of the window sill and there were marks on the pine window frame.

She was aware of standing, of smelling the pungent, slightly sweet smell of the butcher's shop and then of floating across to the window. She curled her fingers into the dished brass plates set in the window frame and hauled. Rain began to drift into her skin. She saw the lights of the Post Office tower again and then she looked down into the scrapyard.

Below her, rain was swilling through a heap of ancient cold water tanks. She could quite clearly see the hand protruding through the centre of the pile. The fingers hung limply, a burlesque of limp-wristed gesture.

11

She raced into the hall and picked up the telephone. Are the wires cut? She turned this way and that as uncoordinated fingers slithered over numbers. The phone rang out. The noise deafened her. Thought reeled. Her hand spread over her face.

' . . . which number do you require?'

She squeezed her eyes together, trying to shut out of her mind the sight of her kaftan on the bed.

Very slowly, she let the receiver sink back into its cradle. As she did so, her legs began to bend. Back to the wall, she slid down to the floor. Her arms wrapped her legs, her head sank into the soft denim of her jeans.

The dead hand rose out of the dumped cold water tanks. It extended on an ever-elongated arm and as it got nearer the hand grew. All the fingers pointed at her.

I'm being railroaded into the dock. That's what those stolen bits and pieces mean. That's why they are here.

I'm the guilty one.

I didn't even know the man. No one's going to believe that I . . . that . . . My God.

206

His blood is all over the bathroom. The smell is still in my nostrils.

He's been murdered.

But what if that thing out there isn't dead?

In her mind's eye the hand began to move again; scarcely recognisable flesh emerged out of the tanks.

She separated her hands from her knees, digging fingers into her palms, using pain to snap out of spiralling panic.

The vortex began to recede. The calmer she grew, the more distant the world became. Time, too, was slowing.

But now she was able to think. Each thought seemed very long in the conceiving and when it arose it was entirely without the weight of emotion. It seemed to float, almost ghostlike, as if no longer tethered in her being.

What she thought was that gaols were full of people who had not done it. What she remembered was that the West Midlands Serious Crimes Squad had been broken up because of detectives who had fabricated evidence. Ten people had already been let out of gaol; twenty more cases were waiting to be heard. And that could be the tip of an iceberg.

No one need fabricate evidence against her.

That had already been done for them by an unseen hand.

But I didn't even know the man. Dear God. I never met him. Why would I kill him?

You're here, aren't you?

Your kaftan is on his bed.

Are hairs from your stolen comb deep in the crevices of mattress and sheets?

Your fingerprints are certainly all over the flat.

They are on the bathroom window sill.

'Poking you, was he?' she heard a detective say. 'What went wrong? What did you quarrel about?'

'It's untrue. I have a boyfriend. I — '

'Bit young, wasn't he? Like 'em young, do you?'

'No. No. No!'

'Like more than your fair share? Is that it?'

She opened her eyes, sitting stone-still in the fluorescent bar of light thrown by the street lamp.

I must collect what I can find and get out of here while the going is good.

That would not do. She must come up with something better than that. The evidence showing she'd been here would now be in the cracks of this place, on unseen surfaces, hidden in the pile of rugs.

Think.

Fingerprints quickly decay. She was recalling evidence in a court case she had covered once. For twenty-four hours they are readily recoverable. But they are ninety per cent water and after that they begin to evaporate . . . Nearly all forensic evidence is perishable.

I must delay the finding of the body if I can, she decided. I must give myself a chance.

But I didn't do it.

What sort of a defence is that?

My best defence is to find the killer. If I can.

Am I really just going to cover my tracks and get to hell out of here? I don't even know for sure who is dead.

Or if he is dead.

The import of that now hit her. The thing really could be alive.

Hold on. Don't panic. Hold steady.

This is what I must do. Check the body. If he is still alive I call the ambulance and then the police. It's OK. I can do it anonymously if I have to. Anyway, if he comes round he will be my witness.

If he is dead — or she! — I make sure the body is well hidden under those tanks in the hope of delaying its discovery. I collect my things and get out.

But at the moment you are totally innocent. You haven't done anything. If you conceal a body, obstruct justice in any way, surely you are breaking the law?

I've got to take my chance. This is murder. I'm looking at twenty years or more.

But . . . And yet there were no more buts. She saw clearly that this was a murder with its killer attached.

'Me.' She said it aloud, not believing it and yet feeling sick enough to know it was true.

Mitch — who had been around the courts long enough to know that truth and justice were all too often distorted in the fairground mirror of human nature — tottered to her feet. She was much steadier when she'd got herself down two flights of stairs. She slipped through the door. It was quite dark now, but lights from the flat and the street lamp illuminated strips of brick and tarmac. The street was empty, and, though she listened out for footsteps, she could hear nothing. But she'd have to be vigilant. She was pretty sure there was a pub in nearby Camden Street — was it the George and Dragon? — and it couldn't be far off closing time.

She studied the scrapyard. Though from here she could see the pile of rusting tanks, the hand was obscured. The yard was railed in. A single-sized mattress had been abandoned near the massive gates. The eight-foot-high railings had not been purpose built. The bottom sections were low and did not match the higher top sections. One piece had been patched with planking. Girders were piled just beyond, some jutting very near to the iron bars.

Were the bars wide enough apart for her to get a toe-hold on the girders and use them as steps? She thought so. On her way back over the railings she would jump, using the abandoned mattress as a landing pad.

She looked up and down the street again. The rain had almost stopped. Wetness seemed to be oozing out of the bricks and tarmac and not from the sky. She breathed deeply and walked rapidly to the spot she'd chosen. Turning her foot sideways, she eased her trainer through the bar. Sections of railings slid a little, grinding together as she swung her body upright. She grasped the spikes at the top. She repositioned her hands, manoeuvring her body over the spikes. The top of one caught in a buttonhole. She freed her hand, balancing herself precariously on the shaking bars. She fumbled with it, her straining muscles beginning to tremble. Free, she lowered her right foot on to a girder. Moving her hands down the railings, she lowered the other foot.

She stood at the bottom, rubbing her rust-burned palms. Her heels were rising. She was ready for action the moment an alarm sounded. All she heard was the rattling of her skidding heart. She cautiously looked around, taking bearings. The scrapyard was oblong, bounded by offices to the right and a high brick wall to the rear. Beyond that was a workshop, unevenly cropped stove piping protruding through the roof. The cold water tanks had been dumped within feet of the More Walls factory. She picked her way round and over wooden pallets, circling towards the back of the tanks. If someone did come down the street, she wanted to be sure she was hidden from view.

She saw the hand. It was caught in a beam of light from the bathroom window; the half-mast fingers trailed against rusting iron.

She tackled the twelve-foot-high pyramid of tanks from the side, testing each foothole before easing her weight upwards. The noise boomed dully through the drums. Water from a sudden downpour rolled into her eyes. She carefully clawed her way over the top layer of tanks and then her hands reached out and she gripped the sides of an uneven hole. The whole pile swayed and settled. She froze. Not far from her nose was the hand. Fingers and nails were beaded with rain.

She looked into the hole.

Robin Pemberton was sitting upright,

knees wedged into his chest, one arm hanging above him, the wrist trapped between two tanks. He looked much younger than the chancer she'd seen in photographs. Death robbed him of his manhood; muscles had relaxed into the smoothness of childhood. His blue eyes were open but already beginning to sink. Because of the thatch of his dark hair, it only slowly became apparent that there was a gaping hole where once an ear had been. A glistening rime of bone splinter and brain crusted his left shoulder. Runnels of blood stained his Save the Whale T-shirt. Blood covered his chin and most of his neck, leaving only the bump of his Adam's apple to gleam through a whiteness of skin. There was a buzz about him. A vibrating halo of bluebottles. Even in the wet chillness of this night he had been found out.

There could be no doubt at all, but she took his wrist and felt for a pulse. There was none.

Poor Robin. Poor Cock Robin.

His lips moved as gases blew gently through them. Muscles contracted. The corpse groaned. She found herself answering his distress, sighing towards him. When she became aware of herself again, she was holding his hand, quite tightly, as if she were helping a child across the road.

' . . . we praise you that men are made in your image and reflect your truth and light. We thank you for the life of your son, for the love and mercy . . . ' The priest's words had stolen into her mind. Words spoken at the funeral of Jon Stanton. She reached down and closed the young man's eyes with her thumb and forefinger. She worked his hand free but she did not let it drop into the hole. She laid it carefully across his knees. And then she looked around for a tank to seal the top of the grave. Very carefully she began to edge the nearest one across the hole. Iron screamed against iron, multiplying in the echoing drums. The whole pile vibrated. With one big heave she shut him in.

Her belly slid over the tanks as she carefully lowered herself. It wasn't until she reached the ground that she realised the noise she could hear came from her teeth. The clattering spread through all her bones. She sat down abruptly.

I'll get the bastard, she thought. I'll get him. She hung on to her sudden anger, using its force to drive her back on to her feet. But she tottered like an old woman as she made her way to the railings. She eyed them with despair. How will I ever haul myself back over them, she wondered.

Help me, someone! she wanted to scream.

But there was no one out there, only the wet night, the distant glow of the silent neon city.

You'll have to help yourself. And she eyed the railings again.

She took several deep breaths before driving her limbs up the girders. She turned as she reached the top and lowered herself backwards over the spikes. The cuff of the riding mac ripped as she jumped on to the mattress beneath.

She stared down the street. A soft whistle of wind, the suck of water in drains, the squeak of telephone wire rubbing against brick.

Who cares what happens? she thought as she climbed back up to the flat. Why not just ring for the police?

No. Just keep moving. Keep doing. Keep going.

Poor Robin. Poor child. I closed his eyes. I shut out the world. I did it.

She knew he was dead and yet could not feel he was. Why had she drawn his eyelids down? Why had she plunged him into endless darkness? In her distress she gripped the door post to the flat. Spasms of shudders left her hot and weak.

When she'd recovered enough to go about her tasks, she could no longer remember the reason for them. She put the things she collected in a Marks and Spencer bag she found in the kitchen. She discovered a pair of her ear-rings — again, she'd not known they'd been taken — in the lounge. When she went into the bathroom, she was shocked to find the blood was still there. Because she could not really comprehend what was happening, she found she was questioning what she'd seen previously. She stared at the hook of stains over the bath, stared at the pinkish sheet shrinking into the taps. And then there was the pool on the thermo-plastic tiles. She stared at that. Blood. Her hand moved to touch her own skull, feel her ear. Such a child, she thought. She saw his lips parting, as if to whistle, heard his groan as his muscles contracted. Rigor mortis begins after three hours, she found herself thinking. Confirming his death to herself as she did again and again that night.

It was in the bathroom that she found her lipstick. Who knew what else the bastard had tucked away, waiting to be pounced on by the forensic experts? The only thing she did know was that in general evidence deteriorated and the longer it was before the corpse was found, the better her chances.

Suddenly she broke through the window of

the almost trance-like state which had overtaken her.

Anyone who comes in the flat, in here, sees the blood, she was thinking . . . But she realised she wasn't going to attempt to clean up the mess; the thought repulsed her. Somewhere out there was Robin Pemberton's killer. She would not actively destroy evidence which could be used against him rather than her. She knew this was a compromise which didn't bear examination but found she couldn't budge herself. She wasn't going to have Robin Pemberton's blood on her hands. She would seal off the bathroom as best she could in the hope of delaying discovery. That was as far as she was prepared to go.

It was only when she turned to the window to make sure his body was hidden from view that she realised it was still open. A brisk dampness played with the bottom of the curtains. She could hear the distant hooting of an express train. Skirting the puddle on the thermo-plastic tiles, she moved over to the window and looked out. There was no sign of him. He was completely covered by the dripping tanks. She shut the window and then went into the kitchen to look for some fuse wire.

The bathroom door was a new one, made

from planks of pine wood. A small round plate with a ridge across operated the lock. She looped the wire round it, drew it towards her and then shut the door. She tugged the wire. The lock moved. She tugged harder. As the lock snapped shut she jerked backwards, the complete length of wire in her hand.

Done.

Now I can go.

Relief sank to her knees, made them wobble.

Done.

It was at that moment she realised she'd childishly supposed she'd never get away from this place, that she would be trapped here for ever, bound by subtle and devious threads of emotion to a dead boy she'd never met. After all, it was I who shut his eyes. She still found herself unaccountably distressed by this action of hers. It was as if she dared not contemplate the larger horrors. The hand, the hole where an ear should be, the rime of exploded matter on the shoulder; they were sucked of their reality, two-dimensional images in a world of three dimensions. But would they become real again in her dreams?

She picked up the Marks and Spencer bag, switched off the lights, clicked on the dead lock and let herself out of the flat. She found herself monitoring her legs as she went down the stairs. Her limbs now felt plastic enough to turn inside out. She wasn't sure if she could make it to her car.

She closed the door and stepped back into the night. Though she was in the heart of a city which held a million souls, she could be in the Gobi desert. Moonlight was beginning to break through; the eerie glow shone out of puddles and watery cracks.

It was only when she reached the car that she remembered the photographs. But I turned the flat over, she thought. If they had still been there I would have stumbled across them. She climbed into the TVR and switched on the engine. She nervously looked at her feet. Could she trust them to push down the pedals? She took a deep breath and let out the clutch.

She found the shot-gun the next morning. It was in the conservatory, balanced across the brass top of the Indian occasional table. Snout and butt projected over the rim. It was double-barrelled, one ugly mouth squatting down on the other.

Eyes widening, she put down her coffee cup next to it. She found herself picking up the gun. Though the weapon was about four feet in length, it was surprisingly light. It weighed less than a ten-pound bag of potatoes.

The barrel slipped between her fingers. She leapt as it snapped apart. Two cartridges ejected, rattling across the tiled mosaic floor. Dismayed, she stared at the two halves of the gun, one held in each hand.

She carefully put the gun on the floor and stooped to retrieve one of the cartridges. She turned it over, letting it roll across the palm of her hand. It was no more than three inches long, bright red in colour, a brass cap sealing each end. It appeared to be intact. She picked up the other one.

An explosive force had turned this cartridge into a flower, the stem empty, the head a frill of tiny reflexed petals.

IN JUNE

WEDNESDAY

I have been reading about female gaols. One stands in a queue with one's chamber pot and then empties the contents into a large sink. What if it sticks to the sides? Does one have access to Jeyes fluid? The stench, one learns, is enough to make one faint.

I could, though, go to a Church of England service in whatever room is designated as the prison chapel. It is, I have to admit, doubtful that the thought of God would comfort me. I am a very fastidious person. God, don't you think, is somehow all about keeping clean?

Apparently one sews gym shorts for male prisoners — even in gaol, it seems, one services men — or makes cardboard boxes.

However, there is other work.

After putting rubber gloves on, one is expected to take a large shovel and clean concrete paths beneath cell windows. The paths are — I found this unaccountable but it is apparently true — littered with burst bags of faeces and soiled sanitary towels.

Hell on earth always seems so much worse

than anything which may occur in after-life, don't you think?

All this, and much more, I found out last week. It made me think of whipping boys. You know, those creatures who were kept so that they could be punished for the childish sins of infant kings. What if I have my own whipping boy? My own creature? Someone who could shoulder my guilt, take my punishment? I would, after all, be doing what most people do without even pausing to think about it. Blame others.

Yes. It is a thought.

Or perhaps one could take a giant step forward and divorce crime from punishment?

Almost anything seems better than having to deal with the problems presented by Her Majesty's plumbing.

Thursday
My diary tells me this is National Day in Sweden. One can't help feeling that the Swedes would provide their prisoners with proper sanitary facilities. Really, I think the Swedes have had a very bad press. They seem quite civilized to me.

All that reading about gaols has made me hit the gin bottle rather. I cheered myself up by learning what four weeks of death would do to the bastard.

Listen to this.

By the third and fourth week the body has decayed so much the hair and nails can be pulled out. The flesh is a greenish purple and is bloated. The tongue — that clack, clack, everlasting clickety clack machine — is so swollen that it sticks out through his lips. Then there is his trunk, never very prepossessing. Well, that blows up like a balloon — it is three times the size it was at death.

When I sink his face into his future flesh the pain in me eases. I find some peace.

Saturday

This week we've had an Irish Bank Holiday and the constitutional days of Denmark and Sweden. But today, nothing.

I have been thinking again of Daddy's trophy. Convenient, yes. Absolutely certain, yes. But if I used that then I would certainly go to gaol.

And I don't see why I can't let myself off the hook. After all, it is not as though he doesn't richly deserve it.

There are, of course, so many other — often totally bizarre — ways of killing him. But could one be sure of their efficiency?

Cantharis vericatoria, Spanish Fly, used as an aphrodisiac, for heaven's sake! But two women given it died and it really has one absolutely splendid advantage. There is no antidote. It apparently has a nice smell, too.

Monday
National Day, Portugal.
　He is coming.

224

12

'You look like the vampires got you,' Josh Hadley told her. 'Christ. Do you look terrible.'

They were in Josh's warehouse which was east of Spaghetti Junction, sandwiched between the Saltley Trading Estate and one of the many gas works which had been shoe-horned into this small area of the city. The warehouse itself had once been a Unitarian chapel. Now it was fenced in by high concrete walls topped with broken glass and travelling rings of barbed wire. The gates were made of inch-wide iron bars, windows were covered first with fine wire mesh and then the same bars as the gates. 'My belief is that thieves would have to take the roof off to get in,' Josh had told Mitch two years ago when he'd been driven to rebuild his defences. He'd been proved right a year later.

Dusty bars of sunlight filtered through the arched windows on to the oak-planked floor. The furniture was stored in alleys. These pieces rarely went into Josh's city-centre showrooms but were bought by dealers serving the American and Continental markets. He was showing Mitch some black lacquer pieces.

'For Christ's sake, stop staring at me, will you?' Mitch said. 'You looked at me like that when I was in hospital that time. It made me think I was going to die. I'd only gone in for a D and C. By the way, honeypot, here's your cash.' She opened her handbag and gave him the wad of notes.

'What on earth's happened, chickadee?'

'Nothing much. As I said on the phone, my trip got called off at the last moment. I was then supposed to meet this chap I'd been flying out to see at his flat. Here, in Birmingham. But he never showed.'

'All seems dodgy to me. Where is he, then?'

'I wish I knew.'

'Are you saying he's disappeared? Done a bunk?'

'I don't know!'

'What the hell have you got yourself into?'

Tears welled up. She swallowed hard, turned away and pretended to examine a narrow, shoulder-high cabinet.

'It was an old gramophone cabinet. 1920s I'd say. It's been turned into a little cupboard,' he told her.

'It's very pretty. I love the panels.' Mitch was surprised at how firm her voice sounded.

'Just a gewgaw, chickadee,' he shrugged. 'You can have it for fifty quid. The dealers won't want to know. It came in a job lot.'

Mitch opened the small doors and looked in. 'Done. I'll use it as a bathroom cabinet. Get rid of that frightful thing on the wall. And, of course, I must have that wardrobe. I'd no idea you could get Chinese lacquer wardrobes.'

'People will make anything. For money . . . '

'I can put my mahogany one in Cassie's room and hers can go in the guest room.'

'Don't you think all these ladies with fans are a . . . well, a touch over the top?'

Mitch could see he was picturing the wardrobe in her bedroom — a bedroom he'd spent many a night in — and suddenly that made her feel like crying, too. She assiduously opened doors and peered into interior drawers and hanging space. 'There's almost more decoration on the inside than the outside. I'll have it, honeypot.'

'I suppose it is a nice piece. If you like that kind of thing.'

'And I do,' Mitch reminded him.

'How about two hundred quid then?'

'What! Oh, you are an angel. I could hug you to death.'

'You need a pick-me-up,' said Josh. 'You

look as though you've had a run in with a JCB. A bit of Chinese lacquer is better for your liver than gin. But can you even afford my prices?'

'I keep telling you, Josh. At the moment I'm flush. Oh Lord. That can't be the time . . . ' Mitch had caught sight of her wrist-watch as she opened her handbag.

'Where are you off too in such a hurry?'

'I'm actually on my way to see Ann Wellesley. She lives in Sutton Coldfield.'

'The Green for Good woman? I wouldn't have thought saving the planet was your scene.'

'Why do you say that?'

'You're such a doubter, Mitch. If you saw a five-pound note on the pavement you'd leave it there. You wouldn't believe your eyes.'

'You exaggerate,' she said, ripping off a cheque and giving it him. 'And what about you? Look at you! Checking I've got the date right, the sum right and I've not signed the damned thing Diana Windsor.'

He laughed. 'Long habit, chickadee. The fruit of much painful experience.'

'You haven't counted the cash I gave you back!'

'That just shows you I trust you really. And I worry — ' But, seeing the look on her face, he said, 'All right. All right. None of my damn business. I'll give you a ring and let you know when I can get the pieces delivered.' He escorted her back out into the sunlight. He turned to say something but bit it back. What he did say as she got into her car was, 'Take care.'

The remark she swallowed was, 'Love to the blonde bimbo.' She substituted, 'Could be quite hot this afternoon.'

She took the A5127 out to Sutton Coldfield, a Birmingham middle-class enclave which vied with Edgbaston and Solihull. Here lived people who talked about their landscape gardeners while out riding bikes in health clubs, who drove their Range Rovers through tree-lined suburban streets to pick up their children from preparatory schools, who competed with each other to unfit their kitchens.

Hardly the setting, Mitch thought, for a Green feminist lecturer. But when you came to think about it, you rarely found even the most extremist lefty MP living among the poor. And who can really blame them, she further thought, as she nosed the TVR through heavy traffic. Real poverty must be even more corrupting than real power.

How are you going to approach the Wellesley woman? She asked herself. She found she didn't want to tackle her at all but go back home and hole up in her bed. Shut the world out.

The west front of the District General Hospital bordered one side of the street on which Ann Wellesley lived. Much of the other was taken up by the boundary wall of the cemetery. It was not an approach most people would have chosen to their home, Mitch thought, but certainly better than the traffic mayhem which faced her at the bottom of her own drive. The street turned into a cul-de-sac of small 1960s detached houses. Most windows had nets up, or festoon blinds, and were crammed about with flat-roofed extensions of one kind or another; some sprouted burglar alarms and satellite dishes. Ann Wellesley's house was pristine. The front door, like that of Number Ten, was painted black.

Mitch rang the bell.

The door was opened by a woman in a gunmetal shell suit. There was half an inch of air below the heels of her old-fashioned gym shoes. Ann Wellesley obviously liked to keep on her toes. 'Miss Mitchell?' She'd been to the hairdresser since Mitch had last seen her. Thick curls still adorned the crown of her head but from the top of her ears down, her skull was clean-shaved. The style made her look aggressive.

'Good morning, Miss Wellesley.' Mitch found herself anxiously surveying the woman's hands. They held nothing more lethal than a pair of extremely large-framed glasses.

'Come in.' There were no rugs on the stripped and sealed pine floorboarding in the hall but a large kelim covered the floor in the seating area of the through lounge-diner. Books lined most walls; the rest were off-white. On the opposite wall to the gas fire, above a black and chrome leather settee, was an oil painting. There was something familiar about the vigorous brush strokes. A picture of a limp-wristed hand came into her mind.

She became aware of Ann Wellesley watching her as she looked at the painting. 'It's so striking. It's of the bird of paradise plant, isn't it? It's so strong,' Mitch found herself saying.

'It's by an artist called Robin Pemberton. He will certainly make a name for himself,' Ann Wellesley said and indicated a seat. It was some seconds before Mitch, sinking on the couch, arranging her handbag and scarf on the floor, realised that Ann Wellesley was going to remain standing. After putting her glasses down on top of the ledge over the gas fire, she was swinging round to confront her.

Mitch felt increasingly dismayed. She said, quickly, 'I was at your recent lecture at the

Mechanics Institute. I found it very interesting. You're a good speaker. If you don't mind my saying so — '

'From what I hear you weren't there because of any interest in Green for Good.'

'I don't know what you mean — '

'Oh, can it. You've taken it on yourself to investigate my poor cousin's death. Haven't you?'

Mitch stared straight into Ann Wellesley's eye. She had to look up so far her skull almost rested on the nape of her neck. 'Why on earth should you think that?'

'I find it sick. I find it really sick. And you can take that look of injured innocence off your face. I couldn't believe it myself when I first heard. I thought nobody would be capable of . . . Well, I found out. I rang Mrs Stanton's housekeeper. So don't you try and bullshit me. You've conned that poor old lady, haven't you?'

Mitch began to stand up.

'Sit. You sit this instant. I haven't finished with you. Not by a long chalk. Sit. Now.'

'It seems we've nothing to say to each other, Miss Wellesley — '

'I've a lot to say to you, you bitch — '

'Actually, I came out to see you to discuss the possibility of you appearing on my show 'City Talk.' I thought we might discuss the

232

campaign to save the Shakeshaft Nature Reserve. I've not the slightest idea what you're talking about. But it appears to me — '

'Bullshit! How the hell can you look yourself in the face? Taking money off that poor old cow half mad with grief? Callous little shit. If you think — '

'I'm afraid you've had your leg pulled, Miss Wellesley.'

'Come off it! I'm telling you to lay off. I won't have her conned by some hard-hearted old bat who — '

'Move out of my way.'

Ann Wellesley didn't move an inch. Her lips and fists were curling.

'Unless you intend to hit me I think you'd better get out of my way.'

'That's what you need. A bloody good hiding.'

'I hadn't heard that you were violent, Miss Wellesley. Please stand aside. You're surely not suggesting we indulge in fisticuffs.'

'Fisticuffs! Jesus. What century were you born in! You old cow. If I ever catch you — '

'Catch me what? Just what are you talking about?'

'Don't think you can wriggle out of it just like — ' but she was moving aside. Mitch, walking slowly, went out of the door. As she moved down the hall she could hear the other woman gasping through the thin wall. She opened the front door and closed it quietly behind her. She wouldn't allow herself to trip down a step or run along the drive to her car. She only became aware of her squealing heart as she jerked the TVR into gear.

I'm too old for this, she thought. My cardio-vascular system's not up to it. My wiring's coming loose.

A tear ran down her cheek. And then another, and another. Alarmed, she realised floodgates were about to open. She turned off the street into the hospital driveway and managed to reach the car-park before the monsoon claimed her.

When her heaving body at last began to calm a little she knew her devastation had little — if anything — to do with what had happened in Ann Wellesley's lounge.

I saw a man with his ear blown off.

I sealed him in his grave.

I have the weapon which killed him.

If the police got a search warrant they'd find it.

Stop this. Stop this. Take a hold of yourself. You've got to keep going.

A torrent of fresh weeping swept her. Back and forth she rocked, back and forth, her arms sinking and rising against the steering wheel.

I closed his eyes with my thumb and forefinger.

Gradually, though, she gained enough control of herself to start the car again and drive home. But her weeping had not cleansed her. If anything, she felt worse. It was all she could do to manoeuvre the car against the pressing wall of traffic into her driveway. Not crying now, but exhausted, she leaned back in the driver's seat.

Am I in delayed shock? she wondered.

Well, you'd better get yourself out of it, she told herself grimly. You've work to do tonight.

But when she got into the house she found she was too exhausted even to make herself lunch. By the time she sank on to the couch she decided she was coming down with some sort of bug. Her jacket still on, she fell asleep.

It was dark before she ventured out of the house again. She'd showered, eaten and fortified herself with brandy. She still felt a bit groggy, but what she had to do wouldn't wait.

She'd now transferred the shot-gun, which she'd put in one of Max's fishing bags, under the passenger seat. It had spent the day on view, with the rest of Max's fishing bags and tackle, in the attic. She had thought it too dangerous to try and dispose of it in broad daylight. She had known the risk she was taking; the killer could ring the police at any time and tell them where the body was and who had the gun. She'd reasoned he'd see that an anonymous tip-off might strengthen her story — that she had been framed — and would keep quiet, at least for a day or two.

She had considered the possibility, too, that this wasn't a serious attempt to frame her — after all, she had Madeleine Stanton to back up most of her story — but a diversionary tactic, something to keep her occupied while . . . while what? To break into her house, the killer — if it was him — must be worried about what she knew. He could not know that the few pieces of the jigsaw she had made no sense.

And there was something else, she felt, behind this attempt — serious or not — to frame her. An element of malicious fun. Someone was playing with her, pulling her strings, making her twitch.

She had no doubt at all now that Jon Stanton had been murdered as well as Robin Pemberton. But why? She must assume that the photographs Jon Stanton had taken were the key to both deaths. The identity of one of the people on the photographs was known. Just what did Bettina Mayo have to do with all this? I must, she thought, concentrate my efforts on that kid.

I'm missing something. I know I am. I

must look at that earlier evidence in the light of what has happened now. All these events connect in some way.

But for most of the time, the effort of marshalling thought was beyond her. Her shocked brain couldn't seem to concentrate. To get going at all she found she had to resort to mental tricks. The only way she'd been able to cope with the gun was to handle the fishing bag as if there weren't a weapon inside.

Unable to deal with thoughts of what might go wrong when she tried to dispose of it, she focused on her driving, on details of other vehicles, traffic lights, slipways. She took the second left at Holloway Circus, easing the TVR down Queensway into Suffolk Street and then, aware she was approaching the inverted pyramid of the library building, changed down, ready to turn left into Broad Street.

Summer had crept out again. The fluorescent glow of the city sponged away the stars, but the night was soft, balmy, promising a blue tomorrow. Mitch knew it to be a false promise. She'd heard the weather forecast before coming out.

She turned off Broad Street into Gas Street and parked in a Pay-and-Display space across the pavement from Arthur's Bar. The lights from the building illuminated a row of 'No

Parking' signs fixed to the walls of the darkened motor business premises across the street.

She snapped on the car's interior light and looked with some surprise at the pair of plug-holes which stared back. She blinked and twisted the driving mirror so she could get an extended view of her face. A night for slapping on lipstick, honeypot, she told herself, and felt a bit better when she'd applied plenty. She stuck Cassie's baseball cap over her curls and zipped herself into her daughter's denim jacket. Well. Now or never. She got out of the car, locked it, and took the fishing bag from under the passenger seat. She bent to heft it over her shoulder. As she looked up she saw a group of dancing youngsters turning into the street. She hurriedly slipped down a narrow passage into the Gas Street basin.

Just beyond a humped footbridge two rows of narrow boats, facing each other across a pathway, rocked gently in the light-splattered water. Much of the basin had been restored, but to her left a line of derelict buildings straddled the canal. Across the water people were sitting drinking on the wharfside in front of a neo-Edwardian pub. Lovers stole along a complex weaving of towpaths. Her heart sank. She'd chosen an idiotically busy place to get rid of the shot-gun. When she'd first thought of the Gas Street basin she'd congratulated herself; she'd told herself she was thinking straight again, climbing back on top of the situation.

She stood for a moment, hesitating. Too late now. She'd have to make her plan work.

She turned away from the waterways and pools of the basin and walked past a canalside antique shop. Here the water was a river of light cast by wharfside steak bars and housing units. Weeds broke through granite paving setts. The hum of music, voices, laughter grew more distant. Darkness intensified.

Do people fish these waters? she wondered, belatedly, as she looked across the canal at a man who was watching her. He was haloed in the light of an open doorway on the ground floor of a stepped three-storey apartment block. He threw a cigarette down before going back in, shutting the door behind him.

The bag was banging awkwardly into her buttocks, occasionally jarring against the back of her knee. She paused to shift it before turning a sharp bend. Now the canal cut westwards through the brick and tile industrial heartland of this city of a thousand and one trades. Three hundred yards down this section of the canal, narrow boats were moored by a fuelling point on the opposite bank, but none showed lights. Their outlines loomed out of the dim city glow; the illumination died as soon as it touched the water. She strode towards a distant iron bridge. The chainlink fencing on her left ended; Victorian workshops loomed. She ducked into a doorway and slung the bag off her shoulder, pausing to rub the bone. She fumbled as she undid the straps of the bag. She drew out the gun. It rested black and hard in the palms of her sweating hands.

Leaning forward she quickly viewed this stretch of towpath. She took a deep breath and then emerged from the shadows, quickly walking to the canalside. She dropped on her haunches and lowered the gun, barrels first, into the inky cut. Water glugged up the twin snouts. The gun disappeared quickly, leaving only a few bubbles, a widening ripple. Staring at the water, she could hardly believe she'd got rid of it at last. She was rubbing her hands together, washing them in the warm, dry air of the night.

She heard footsteps. She rose quickly, looking up and down the length of the canal. She could see no one. She hurried back to the doorway, pulling a blue and white Tesco bag out of the denim pocket of the jacket as she went. She rolled up the canvas fishing bag and dropped it in. As she walked back along the towpath a couple of boys, beer cans in their hands, came round the bend.

'You got the time, babs?' a white boy, no more than twelve, sang out as he skipped towards her.

''Ave we gorra big surprise for you!' laughed a bullock-muscled baby Rastafarian. His white teeth gleamed in the darkness.

'Bugger off.'

'Oh. Oh. Cunt's got a gob — '

Mitch, the tensions of the last twenty-four hours releasing themselves in fury, lashed out with the Tesco bag.

They peeled past her, dancing away down the towpath. 'Stupid cow!' 'Fuckin' bostin bonkers!' Their jeers squealed over her head as she walked rapidly back towards the basin.

As her anger ebbed away, she became aware once again of her terrible tiredness.

God. What I would do for a drink.

She looked across the basin at the drinkers on the wharfside. She took off her daughter's baseball cap, dropped it in the plastic bag and shook out her curls.

A double gin, she promised herself. Jesus. I'm going to murder it. She crossed the hump-backed footbridge and hurried along the pathway which separated the two rows of moored narrow boats. Pushing through noisy drinkers round tables on the wharfside, she was grateful to find that it was quieter inside. The pub was bisected by a narrow glass arcade hung about with brass lanterns and greenery. A fat brass railing ran round the brick and mahogany bar.

She'd downed a drink and was on her second when she heard a voice behind her. 'I thought it must be you, though all that denim had me fooled for a mo. You look like a dwarf brickie.'

'Freya!' she discovered as she turned. 'I'd no idea this was one of your watering holes.'

'I thought you were in Malta. You can't keep not flying off. This is Lygo Pim, the Green for Good press bod. We're all meeting here for a bit of a knees-up.'

'Mitch Mitchell, isn't it?'

The cast in Lygo Pim's eye made Mitch's eye wander too as she strove to make contact. She suddenly became aware of the Save the Whale T-shirt he was wearing. She tried to disguise her shocked start. 'I saw you at the lecture on Saturday, didn't I?'

'And I know all about you . . . ' A small smile produced a babyish dimple.

'Why didn't you go to Malta?' Freya asked.

'Last-minute change of plan.'

'I'd stop having them, kiddo. No one ever knows where they are with you. But at least it means our Friday night din-din is definitely

242

on.' She was looking around. 'Seems we're the first to arrive, Lygo. The others better hurry. They'll be calling time soon.' She turned back to Mitch. 'It's all very last-minute. Ann announced at our meeting tonight that she's Jon's heir. She's giving the movement a hundred thousand. I mean — wheeee. You've got to drink to that. We can really put some muscle into things now. Why not stay and join us?'

'Sorry, Freya. Got to go . . . '

'See you Friday, then. Fish for us, kiddo. That's the thing. The Japs live for ever because they eat mounds of raw fish.'

Mitch, moving towards the door, looked back in horror.

'Don't worry. I like mine cooked, too. Sometimes, Mitch, I believe you think I'm capable of anything. And I worry because I'm afraid I'm just a boring old company workhorse!'

Lygo Pim caught her as she escaped through the door. 'Your bag, darling . . . ' The dimple grew as his smile broadened.

13

Mitch saw that Tommy Hung took a pragmatic approach when dealing with the English summer. Though it was eleven o'clock on a June morning, his lounge was lit by a softly glowing standard lamp and the central heating was purring. Rain, mixed with hailstones, was beating a tattoo on the windows.

'The test match at Old Trafford is off,' he'd told her as he'd led her down the hall to his lounge. 'Waterlogged pitch. Perhaps it's as well. England aren't what they were.'

As he brought their tray of tea in, she asked him, 'How come you speak English so well?' Her cheeks suddenly flamed. 'Oh Lord. Now you're going to tell me your family have lived here for generations and you went to Rugby.'

Laughing, he shook his head. 'Not at all. Actually, it's entirely down to Paul Temple and Dick Barton.'

'Good Lord. That's going back a bit. Radio detectives, weren't they? Snowy, Jock and that music which broke all speed records.'

'I told you — didn't I — that I was an Unofficial? One of Her Majesty's Chinese laundrymen? I first worked on the aircraft carrier *Ark Royal*. Keung Shun Shao used to tell us the most ripping yarns. My dear, you simply can't imagine. Awfully good. It was some time before I learned he'd worked with his brother in a restaurant in Birmingham. He'd heard the tales on the radio, d'you see? Sugar?'

Mitch shook her head.

'Well! Nothing would do but I must learn English. I must listen myself. Keung Shun Shao explained to me about the different grades of English. He told me I must acquire the pukka stuff. But how? Another bikki?'

'No thanks.'

'H.M.'s captains get their dhobi done free but each Chinese New Year there's a small celebration on board. The captain hands out little red envelopes containing nice new banknotes. '*Kung hei fat choy*,' says the captain. 'Happy New Year.' Let me tell you, my dear, there are no shirts in the suds that day. I refused my little red envelope. Keung Shun Shao explained to the captain that I wished to learn top-grade, number-one English. The chaplain took me over. Mr Barton. Bets were laid. Unofficials, ratings, officers . . . even the captain. I had to achieve BBC standard English in a year. Most thought it was impossible but I'm proud to this day that the captain placed his money on me. And I bet two years' wages on myself. So you see I had no option, Miss Mitchell — '

'Do call me Mitch.'

'And when I really started to get into my stride Mr Barton used to finish off his daily lesson with a bit from a book. He'd learned about my love for the Paul Temple and Dick Barton stories so he chose Sherlock Holmes, Peter Wimsey . . . people like that. He wouldn't read me the end of *The Monkey's Paw*. Really, even though he was a jolly nice chap one's thoughts were alarmingly murderous . . . '

'What happened?'

'Mr Barton made me learn to read English. One detested it at first but what could one do?'

'And then you started reading detective stories yourself and that's why you've got shelves and shelves of them.'

'I even took a sneaking liking to Mr Marlowe,' Tommy Hung admitted. 'Though in my opinion his English is a trifle off colour. But of course one's first enthusiasm does tend to dull a little over the years. Another cup?'

'Please.'

'One does so fancy putting a toe in the water oneself . . . ' He looked at her and then shook his head, as if impatient with himself. 'But I have to say I haven't managed to come up with much yet.'

'At this stage anything at all would be a marvellous bonus.'

'Well, I told you I made the acquaintance of Jeanie Campbell, didn't I? A charming person. She's on the Green for Good executive committee. Now, you mentioned to me some photographs Jon Stanton took which had a van in the background.'

'That's right. Edna Cowley, who saw the pictures being taken, said it was green.'

'Well, Green for Good use a van. A green one. Apparently it belongs to Quentin Plunkett.'

'Quentin? Radio Brum's serious music man?' Mitch was stunned.

'His wife is chairman of the movement,' Tommy Hung reminded her.

'Quentin, Bettina Mayo and Freya Adcock . . . ' She was counting them off on her fingers. 'They all work for the station and are members of Green for Good. They all knew Jon Stanton.'

'You believe now that Jon Stanton was killed, don't you?' Tommy was watching her closely. 'What happened to change your mind? Did you see this chap Robin Pemberton? What did he say?'

'He rang and I went to his flat as arranged. But he didn't show up.'

Before coming to see Tommy she'd decided she'd tell him the same story she'd told Josh Hadley. This was the version she was also going to give Madeleine Stanton when she returned her call. She felt it reduced her chances of ever landing in the dock if she didn't produce witnesses for the stand.

'I learned something else last night,' she said. 'Ann Wellesley is giving the Green for Good movement a hundred thousand. She is, as you know, Jon's heir.'

Tommy didn't pick that up. He was obviously still thinking about what she'd told him earlier. 'Why have you changed your mind? Why do you now think Jon Stanton was murdered? Are you beginning to see some kind of shape to it all?'

Oh, if only I was, thought Mitch, and almost groaned out loud. 'Perhaps.. but it is a bit early to say yet . . . '

'How important do you think these photographs Jon Stanton took are?'

'Very.'

Tommy stroked his chin. 'There must be negatives.'

'If there are they are certainly not in Jon Stanton's flat. I've gone through that place twice, once very thoroughly. There are some

248

negatives — but not the ones we're looking for.'

'And you're still trying to track down the whereabouts of this Robin Pemberton?'

'Among other things.'

It was some time before he replied. Mitch realised that he knew she was keeping something from him. 'I suppose that as I saw Jon on the afternoon before he was — as you now believe — murdered, that I must be a suspect.' But he was smiling. 'I see I must prove myself, yes? Perhaps if I can be of real help — find those negatives or something . . .'

'Mr Hung . . . Tommy — '

'No, no. You needn't explain. One must prove oneself worthy. One will certainly have a jolly good bash at any rate.'

It was still raining when Mitch got up to leave a few minutes later. Tommy insisted on ushering her out to her car under his black and canary yellow golfing umbrella. As she settled into the driving seat he said, 'You know, I still like listening to the radio. I've always been a fan of yours, Mitch.'

And before she could reply he was scurrying away, so overwhelmed with anxious embarrassment that he splashed through a puddle on the tarmac. For the second time that morning, Mitch felt her cheeks flame.

But as she drove back home she felt enormously cheered.

The telephone was ringing as she went in. Mrs Stanton, she thought, as she ran down the hall.

'You're never going to believe this, Mitch. Never, never, never. Your wig's going to drop off.'

'I'm holding on to it,' she said.

'We've got him! Yad-da-dad-a-doo!'

'Shaun, for Christ's sake come down from the ceiling. Got who?'

'Who? Who! The Chancellor, of course. The hasn't-the-boy-done-good member for Birmingham East. The balls driving the British economy.' He began singing. 'Shaun's a good boy, good boy, good boy. Shaun's a good boy, the best there's ever been! Week twenty-eight, kiddo. Three days after you get back. Start swotting up your hard ecus and currency baskets. Fuck around with little Emu. You lucky, lucky creature, you. I've just told Freya. Did her boobs bounce. He's coming on Wednesday evening but no phone-in. Our Rev doesn't want to hear from the voters. Can't blame him. Not when the economy's neck deep in shit. As usual.'

'Let me get this straight. Revell Ullman's coming into the studio week twenty-eight to be interviewed by me?'

'And isn't Miss Bettina green. But our Rev isn't coming down to his constituency until you're back in the saddle.'

'Even Freya wouldn't let a monkey-booted kiddy in the ring with the Chancellor — '

'Bettina may be young but she's no push-over.'

'Freya is an organisational woman. Right down to the last button and bow. She'll play it safe.'

'Like you?'

'We're not going to quarrel, are we, honeypot? Not when you deserve a bottle of champagne. I'm going to take you out for a super lunch this week. Or next. Lots of gobbly goodies. And I see no reason why you can't get in on the act. Grab some of the glory.'

'How? You're the presenter.'

'We'll work on it. There'll be a way. I promise.'

'Honestly? Ace. Really. You're the best. The bestest best.'

'A better bet than any other at this moment in time. Even if my legs don't grown out of my skull.'

'There's more to life than long legs. You don't have to tell me. I know that.'

'You won't know it until you feel it.' Mitch sighed. 'And when you're old enough to know better you're too old.'

'Hey! This is happy time. Put the champagne on ice. See you soon kiddo.'

Mitch put the phone down before she told him, 'And don't call me kiddo.' I mustn't allow him to irritate me, she thought. After all, he's got me a scoop, the little darling. If I'm not careful I'll get as bad as Quentin Plunkett. There's nothing wrong with the young. In small doses.

She spent the afternoon reading back over her earlier notes, trying to fit them with the information she'd mentally filed on Robin Pemberton's murder. She'd have liked to have written it down, but dared not. There's such a lot of information already, she thought. It's all around me. It's just that I can't get a line in. By this time her head was beginning to ache and the terrible tiredness she'd experienced yesterday was creeping back.

In the hope of revitalising herself, she had a bath and made herself some tea. Before going out, she decided to face the task she'd been putting off all day. She picked up the receiver and dialled Mrs Stanton's number.

Mitch was always alarmed at the ease with which she could make some people believe her lies. She was almost ashamed of herself by the time she and Madeleine Stanton said goodbye.

It must be something to do with having a good broadcasting voice, she thought, as she hung up the receiver. Received English. But just what is the timbre of sincerity? What decibel implies truth? Why do I convince as I lie through my teeth? This talent of hers had a downside; aware of her own skills, she found it impossible to believe anyone else. Discounting what they said, she was forced to watch what they did. What they did was very truthful indeed, often fiendishly so. Well, you don't fool everyone, she reminded herself. You didn't fool Tommy, did you? He sees no truth in received English.

By some peculiar sideways jump in her thought processes she came to Charlie, who had not left a message on her answering machine. She tried to shake off his shadow as she climbed the stairs. She made herself think of the unlawful activities she was about to get up to. She needed to be anonymous. That, she felt, was always the best disguise. Jeans and an anorak, she decided. But her real inspiration was the helmet her daughter Cassie had worn during a brief but torrid affair with a motor cyclist. Cassie had been quite unrecognisable. Mitch hoped she would be, too.

It was still raining heavily when she set off for the house in Templar's Rise. She parked two streets away and turned on the radio. 'Style is the most important thing, Bettina. The people I know who are truly stylish actually always look the same. They achieve true style because they are truly integrated into their own — you know — being.'

'You think then that leggings by Gianni Versace are more than just an item of clothing?'

'One loves them, darling. I even wear them in the evening, you know. Velvet or satin. Simply scrumptious. Of course one wears one's Ralph Lauren jackets if one's writing one's novels. Such an inspiration. One really finds that, you know. And absolutely not a touch of make-up. Not before the blank page. No. No. No. Absolutely no, darling. Yeats — what a pet, don't you think? — I mean, he has it when he says one is looking for the face one had before the world was made . . . '

Mitch, who had only intended to hear a word — enough to assure her Bettina was in the studio — had found herself listening with growing but appalled fascination. My poor, poor show, she inwardly wailed. In her mind's eye she saw this huge elm shrivelling under the mighty mite of Dutch elm disease. She hurriedly turned off the radio.

No time to think of that.

Can't think of that.

Oh, the bitch.

Mitch jammed on the helmet and locked up the car.

The rain had slackened but it was such a murky evening that lights were already on in one or two houses. Mitch, walking down Templar's Rise, was not foolish enough to suppose she'd escape being seen by Edna or her husband. But surely they wouldn't recognise her? She turned into the driveway of the house Jon had lived in. A watery mist wreathed the building at waist-height. Two or three doors away a woman was screeching, 'You can sod off!' A door slammed, a car engine started. The drip, drip, drip of soaking silence closed in again. Mitch, skirting puddles, went round to the back of the house and checked all the windows of Bettina's flat. They were shut. She tentatively poked her own front door key into the kitchen door. She heard a tiny but satisfying grating sound. She unzipped her anorak and pulled out a short roll of pedal bin liner and ripped off a length. She used some to protect her knees from the wet brick step, manoeuvring the rest under the kitchen door. She then took out the skewer she used for testing roasting meat and inserted it into the lock. The key clanked as it hit the pedal bin liner. Kneeling again, she teased the liner from under the door. 'There's my beauty . . . ' she crooned as the key fell down the step. She seized it triumphantly.

Breaking the law, she was discovering, was thrilling. Just as good as being on air.

She let herself in.

The kitchen was a mess, much, much worse than her own. Mitch found herself looking around with happy disapproval before checking the other rooms. The place was full of stale smells. An apple core, a banana skin and a half-full can of Diet Coke were on the sticky glass top of the coffee table. The fabric-covered waste bin in the bathroom contained, among discarded tissue and packaging, strips of perforated plastic which indicated Bettina was on the pill.

Mitch explored the bedroom. There were faint but easily discernible grease stains in the centre of the pillows and a musky animal smell lingered about the duvet. Clothes were scattered on the floor and over the chairs; unlike the bedding, though, these were clean. Bettina, perhaps, had not reached the stage where she was prepared to admit pillow slips and duvets needed to be tubbed as often as clothes. Mitch well remembered the time when her daughter Cassie had looked her straight in the eye and told her, 'But I didn't know you had to wash the kitchen floor. No one ever told me.'

She opened the wardrobe and then took a look in drawers, most of which were filled with an extraordinary assortment of loose change, cassettes, ear-rings, empty boxes of tampons, tennis balls, biros, bras, holey knickers, a pair of earphones. Most of this was so similar to what she was used to finding in her daughter's drawers that her heart momentarily softened towards Bettina. After all, she's just a bit of a kid, she thought.

One who is at this minute trying to oust me out of my job, she told herself. And one who is very likely implicated in Jon Stanton's death. Just what, though, am I looking for besides those photographs and negatives? Something that will give me a line in. Will point me in the right direction, she told herself.

It was when she explored the kitchen that she began to wonder if Bettina had used the flat in the last day or two. There was no milk, no bread, and mould was forming on a half-eaten can of baked beans.

Where did she stay when she wasn't here? With whom?

Before she left she locked the back door and went out of Bettina's front door into the cavern of a hall. She picked up Jon's mail and pocketed it.

Plodding back to the car, she felt dispirited.

Zilch. That in itself was odd. If she does have a lover, why isn't there a letter from him, a snapshot, postcard . . .

Something, though, was nagging her as she got back into her car. She wrenched off Cassie's motor-cycle helmet, shaking out her hair. She mentally reviewed her search of Bettina's flat.

Cans. It's those cans. But lots of people have back-up earphones, she thought, though they don't often keep them in the same drawer as their underwear. And then she knew.

Those cans had been Jon Stanton's. Since Mitch had searched his flat Bettina must have gone upstairs and nicked them.

14

'Is it you?' Mitch was relieved to hear the voice of Radio Brum's secretary. 'I got put through to the engineers. Listen, have you seen Freya Adcock? Is she in? No one seems to know.'

'Mitch? I thought you were on holiday. Catch me ringing work,' said Trish. 'Freya was off at the beginning of the week. They held the boards for the manager's job in London. But I did see her briefly yesterday . . . Hang on.' She came back. 'No. No one's seen her today.'

'Oh God. I really must try and get hold of her. I'm supposed to be having dinner with her tonight but I feel a bit ropey. Perhaps I've picked up a bug or something. Listen, can you give me a shout if she comes in?'

'Will do.'

Mitch's heart skittered. 'Did Freya get the job?'

'No one knows yet. I think they were interviewing a late candidate yesterday. Just shows you how popular we are.'

'Doesn't show in the ratings.'

'Hang on a sec . . . ' Trish came back to

her: 'Digger has told me to tell you to hurry back. Has he got a surprise for you . . . '

'I've gone right off surprises. What else did he say?'

'I'm not going to tell you that.'

'Why not?'

'Because he's a little shit and it's rude.'

'Well, if it was about my age tell him it's an underestimation. Either I've become completely unglued or in reality I'm a hundred and two. Anyway, I'll be in to see Shaun at some stage if I feel up to it. We've got this Chancellor thing to get on the road.'

'Two lovely chaps from Special Branch came yesterday to case the joint. Well, Digger said they were Special Branch. He was practically drooling. You know how he admires anything big, butch and beautiful. I must say I was quite taken myself. Well smart.'

'Case the joint?'

'Looking us over from a security point of view, I suppose. Got to dash. Every phone in the place is going off. I'll give you a ring if I see Freya.'

Mitch put the phone down and poured her coffee. Her steps faltered as she carried it through to the lounge; she put out a hand to steady herself. She'd had a dreadful night. In her dreams the fingers protruding through

260

the cold water tanks had fluttered upwards. 'Help me!' The wail had echoed through and through the drums, through and through the membranes of her being. She'd woken in horror, convinced she'd buried Robin Pemberton alive.

How do I know he's dead?

How can I be sure?

Because his brains were spilled on to his T-shirt, reason screamed at her. She'd tottered to the lavatory to be sick, tears streaming down her face.

Poor Robin. Poor Cock Robin. Hot and sweaty and terrified of going to sleep again for fear he'd stir to life.

When she'd woken in the morning the almost paralysing tiredness had once again settled in her limbs; it was as though she'd moved into a dense wall of fog. Mitch knew she needed to think about the van and Bettina. Surely she must know who the mystery figure in the photograph was? He must be connected to the radio station, or Green for Good, or both.

The murdering bastard was there, right there under her nose; if she could see more clearly she'd recognise his face.

But she dozed away the morning on the couch. At lunchtime, she tried the office again and then, late in the afternoon, rang Freya's home number once more.

'My name is Hermes,' the telephone told her. 'Why am I answering your call? Simple, son. I'm the only one here. You can leave your message with me. Wait for my tone.'

But Mitch couldn't quite bring herself to do that. More than once she'd cooked up a feast and never known why the guests hadn't turned up until she'd checked with her answering machine.

I've simply got to get going again. Snap out of it. I could learn a lot from Freya about the Green for Good people.

Hoping to wake herself up, she went to have a bath but she dozed until the water got cold. She jollied herself along by choosing a comfortable outfit to wear, one she often went to work in; electric blue culottes and a shirt with a matching print jacket. Though she normally stuck to her fiftieth birthday vow to wear less make-up, she felt tonight she needed some armour-plating and proceeded accordingly. She finished by spraying a bit of golden glitter on her eyelids.

When she surveyed the results in the mirror she realised she'd been striving to look like Wonderwoman. She'd achieved something quite different. She told herself she'd be lucky if she didn't get rounded up with the city's whores.

Oh Christ, honeypot. Too late to change it all now. She'd have to do. But she did have time to dig out a different pair of shoes; ones she could run in. Run? Some hope, the way I'm feeling. And yet she was better now than she had been all day. Just keep on the move. Keep going, she told herself. The rest will follow.

She decided against taking the car. The block of flats Freya Adcock lived in was a good ten minutes' walk away but she didn't see how she'd get through the evening without getting pretty drunk.

Even for June in England it was chilly. The sky was in blood red tatters; coming night wielded a club and light lay bleeding. Trees sighed, too; buttock wrung squawks swelled in some. Baby bright leaves, torn from their branches, whirred about her head.

She was aware of wearing the cosmos like a too-large overcoat; often tripping, sometimes almost breaking her neck. It was all too obvious. None of this had been created with Mitch Mitchell in mind. When she'd been very young indeed the indifference of it all had practically reduced her to a speechless rage. Some day, she'd thought then. Some day. Well. I'll outsing the birds for a start. Put that in your pipe and smoke it.

Outsing the birds? Raising any kind of tune

seemed a triumph these days. Tonight, she thought, even a croak would be an achievement.

Croak? She was alarmed.

You're not going to croak, she told herself.

The sky bled more freely overhead, the trees whinged more persistently. She found she was glad to reach Freya's block of flats, an elegant curve of 1920s Odeon-work with a flat roof and interstices breathing the silent melodies of the Wurlitzer.

Already a little out of breath, she took her time about climbing two flights of stairs. Trying to gather up protesting bones which wanted to be nursed, to be rocked in caring arms — she was ill, damn it — she rang the bell. She didn't notice Freya at first because she was knocked back by a pungent feline aroma. When she did she thought for a moment she was looking in a mirror and was truly horrified by the picture she presented.

Blown-out, distorted; a fairground image of electric blue culottes, jolly print jacket, strawberry jam mouth.

'Good heavens,' said Freya. 'I say. You've got my clothes on.'

Mitch was too stunned to speak.

'How extraordinary,' said Freya 'Do come in and meet Mummy. She's my puss.'

She was introduced to a Persian cat with

haughty manner and snooty blue eyes. It immediately showed her its buttocks.

'There. She likes you. She doesn't take to everyone, you know. She can be very choosy, can kittiwitikins. I thought white wine. It's fish. A new recipe. One likes to be a little adventurous at times. Pike. Mummy likes pike, don't you, dear? Meaty. A good gobble.'

Freya had stopped to crimp at a long mirror on the wall. 'I've been thinking for a while that I might change my style. I mean, kiddo. One can't keep going on in the same old way. Can one? Strange we should pick the self-same outfit, though. Mind you, I've always thought we had a lot in common.' She turned. 'Sherry?'

'Gin, I think.'

'Actually, I've always rather admired the way you dress. But picking the same things! Where did you buy that?'

'It must have been the same place as you.'

'You must be more careful in future,' and Freya wagged a playful finger before pouring drinks.

The Persian, now on the mantelpiece, half closed its eyes.

'Oh Lord! The sauce!' Freya dumped a glass of gin in Mitch's hand and dashed off to the kitchen.

Mitch grimly poured it down her throat

and got up to get herself another. As she turned she saw the cat was laughing at her. It could have been a yawn but Mitch was pretty sure it was a laugh.

She looked in the long mirror, hoping to confirm her own picture of herself. A second image loomed up behind her shoulder. Christ, thought Mitch. That woman is stealing me clean away; that bag has bagged my image.

'They have a story about pike.'

And she's going to give me pike to eat.

'German, I think.' Freya had stepped back and picked up her drink. The cat leapt on a chair, goose-stepped across and took a second jump up on to her mistress's shoulder. Two pairs of blue eyes now looked at Mitch; Mummy's were indolent and snooty, Freya's earnest and school-ma'mish.

Mitch began to feel dizzy. She retreated to a brown corduroy covered armchair which smelled of cat pee. Why don't I tell that woman where to get off? Tell her to damn well come out of my clothes? But she knew where she'd land up if she did that, didn't she? A boot up her backside and a very hard landing on a cold wet pavement. She'd been there too often in the past to have any illusions. In broadcasting — as in life — when one door closes, another slams shut.

No one likes a loser.

'Yes, Germanic,' Freya said, nodding in agreement with herself. 'They have a tradition that when Christ was crucified all the fishes dived under the water in terror . . .'

Mitch, seeing how Freya's dray horse of a figure distended the lines of her print jacket, still found herself sorely tempted to let rip. She clutched the corduroy seat with her hands, as if this would somehow pin down her tongue. Nothing on earth, she warned herself again, is more unemployable than a fifty-year-old female broadcaster. I carry my age like a leper his bell.

'Kiddo, is something the matter?'

'Not at all. You were saying . . . all the fishes diving . . .'

'Except the pike. A chappie with a lot of curiosity. It lifted its head and saw the lot. For its pains it was marked with the crucifixion. The cross. Three nails. A sword. Distinctly recognisable parts of a pike's noddle.'

As often happened when talking to Freya, Mitch found herself floundering around for a reply.

'One marinates the flesh for an hour. White wine, mushrooms, shallots; you know the sort of drill. Filets de Brochet au Pouilly.'

The gin was now stiffening her up. 'I'm surprised you can buy pike in Birmingham.'

267

'One has to know the right people, kiddo. Let me freshen your glass . . . ' and Freya brought the gin bottle over. She suddenly sat down next to Mitch, so close that their identical culottes and jackets collided. She put the bottle on the floor and turned to look at her.

Like a fox eyeing a chicken, Mitch thought, alarm increasing as Freya took hold of her hand. 'I know I can trust you with my secret.' The pressure on Mitch's hand increased. Mitch, horrified, found her fingers had taken on a life of their own. They were returning the pressure. Freya leaned closer; identical fabrics sighed against their soul mates.

She's in love with me.

' . . . of course, everyone will know next week . . . I've made it, kiddo. Station manager . . . ' A tear trembled on the edge of her eyelash and then rolled off.

Mitch found she was almost in tears herself.

'Wonderful . . . ' She pushed herself up, walking over to the window. She pretended to look out.

'Why, you're overcome,' said Freya. 'I've always been aware . . . well, of your support . . . that . . . Well, I must say it's helped me through. It's not easy being a programme organiser, kiddo. But no more of that. Let's get stuck into Mr Percy Pike.'

Mitch had recovered herself sufficiently to say, 'Congratulations.'

'Of course, Mummy's not going to be pleased. I'll be seeing less of her. Won't I, dear?'

A gust of wind rattled the window pane. Mitch moved back a pace.

'Here we are.'

She turned as Freya carried in a large steaming dish. The cat jumped on to a dining chair. Freya put the dish on a large ethnic mat, realigned the other mats on the pine table, then walked round to the cat's chair. Seizing the back with her hands, she lifted it two feet clear of the table. 'Mummy's allowed to watch but not to eat,' she said. 'She has to wait and have hers in the kitchen afterwards. One wouldn't want to give her titbits from the table, Mitch. Please refrain.'

'Why do you call her Mummy?'

'I saw one just like her in a mummy's tomb. I was in Eygpt, you know, just before I got her. One never really cares for these foreign places. Travel, don't you find, is a continual let-down? One has these splendid pictures in one's mind and when one gets there . . . ' She shook her head. 'Reality's never up to much. Now . . . what are we going to do with the Chancellor? I expect you've got lots of jolly bright ideas?'

Mitch, who hadn't thought about the show, did what she always did when caught out in this way. She widened the discussion. 'I should imagine he is the act that absolutely no one wants to follow.'

'What do you mean? Help yourself to rice. More spinach?'

'Environment, education, transport, health. He gets his feet under the table, initiates invigorating changes and then leaves in the nick of time. The next man in opens the door and falls head first into a hornets' nest.'

'One hopes, kiddo, you are thinking in terms of positive radio. Minister bashing is all very well, but where does it get one in the end? To be frightfully frank — and shockingly ungrammatical — nobody gets nowhere with negativism . . . One simply throws that in . . . a thought . . . something to chew on. And, of course, one mustn't forget the man in the street. Or the woman in her kitchen. Those are our listeners. Good, solid citizens. If not quite Ph.D. material.'

Mitch got her teeth into more pike.

'One must always have a high regard for one's audience. A negative approach is always a turn-off.' The bloated mirror image of herself, fork in hand, waved a morsel of pike so freely it went right under the cat's nose, out the other side, and was snapped up between two rows of very well-kept teeth. Freya washed it down with two sips of wine and then dabbed her mouth with her napkin.

Mitch found she wasn't dismayed to see the cat hissing at its mistress. She couldn't bring herself to call it Mummy. She felt the implications of that were too macabre for anyone half-way normal to contemplate.

She'd also rejected the notion that Freya was in love with her. Unthinkable because Mitch had absolutely no intention of thinking about it. Ever.

'You're not eating much, kiddo.'

'To be honest, I'm a bit under the weather. I think perhaps I've caught a bug.'

'Does one really want a holiday? Even if one's not going away? One always falls ill, or is bored or finds oneself caught out by British Rail. Such a worry. One must forget such nonsense and rely on the satisfactions of one's job.' She leaned forward. 'Never go to Egypt. It pongs.'

Mitch laid down her fork and emptied her wine glass.

How drunk would she have to be to cope with Freya?

'You know, now you mention it, you do look a bit peaky. Quite green around the gills. I'd go easy on the alcohol, kiddo. Doesn't do when one's not quite the thing.'

'Nonsense!' Mitch did find she had some fight in her after all. 'My father was a great believer in the medicinal properties of alcohol.'

'One's sire rarely turns out to have been a wise man.' Freya stood up and began clearing the plates. 'I was very lucky. Not many kids have the kind of parenting I had.' She swept into the kitchen. The cat goose-stepped behind her, close enough to be her shadow.

Mitch glanced at her watch. Another hour before she could go? I'll never make it, she thought.

'Mummy mustn't be greedy. She's going to have to wait like a well brought up little girl,' she heard Freya tell the cat in the kitchen.

Mitch got up and wandered over to the window again and then began to pace the floor. It was a drab room, a grey tweed carpet, functional pine furniture, and the brown corduroy suite making Mitch think of a time share apartment in the blustery braes of Scotland. It seemed to have no connection whatever to the person Mitch knew as Freya Adcock. Perhaps, like my clothes, she's pinched it from someone else?

It was when she was passing a shelf full of filed radio programmes — the thin white boxes containing the spools of tape labelled only with initials — that she saw *The Brandons* sitting there, flat and face up on top of a short row of books whose weight was being used to keep the tape boxes upright. As she bent she saw that there could be no doubt. It was her copy of Angela Thirkell's novel resting on Collins English Dictionary and the hardback edition of *American Psycho* by Bret Easton Ellis.

'*Bombe surprise!*'

Mitch, snatching up the book, turned, eyes widening.

Freya held the dish high on the tips of the fingers of one hand. The cat, still licking a paw, was draped about her shoulder.

Mitch was raising the book in her right hand. 'Where did you get this?'

'Actually Digger is always recommending her stuff so when I saw it on the book table I thought, 'Well, it won't kill me to have a go.' Are you a fan too?'

'Book table?'

'Oh, a Green for Good cheese and wine last night. They always do a stall of books and bric-à-brac, too. Every little helps.'

'You don't happen to know who brought it along?'

'Well, as a matter of fact I do. Ann Wellesley, actually. Someone gave it her but she's not a Thirkell fan. Tea-cosy literature, she calls it. Still, one can't always be reading rigorous stuff, can one? A box of chocs, gin and a good book . . . can't be any harm in indulging occasionally. Of course, one wouldn't expect a woman like Ann to waste her time on entertainment. Her input is only ever of the highest quality. Why are you interested?'

'I'm a fan myself.'

'Really? A cynic like you? One's a tad surprised. Do come and gobble, my dear. Though I say it as shouldn't, my puddings aren't to be forgotten.'

'I wonder who gave it her? They might have others . . .'

'Well, I'll ask her if you like.' Freya sat the cat down on its dining chair, wagging her finger. 'No pud pud for the pud pud.'

'That's kind of you.' But Mitch again had a strong feeling of strings being pulled, of laughter just out of earshot.

'Do get stuck in.'

'Why do you call me cynical?' Freya's confection slid down between her molars; a shock of cold squealed along her gums.

'Because you are, and cynicism is so negative, kiddo. It's a fault in a broadcaster. People like plenty of bounce. They like lots of jolly, jolly. Even if it's lots of jolly awful. That's what's bankable in a performer. Look at Esther Rantzen. Look at Terry Wogan. People warm to yo-ho-ho-what-fun.'

'I've never thought of myself as cynical.'

'It's all right in a foreign correspondent. They're supposed to be world-weary. I think you should try to cultivate a more positive approach — without, of course, losing your touch. You have a very nice acerbic touch at times . . . Something to think about, yes? I just toss it in . . . one can't stay the same, you know.'

'Apparently not,' said Mitch, horrified that she was no longer horrified this woman had thieved her look. And how could she have adapted to that without a measure of cynicism? And if she didn't keep adapting where would her monthly pay cheque come from?

There was another — quite separate — question.

What if Freya had lied?

What if she hadn't picked up *The Brandons* on a Green for Good white elephant stall? What if it were Freya's laughter she detected just out of earshot?

By the time she finally escaped from the flat she knew quite positively and absolutely that she'd never be able to face another dinner with Radio Brum's new station manager.

She took in a very deep breath.

Some time very soon she'd be forced to fire her boss.

The thought was completely unnerving. Bosses fired her, not the other way round. It was a completely unnatural thing for her to do. The height of folly.

Her bank manager would regard it as a wholly irresponsible act. So would the DHSS, who would probably refuse her dole money.

What was it like firing people?

How could firing Freya not be anything but wonderful?

Though she was tired and still feeling ill, her steps became more positive until a squall of rain hit her in the midriff and knocked her off her stride.

By the time she reached home her hair was too heavy with water even to flap in the strengthening westerly; ears and nose tingled and there was an ominous squelch in her left shoe.

It wasn't until she let herself in that she was aware that there was someone else in the house. A footstep. A drumming which started and stopped. She looked down the hall and saw light seeping round the frame of the lounge door.

She was more angry than frightened. I've had it, she thought. I've had it up to here. I'm fed up with people just walking off the street and into my house. It's outrageous. I won't put up with it. She snatched a walking stick out of the umbrella stand. Her knuckles whitened about the handle. She flung open the door.

'My God, you're wet,' said Charlie Collins. 'You look like a drowned rat.'

'How the hell did you get in?'

'Well, I wouldn't have done it. Honest injun. Not if it hadn't started to bucket down. I'd have sat on your front door step for ever. But as it was . . . ' He shrugged. 'You'd left the kitchen window open. The little one at the top. I just reached through and opened the big one. Easy-peasy. You know, you leave yourself wide open. You shouldn't do that.'

'Why didn't you ring?' But already her tired nerviness was dropping from her, already the Grand Guignol dinner for two was becoming a memory.

'I was at a meeting but it finished early. Better give me the walking stick, darling. Here! I'll help you with that coat . . . ' and she stood and let his hands play about her. 'The only thing is — can I stay the night? My car's in dock. And could you give me a lift in to school tomorrow morning?'

'It's Saturday.'

'The school's doing *The Canterbury Tales*.

It's the end-of-term offering. The Art Department's got volunteered for the backdrops. Do you mind?' A finger was sliding over the nape of her neck, parting wet hair. She shivered. 'Cold?'

Not for much longer, she thought, as she turned to him. 'Wet.'

'I mustn't eat your ear,' he said. 'That wouldn't be nice. But I'm so hungry. Can I raid your larder?'

15

She'd parked her car behind the broadcasting centre. Tuesday morning and she was sizzling with energy, quite ready to take on image-bagging Freya Adcock, young Bettina Mayo, and she didn't mind if Quentin Plunkett was thrown in for good measure. She'd spent another night with Charlie Collins.

It just shows you what the pleasures of the flesh do for your ego, she thought. It's probably unchristian.

Not that I'm in love with him. Rubbish. You can't keep your hands off him. You've only got to conjure him up in your head to sound off the whole of this city's fire alarms.

'Charlie is my darling . . . ' she hummed. Yes. Definitely. And she bounded across the car-park, not a fifty-year-old bone in her body.

All of which, she feared, boded no good for her future. Who cares? she thought. Jesus. Who gives a damn?

She was not so bewitched, though, as to be entirely lost to the world. The electric blue outfit with the print jacket had gone right to the back of her wardrobe. She wore a dress she had bought three years ago. Let Freya try to replicate that.

Though early morning rain had cleared, there was still a strong wind about; the sappy smells of freshly mown grass were batted back and forth across the tarmac. A Coke can rattled in a grid and a discarded Kit Kat wrapper butted her heels, soft and squashy, like the moist nose of a dog.

Buffeted by sly draughts, her skirt billowed and rose to tease her thighs. 'Charlie is my darling . . . ' the wind breathed as it tickled the hairs at the nape of her neck.

She took the concrete steps two at a time and sailed through the back entrance of the broadcasting centre, down past the caged props which lined the corridor. The building was settling into its summer quiet; no new drama or laughter, chat shows coasting towards their summer breaks, tanned faces beginning to appear among the white or alcoholic shades of pink.

Wheeling towards Radio Brum's production office on the first floor, she could hear moans coming from the engineers' rooms: 'Shit. Shit. Shit. Mega shit sod shit . . . ', the engineer's distress a perfect replica of rapping rhythms. Mitch felt so stuffed full of herself that she almost popped her head round the door, crazily confident that she could magic any bit of broken equipment back into working order.

Oh, the illusions loved and loving flesh created as it shinily sat on evergreen bones.

The morning's work in the production office was in full swing. Digger Rooney was on the phone, frantically scribbling away on a pad, but he managed to wave a pale green shoe sporting a lemon lace.

Quentin Plunkett, yellow leader wrapped about his neck, was hurrying to the studio but he had time to say, 'It makes you look quite the matron, dear. Can it really be your kind of dress?'

Mitch, who felt beautiful, looked round to see this drab, porky person Quentin was addressing. Only when she saw that there was no one there did she realise he was referring to her. By then he was shutting the production office door behind him; the wood was impervious to her bared teeth. He'd made her quite angry enough to toss any monkey-booted kid out of the window, but Bettina Mayo was not using her desk — in fact, she wasn't in the room. Still growling, Mitch picked up the phone and dialled Woody's number.

'The wife's left me,' he informed her.

'But you're the most devoted couple I

know.' She was astonished.

'I'm the most devoted couple I know, too.'

'Oh dear.'

'It's a bugger, isn't it?'

'I really am terribly sorry.'

'Listen, poppet, don't take this amiss, but sod off, will you?'

'You're not crying, are you?'

'Of course I'm not!' he screamed at her. The phone went dead.

She put the receiver down and then picked it up again. 'Oh hell,' she muttered, dropping it back in the cradle. She decided to ring him the next day.

When she looked up she saw Digger beaming at her from behind his desk. 'That's got that all buttoned up.'

'All what buttoned up?'

'Miss Karlie Kustard. The kid who never sings a note without thrusting the hairs of her fanny up your nose. Which reminds me. You can open your purse and give me twenty quid.'

'I don't like your word associations, Digger. Apart from that, I don't owe you any money.'

'Next Tuesday night we've got a date at Lord Carr Lyons' place. You and I, blossom, are going to storm the upper reaches of society.'

'Just what have you got me into?'

'Cinders and Buttons are going to the ball. Don't look at me like that. It's all in a good cause. They're holding a fancy dress party at Coomb Abbey. Green for Good are fund-raising for their campaign to save the Shakeshaft Nature Reserve.'

'Listen, honeypot. I'm going nowhere as Cinders.'

'To be honest I'm not mad about Buttons. I'm leaning slightly towards a Greek toga. And you can forget your wooden-top Spartans. I want to be a genius. But I can't quite bring to mind what Sophocles did.'

'Wrote *Oedipus*.'

Digger thought about this and then turned his thumb down. 'One wouldn't tempt fate. There's Socrates . . . what do we know about him? Apart from his name, I mean.'

'He was indicted for impiety and the corruption of youth.'

'Hum,' he said. 'Pretty devilish lot, these Greeks.'

'Is that shit Quentin going?'

'He'll be our Saddam Hussein, I expect. The Lord God Almighty has become far too namby-pamby for Quentin. Anyway, blossom, stop straying from the subject. I had to fork out for your ticket and if you don't pay me I can't have my lunch.'

'How did you know I'd want to go?' Mitch

asked, digging her purse out of her handbag.

'Darling, how could you not go?'

'I suppose you're right. And Freya?'

'I expect so. I hear she's joined the cause.'

'If she were more normal I'd see her as Lizzie Borden,' Mitch said.

'I don't know why you're so down on her, Mitch. Let me tell you, one or two lads in the newsroom wouldn't mind getting their legs across.'

Mitch, jaw dropping, held a half-opened purse in her hand.

'Who-ah!' Trish was steaming out of the stock room with a pile of copy pads, felt-tipped pens and expenses claims. 'Wh-ahhh!' The pile tipped over Mitch's desk, knocking the purse out of her hand. It hit her handbag. Pens, coins, credit cards and pounds skated over the desk and on to the floor. 'Oh sugar.'

'No harm done,' Mitch said and dived to help her round up escaping stationery and coins. It was when she was re-sorting things into her purse that she realised one of the photographs she always carried was missing.

'You haven't got a snap among that lot, have you?' she asked Trish. 'A picture of me and Cassie together on the beach?'

'I don't think so . . . ' Trish began checking through the pile.

Even as she looked, Mitch knew it wasn't there; it would be somewhere in Robin Pemberton's Hockley flat waiting to be discovered. Mice skittered down her spine. Am I mad? Playing housey-housey with Charlie when at any moment the police could discover poor Robin.

She riffled through her handbag, heaping the contents on to the desk. The photograph wasn't there.

What else was missing?

Nothing, apparently, but she couldn't be sure. How would she know if a supermarket receipt had gone astray, or perhaps an odd note for a programme item?

Gambolling around with Charlie Collins when my head is on the block. I really have gone absolutely loopy. Even though in her mind's eye Mitch now saw the photograph of Cassie and her in a great policeman's paw, even though her stomach was coming loose, she found she was still smiling. Not mice, but his finger, was running down her spine. But panic was beginning to hover. She pushed it back.

'Are you all right, Mitch?

'What?'

'I know it's awful losing a photo but — '

'Oh yes. Fine. It's just a nuisance. It was a favourite picture.'

I've got absolutely no further in trying to find out more about Bettina Mayo, she was agonising. Then there's Freya. But she said Ann Wellesley had had my copy of *The Brandons*. And I'm still back to the fact that only Ann had a motive for killing her cousin. Unless someone plans to take off with the hundred thousand she's handing over to Green for Good. Though that really would make things ridiculously complicated. Anyway, no one could know for certain she would give any money to the organisation, let alone how much.

She began to feel cold. The smell of Robin Pemberton's decaying corpse must be getting overpowering by now. Time was running out. I'm getting nowhere fast. Just where the hell do I go from here?

As she looked desperately about her, her panicky gaze lit on a bright flash of gold. The brass metal studs on Bettina Mayo's tapestry handbag. It was sitting on one of the two shelves running along the wall, just above the desk. She rubbed her healing chin. Perhaps it contained some of the answers she'd been looking for when she broke into Bettina's flat? Letters, a diary perhaps? If only she could get her hands on the bag for a few minutes. Not easy. She'd have to bide her time. But she'd do it.

If only I could get a break. It's all here and it's got to make sense. It's not a stranger. It can't be. It all ties up somehow. I know the bastard who killed those two kids.

'Mine, blossom.' Digger Rooney was plucking two ten-pound notes out of her hand. 'Actually, I quite see you as a Gorgon.'

'What?'

'At our fancy dress bash. Oh, the terrible look you had on your face a minute ago. One wouldn't want one's mummy to look like that. Ever.'

'Oh, do shut up.' Mitch shovelled back the contents of her handbag.

'Hey, you guys. Anyone seen Quenny?'

Bettina Mayo had appeared at the doorway of the production office, a plastic daisy slide securing her two rat-plaits on top of her head. She was wearing an ex-army surplus flak jacket over a sprigged lilac Laura Ashley dress. Her Nikes looked as if she'd run all the way to India and back in them.

'Try the studios,' said Digger. 'He must have been going that way. He was dripping leader tape.'

'I'm expecting a call from the town hall press office. Be a pal, Digger. Get it for me. They're giving me the name of the woman from the Gogo Ahead Project. I'm on in minutes.'

'Busy myself,' said Digger, removing himself from the vicinity of Mitch's desk.

'Otherwise engaged,' Mitch said. 'Permanently.'

Bettina muttered something which might have been 'wankers' and removed her Nikes from the door. It swung shut.

'An empire builder, I see,' said Mitch. 'How many unpaid secretaries has Miss Rising Star managed to drum up?'

'She's certainly had Shaun doing a few handstands.'

'He's a special case. He's got hormone trouble.'

'Has he? I never knew that,' said Digger.

'He suffers from too much of a good thing. Testosterone even leaks out of his toes.'

'*Vive la différence*,' he sighed.

'Quenny?' Mitch queried. 'Is he carrying her spools of tape, too? Shining her cans for her?' The idea of Quentin Plunkett doing any such thing amused her so much that she began to laugh. 'Quenny. Quenny indeed.'

'Seems to lap it up.'

'You're not serious?'

'Cross my heart. Hand on *The Brandons*.'

'You don't mean they're . . . ' Mitch looked at Digger in disbelief.

'What on earth can she see in him?' Trish, coming back in again from the stock room, had caught the end of their conversation.

'Well, whatever you say about Quentin, he is a good broadcaster. Perhaps she's picking his brains?' wondered Mitch.

'When you're that age you already know more than God,' said Digger. 'She probably thinks she can teach him a thing or two.'

'I couldn't bear Quentin touching me,' Trish shuddered.

'He's got to have the hots for her,' said Digger. 'Would you dare to call him Quenny?'

Trish shook her head.

'It's an appalling thought,' Mitch said. She was remembering what Tommy Hung had told her. 'Green for Good use a van. A green one. Apparently it belongs to Quentin Plunkett.'

'When he's had chilli con carne he sits there all afternoon farting while he slices up Mozart on that editing machine,' said Trish.

'I did go for daddy figures myself once,' Digger said. 'But, you know, daddies aren't much fun.'

'I don't think you're as bad as you make out,' Trish told him.

'That's kind of you, blossom. But if I'm not, it is because I'm so lazy. Getting up to naughties is such bloody hard work . . . ' and the thought of all that labour made him yawn.

'Well, I must go and dig out Shaun,' said Mitch. 'We're supposed to be having lunch and deciding what to do with the Chancellor.'

She found him in the gram library sitting cross-legged on the floor.

'Money, money, money . . .' he crooned, then pulled his face. 'I've been thinking of music for our Chancellor show. But all the tunes have been done to death. Do you think it really is a rich man's world?'

'Yes.'

Shaun sighed. 'That lets me out.'

'If the Chancellor won't agree to a phone-in perhaps we could start with a vox pop? Get a few body blows in that way?'

'Might work,' said Shaun, putting records back on shelves.

Mitch sighed. 'The trouble is that politicians are as adaptable as a virus — if they don't have you one way, they'll swing by for a bite at the back entrance. By the way, do you know if Bettina's got a boyfriend?'

'Why do you ask?'

'Well, Digger seems to think . . . Christ, this sounds crazy — her and Quentin?'

'Quentin likes her because she's got the right pedigree. She went to Oxford and got a first and Daddy's some kind of minor league Anglo-Irish aristo. You know what a mega-snob Quentin is.'

'She's got a boyfriend already?'

'Wouldn't know,' he shrugged.

'You not having much luck?'

'None of your bloody business.'

'Sorry.'

He grinned. 'Come on then, kiddo. Take me out. I'm all yours.'

Mitch did some shopping in town after lunch. It was late afternoon when she got home. There were two messages on her answering machine: one from Tommy Hung, who wanted to come and see her, and one from Ann Wellesley. She'd left a London telephone number. 'I owe you an apology,' Ann Wellesley said. 'Please get in touch as soon as you can.'

She dialled the number but was told Ann Wellesley was not in her room. Picking up the evening paper, she went back into the kitchen to make herself a cup of tea.

It was front page news. CORPSE IN 'IRON COFFIN'. The headline ran across three columns. There was a strap head underneath. MURDER VICTIM FOUND IN BIRMINGHAM SCRAPYARD. She sat down on a stool.

She looked in surprise at her trembling hands.

Well, you knew the body would be found, didn't you? she told them.

They'll find the picture of me and Cassie, too.

Poor Robin.

Tears welled.

Poor Robin. Poor me! If I don't start performing and find the bastard who killed him I'm likely to find myself in the dock.

She tried Ann Wellesley's hotel again. She was still out.

She poured herself a stiff gin and got out the file which contained notes and the newspaper clippings about Jon's death.

What am I missing?

16

The pot-bellied north-westerlies which had rolled in day after day from the Atlantic, bursting, seeding mushrooms in lawns, fattening moss in cracks, had waddled away. Soft blue vistas were revealed, lit by a moist yellow eye. In this eye was Tommy Hung, very smart in his linen jacket, his head almost lost in a huge floppy-brimmed sun hat of the kind favoured by West Indies' batsmen. When Mitch had complimented him on the hat, he'd said, 'One has to try to keep up with the times. I thought of a new straw but, my dear, one doesn't want to compete with one's butcher.' He sat enthroned in one of the cane chairs Mitch had carried out on to the lawn, prim as a petunia in winking grass.

Mitch, making tea, was viewing him through her kitchen window. She knew, of course, that her tea wouldn't be as good as Tommy's; indeed, her accent wasn't as good as his. Measuring up to his oriental standard of Englishness would present a daunting task for any native-born soul. But all the same it was more than Tommy's bones which spoke of the East; he was haunted by sampans and joss sticks. As Mitch could not identify with this heritage — to her, all this was unimaginable — she had to go deeper to try and find a commonality. He presented such a problem in understanding she almost felt she'd have to embark on something like an archaeological dig.

As she picked up the tray she warned herself against reading too much into this odd little fellow. He was simply a retired Chinese laundryman.

He told her how good the tea was. She accepted the compliment because it would be unmannerly not to. Both knew the tea fell well short of his standards.

'You saw last night's six o'clock news?'

'I read about it in the paper first,' she said. 'It made the front page.' She bent forward and picked up her sunglasses.

'You knew Robin Pemberton was dead, didn't you? That was why you changed your mind about Jon Stanton. They were both murdered, weren't they? You believe their deaths are linked?'

She silently adjusted the sunglasses.

'This is a jolly nice garden. Really tip-top.' He turned back to her. 'Am I right in thinking . . . ' He paused. 'How can one phrase this? The poor chap's body they've just found . . . is this going to . . . is this . . . will this make things difficult for you?'

'I assure you I had absolutely nothing to do with his death. At least, not directly.'

'You think, perhaps, that someone killed him to stop him meeting you?'

'I think it's more likely he was killed because of the photos. The ones Jon Stanton took.'

'I see.'

'Mrs Stanton thinks it has all become far too dangerous. She rang me last night and ordered me to stop the investigation. She was extremely upset. Not just about Robin. She's absolutely terrified someone else might be harmed.'

'So it's all over then — as far as you're concerned?'

'I'm afraid not. Because of what I stumbled into at Hockley there's a fair chance I'll find myself implicated. It's too late for me to pull out. The awful thing is not knowing what the hell I'm up to my neck in. I've still no real inkling about what's going on. I'm pretty sure it's connected with the Green for Good movement. I've spent the whole morning at the central library digging out what I can about them. But they appear to be as harmless as a bunch of Girl Guides. There's no militant wing, no history of aggression of any kind. Bunnies are more lethal.' She shook her head. 'None of it makes sense. It should do, but it doesn't.'

'I'm afraid I've still not come up with much. Pumping people sounds easy in theory but it's damned difficult in practice, Mitch. I was so afraid of asking one question too many and making Jeanie Campbell suspicious. Bettina Mayo is apparently something of a polymath. Her degree is in chemistry. Seems a rum kind of background for a local radio broadcaster.'

'Did you find out who her boyfriend was?'

'No. I gathered, though, that she and Ann Wellesley had become as thick as billyo and this is causing some resentment. Ann's apparently got quite a devoted following and they don't like a newcomer horning in. It seems to be causing jealousy in some quarters.'

'Sexual jealousy?'

'Oh, no. Nothing like that. The press officer chappie — '

'Lygo Pim?'

'He's Ann's boyfriend.'

'So that means Lygo's unlikely to be Bettina's lover, too. Besides, his description doesn't fit the one given by Mrs Cowley.'

'I can't quite bring to mind . . . '

'She's the woman who saw Jon taking pictures of Bettina and a man who was apparently her lover. It's more than possible that both Jon and Robin Pemberton were killed because of those photos. Though I find it hard to believe, I'm told that Quentin Plunkett's keen on Bettina. But how could photos of those two together be worth killing for? Though Quentin's younger, basically he's in the same boat as me. A broadcaster who has seen better days. And again it is difficult to believe that anyone would think Quentin good-looking. Though one must admit that tastes differ enormously.'

'So it's hunt the boyfriend?'

'That's certainly a top priority. I saw Bettina's handbag the other day and was tempted to raid it for clues even though there was an office full of people.' Her voice was bleak. 'Things are getting desperate. I've got to crack it somehow . . . Mind you, it's just possible a break's coming my way.' She told him about Ann Wellesley. 'I don't know what's changed her mind,' and then she sighed and shook her head. 'I can't be too hopeful. I mean, if she really had something she'd go to the police, wouldn't she? She wouldn't mess around with me.'

'Why don't *you* go to the police, Mitch? I mean, surely it's only a question of time before they interrogate you?'

'After the body was discovered I did consider it.'

'If you wait until they come to you, won't it look suspicious? They'll wonder why you didn't get in touch when you heard the news. I mean, you went to see him, didn't you? He was already dead, wasn't he? That's why he didn't turn up.'

'I've thought and thought about it . . . but if I'm not very careful I could be looking at twenty years.'

'I don't understand.'

'Simple. I don't trust them. What faith can you have in the system? They've just disbanded the serious crimes squad in this region. Every day they seem to be discharging prisoners convicted on dodgy evidence — some of them have been locked up for years and years.'

'But surely — '

'How do I know what would happen if I came forward? How do I know it's any better now than it was? Is there less pressure for a result now? Let's face it, I'd make good, easy, cost-effective dock material.'

'Have you no faith in British justice?'

'I don't seem to have much faith in anything. Look how much society has changed in the past ten years alone — how it is still changing. And the worse the shark the more admired. These are the pillars our society rests on.'

'I don't believe that.' But he sighed: 'Is one still a bit dewy-eyed? Even though it's twenty years since I became a citizen?'

'Tommy, you're just an old-fashioned romantic.'

'Not so romantic that I'll try to dissuade you. But, Mitch, you must know what a . . . sticky wicket you're playing on.'

'That's putting it mildly.'

'Quite.'

'Listen, if I can just get some handle on this . . . well, I'd be practically free and clear, right? I trust myself far more than any bobby. After all, I've got my own best interests at heart. I just need a bit more time.'

'Right then. We'd better look at the priorities. First there's Bettina's boyfriend. But you have considered the possibility that Jon wasn't taking photos of them but of something else within the field of vision?'

'Yes.'

'Perhaps I could go back and question this Mrs Cowley?'

'And then there's her husband, Fred. He might have seen something.'

'Other people in the houses, too. Look, leave that to me, Mitch. I'll take that on. And, of course, there might be more leads after you've seen Ann Wellesley. When's that?'

'This evening. I'm picking her up at New Street station and driving her home. Seems a bit of an odd arrangement but I'll be honest with you, Tommy. I didn't fancy turning up at night on anyone else's door step and finding . . . '

'Finding what?'

When she didn't say anything, he didn't press for an answer. 'I've got to be biffing along, my dear. Your house and garden are delightful.'

'I'm afraid I'm not very good at keeping things in order.'

Tommy rose. Lifting his sun hat, he fanned his face. 'They say that knowing people is to forgive them for not being oneself.' He was laughing.

'Oriental wisdom?'

'Good heavens, no. One of those delightful Anglican bishops of yours who finds himself too honest to believe in God.'

'We're just a great big fairy tale to you, aren't we?' Mitch said. 'We're your Anglo Saxon dreamland.'

'Some would have you believe an individual wouldn't survive without his myths.'

'The bishops again?' She led him back through the house to the front garden where his discreet grey Rover was parked.

He dropped the window before he drove off. 'Do be careful,' he said. 'Remember, two people are already dead. It's far too early for you to be pulling up stumps.'

'You don't have to worry. I'm a terrible coward.'

'Why do you say that? You know it's not true. Being afraid and cowardice are quite separate things. I'll be in touch. I know I shouldn't — but one's enjoying oneself enormously.' The gravel no more than sedately purred as he floated the car down the drive.

Oh God, she thought, as she watched him go. What am I going to do with him? I can't be responsible for a seventy-year-old school-boy fantasist.

She heard the telephone ringing and hurried back into the house. Ann Wellesley? Was she having second thoughts? But it was Josh Hadley, telling her that the furniture she'd bought would be delivered on Saturday morning.

'I suppose you're off somewhere exciting this weekend with whatsit . . . '

'Amanda. It's Amanda.'

'If it's Paris or Rome I'll wring your neck.'

'Far too poor to stir from Birmingham, chickadee,' Josh assured her. 'Mrs Thatcher has galloped off into the blue taking with her everyone's desire for verde-antico marble tazzas and bleu-de-roi pisspots. The bitch.'

Mitch went upstairs, opened her wardrobe and then, faced with the task of clearing it out, shut the door firmly. Surely she couldn't be expected to carry on as if nothing were happening? Didn't madness lie in that direction?

But what should I do?

What do I want to do?

She escaped those questions by running a bath and sticking her head under the water. It's a funny thing, she found herself thinking. If someone in the next room were confessing to the murders I needn't put my ear to the wall. I'd hear every word as long as I kept my head under the water, and her stressed mind crazily ordered her ears to listen out. She sat up, angrily shaking her head. Pull yourself together. No miracle's going to happen. You're just going to have to solve this yourself.

Two hours later — wearing a linen suit she'd bought long before Freya Adcock had got to know her — she eased the TVR on to the Bristol Road. Now the rush hour was over there was very little traffic. City night life took off in the multi-storey flats and seedy back streets which surrounded the bland fluorescent centre. Outsiders, who knew nothing of what went on under Birmingham's lid, thought it a very dull city. Mitch negotiated the Holloway Circus roundabout and drove down Smallbrook Queensway. The sun, too loosely reined by stringy red clouds, was slithering down the right side of a sixties skyscraper. The skyscaper also glowed red. BANKS BEER UNSPOILT BY PROGRESS. But the writing on the wall was largely unread. The figures on the pavement far beneath scurried head down, worried in their worrying worlds.

Mitch turned left by the concrete and granite aggregate wall of the Bull Ring Centre, passing waiting taxis and blue and white railings. Before her were the tiled pillars marking the entrance to New Street station. Three lines of cars were parked under the canopy. The police, she noted, had cleared away the cars which normally formed a fourth line, just in front of the station itself; this had reverted to the purpose designated on signs — SETTING DOWN PLACE.

Like any normal, red-blooded driver, Mitch looked covetously at these wide open spaces, so teasingly placed right under her nose. But then she saw one of the cars begin to move out from the line of vehicles parked nearest the station. She rammed her foot down on the accelerator and raced to claim the spot.

She was a few minutes early, as she'd intended to be. She got out of her car and began to survey her surroundings more carefully. There was a police car, empty, illegally parked beneath an exit sign, and another nearby. Looking round, she couldn't spot any policemen, but knew, by the total absence of the resident tramps, that they couldn't be far away. She was rather startled to find she was comforted by this. After all, in a few hours she could find herself hauled away to an interviewing room or even a cell. She immediately quelled that thought.

She walked across to the station, pushing against an eighteen-inch square door knob. There weren't many people on the wide, creamy concourse; some sat on suitcases, others stooged about ceramic tiled pillars. All seemed to be perfectly harmless. She checked the arrival times on a video screen. The Euston train would be five minutes late. She toured a fabric tree and wandered past a wall sporting sloping lines of yellow, red and pink, perhaps a mural, perhaps born of a thrifty desire to use up left-over paint. But just what am I looking out for? She wasn't going to let herself answer such an alarming question — but all the same she went on looking.

She went back outside and strolled towards the station exit, past the transparent panelled bus shelters with their green supports, past more taxis and leaned against a concrete wall. Not so much as a toffee wrapper stirred. The place was clean, quiet and orderly; downright boring, she thought, and she thought it again because it comforted her. She looked down to the left of the sixties skyscraper, at the tree tops still and tidy in a sunken roundabout. She began to hear a wail; a police car or an ambulance, but it was a distant sound. Nothing that need concern her.

As she returned to her car she checked her watch. The train should be pulling into the platform five minutes from now. It would probably take Ann Wellesley five minutes more to reach the concourse. I wonder why she wouldn't speak on the phone? Am I in for some kind of assessment — reassessment — before she's prepared to say what's on her mind?

She must have read about Robin Pemberton's death.

Before or after she decided to get in touch?

Mitch settled back in the driver's seat and turned on the car radio. Bettina Mayo was well through the programme. ' . . . and our competition question for tonight. Who — are you ready? Got that pencil poised? Which — wait for it — which actor sobs at rehearsals because she — or he, a he, do you think? — felt Shakespeare — the Bard, no less — had maligned the character the actor was playing? Brain-teaser lines open at six forty-five. And the accumulator, my friends, is still ticking up . . . ' Mitch stuck two fingers in the air before switching off.

The doors of the station began to open, spilling passengers on to the pavement. She hopped out of the car and locked up. She saw Ann Wellesley almost immediately. She was wearing a bright green suit which carried all its clout in its shoulders. In one hand she held two document cases, in the other an overnight bag.

As Mitch started to cross the tarmac a red Volvo pulled up. Lygo Pim, the Green for Good press officer, leapt out.

'Miss Wellesley!' Mitch broke into a run.

Lygo Pim had reached Ann Wellesley and taken the overnight bag out of her hand.

'Miss Wellesley!'

Ann Wellesley turned to Lygo Pim and said something to him as they began to walk across the pavement to his car.

'Hey!' As Mitch came up on her, the other woman turned her head. She took off her glasses, not looking at Mitch but past her ear. She swung back to Lygo Pim and the pair of them made their way across to the car. Mitch was so dumbfounded that she stood for a moment gazing at their retreating backs.

'Hey! You phoned!' She rushed across to the car.

Ann Wellesley was already climbing into the passenger seat. Lygo Pim had tossed the overnight bag into the back of the car and had the ignition key in his hand. He didn't look in Mitch's direction but at Ann and they were laughing.

'Hey! We planned to meet!' Sudden fury spat round Mitch's words.

Ann Wellesley extended a forefinger and pressed down the Volvo's door lock.

Mitch, hands curling into fists, rocked with indignation. 'Hey you!'

Lygo Pim started the Volvo's engine.

'You bitch!'

Rubber squealed as Lygo Pim took the bend too quickly. Mitch was racing back to her car. But already other vehicles were backing out, blocking the way.

She slumped back in the driver's seat. Try and work that one out, she told herself bitterly.

An hour later she tried ringing Ann Wellesley's home number. There was no reply.

Half an hour later she went back in the kitchen to try again. The phone rang out as she was about to pick it up.

'Will you be my white nun?' Charlie Collins asked her.

'Oh Christ. I knew it was too good to be true. You're kinky.'

'You sound like you've had a bad day.'

'Frustrating, yes.'

'I've got us two tickets to a fancy dress party at Coomb Abbey. All in a very good cause.'

'Snap. But I've only got one ticket.'

'Sometimes I don't think you care for me, Mitch.'

But Mitch, a Puritan in her heart of hearts, was already worrying about having an extra ticket. 'I'll give mine to Tommy Hung,' she decided. 'It'll be just his cup of tea. Mead and medieval England. I suppose there will be mead.'

'Am I to understand from all this you'll be my white nun?'

'What are you?'

'A friar. I'm bagging the costumes from the school's Chaucer production.'

'I suppose I ought to be grateful you've not cast me as the Wife of Bath.'

'Darling, all the best costumes have gone,' he said. 'I can drop the habit over on

Sunday. Will you come?'

'As long as you don't tell Freya Adcock what I'm wearing.'

'Do I know anyone of that name? Oh, Coomb Abbey. Where the hell is it?'

'Not too far. I'll be your guide. I'm trying, Charlie. But I can't quite see you as Friar Tuck.'

'Wrong legend,' he said and put the phone down.

Mitch, looking at the receiver in her hand, was thinking: what the hell is he doing on Saturday night? Is he dating some other woman? Jealousy, that so physical pain, twisted her face. The pangs reminded her of other pangs, Woody's pangs. And she was ashamed of herself for not having found out how he was coping.

She rang his number.

'Is that Mitch?' It was Isobella, Woody's wife. 'The bugger's out again. Left me twiddling my thumbs in front of the telly.'

'I'm so glad you're back together. I mean, it's marvellous. Marvellous news.'

'Told you as well, did he? Told half the town. I've never been so humiliated. And now he's out getting a bellyful of booze again. Well, Mr Yo-ho-ho-and-a-bottle-of-rum can sleep on the lawn. He won't get in this house, babs, unless he breaks the bleedin' glass.' The

309

receiver going down crashed through Mitch's head.

At least I know now why I never married again, thought Mitch. Loving and leaving might be painful but it is better than round-the-clock warfare. The occasional smart bomb landing on my doorstep is nothing compared to that.

She tried Ann Wellesley again.

No reply.

She found herself scratching her head.

Just what the hell am I supposed to make of that little charade?

It wasn't until Monday evening, when she was back in the studio presenting gardeners' questions on her show, that she connected plant-watering problems with murder.

17

Helen Brierley was sitting at her kitchen table cleaning fiddle patterned Georgian cutlery. She wore a vinyl cloth pinny over her floral dress. On the bib five stars blazed round the legend TOP COOK; beneath, a laughing chicken was trussed up on a well-garnished plate. 'I'm not at all sure why you've come . . .'

Her arms were bare and, Mitch noted with some surprise, muscular. For a grey-haired old lady she certainly knew how to pile on the elbow grease. But she can't be much older than me, Mitch realised again. When I last saw her at that reception five or six years ago she looked younger than me!

'I mean, I'm not sure I heard you *correctly* when you phoned. About the plant? I suppose you know about Robin Pemberton? They were so very close, you see, that poor chap and Jon. Still, one didn't expect him to . . . I'd no idea he even kept a shot-gun. I was always rather under the impression he was a vegetarian.'

'Robin didn't kill himself. He was murdered.'

'Oh, no. Really. Look here, will you? This

thing has gone too far. When Maddy Stanton employed you one was uneasy but inclined to go along . . . it was a *grief* reaction. Can't you see that, Miss Mitchell? Some people who lose those they love found cancer appeals or campaign to get the traffic laws changed. They have to do something. Maddy — well, she needed someone like you . . . I . . . '

'Robin didn't put the gun in his mouth and pull the trigger. Nor did he bury himself in that scrapyard.' Mitch, startled, found she'd banged her fist on the table.

With her forefinger Helen Brierley quietened a vibrating spoon. 'It's been so strange these last two or three years.' She looked about the kitchen as if she were a stranger in an unknown place. 'They were so very, very close, Jon and Robin. Did you know they went to the same prep school? Such a pair of jolly little lads.' She was looking about her again. 'I always wanted a nice cottage. I saw myself in a place like this.' She shook her head, apparently baffled.

'I wonder if you'd mind if I looked at the plant Jon brought you? I want to take it out of the pot.'

Eyes widening, Helen turned back to her.

'I know it's a peculiar request. I'm the first to realise I'm probably about to make a complete prat of myself. But, you see, I think there were some photographs in that packet Jon sent to Robin just before he died. We can't find them, or the negatives, and it suddenly struck me . . . Well, directly before posting the packet he brought you the plant, didn't he? And you told me it needed repotting. You said the crocks at the bottom were too tightly packed.'

'I don't think I did, my dear. I'm sure I didn't, in fact. And anyway, how can that have any bearing at all on . . . One feels the whole thing has gone too far. Got completely out of hand. Can't you understand? Jon committed suicide, poor little thing, and then Robin . . . They were so close, you see. You do see? It's quite ridiculous to suppose — '

'Mrs — Miss Brierley — '

'One feels a trifle old to be a Ms.' She lifted her head. 'But that's what one wants. Call me Helen. That's simple, isn't it? And if you wish you can dig out that palm. Hopefully it'll put a stop to all this rubbish. But don't do it in the kitchen. Or on the patio. The lawn, I think, and then I won't have to sweep up the compost.' She looked round, her bafflement returning. 'What do you do when you have your little cottage in the country?' She immediately added, 'Of course, one has one's friends. One's really frightfully lucky . . . '

Mitch was already opening the french

doors. 'It's still quite warm,' she said, fearing the old lady would suddenly start on about draughts and order her to shut them. She seized the plant pot.

'Lift from the knees. Good grief. The knees,' Helen called. 'That back will go. Knees-shunt-up! Oh fuck a duck,' and Mitch heard a spoon tinkle on the ceramic-tiled floor. Holding the plant pot at calf-height so she could get the fronds under the lintel, she staggered through the door. She dumped it on the lawn and then stretched, prodding her back. Squatting, she carefully laid the plant out on its side and began to ease the roots out of the pot. A small plastic bag was at the bottom. Fingers trembling, she picked it out of damp compost and grit.

'What is it?' Helen Brierley was just behind her.

Mitch's fingers were already in the bag. 'Negatives.' Her smile grew wider and wider. 'Negatives! Do you have something white to lie them on? It should help illuminate them.'

'Yes. Of course.' Helen Brierley suddenly seemed to snap out of her uncertainties. 'White . . . let me think . . . I've a big serving plate. We can use that.'

There were four negatives. Helen cleared a space among her cleaning materials and put down the plate. Mitch carefully placed them against the white surface. The van, two figures and branches of a tree were discernible. 'I wouldn't even know one of them was Bettina Mayo unless I'd every reason to suppose it was.' Mitch's disappointment flattened her voice.

'Let me look.' Helen Brierley came forward, peered at them and then stepped back. 'I'll put on the light. That might help.'

Mitch picked up the negatives one by one and held them under the beam.

'Well?'

Mitch concentrated. The set of that head looked familiar. Didn't it? She shook her heads. 'I'll have to get them printed up. It's that branch being just level with the shoulders . . . '

'It mostly seems to be backs of head,' Helen said. 'Really, my dear, I'm not at all sure where these photographs are supposed to get one. They look perfectly harmless to me. I simply can't imagine what Jon thought he was doing when he buried them . . . I mean, one thinks of his practical jokes but it's hardly funny, is it?'

Mitch was putting the negatives back in the bag. 'I'd be glad if you didn't tell Mrs Stanton about them. Not for now, at any rate. I'll get them printed and then — if necessary — pass them on to the police.'

'Police?' Helen Brierley seemed astounded.

Mitch began to wonder if the woman were on tranquillisers or anti-depressants. It seemed she couldn't, or wouldn't, grasp the situation. Now she was looking at Mitch as if she were uncertain that she was real. 'The police suspect that Robin Pemberton was murdered.' She said it slowly and clearly. 'They don't think it was suicide.'

'They were so close,' said Helen. 'Real friends.' She turned as a marmalade cat stalked through the open french doors. 'One hopes that devil hasn't been at the birds again. Have you been a good puss, then?'

'I'd better see to your plant,' said Mitch and was relieved to escape from the cottage five minutes later.

'I don't care what Maddy says.' Helen was standing on the front door step watching her go. 'I'm not going to the poor chap's funeral. One can simply do too much of that sort of thing. It can all get too, too gloomy and, after all, one must press on, mustn't one?' She raised her voice. 'One jolly well won't keep buying wreaths for young chaps.' The door banged shut.

Mitch stared back at the vibrating knocker, and then dashed to her car. I've got them. She hugged herself. Got them. Amazing! On the way back she stopped to ring Josh Hadley.

'Honeypot — '

'How much?'

'This is important, Josh. Stop arsing around. I'm going to post four negatives through your letter box. First thing in the morning I want you to take them to be developed. I need the prints pronto.'

'Twenty-four hours is the quickest developing service I know of.'

'The best you can do. Then ring me.'

'Mitch, are you having me on? Listen, spam head — '

Mitch put down the phone on him. She felt easier now she knew she wouldn't have to hold the negatives overnight. I ought to get a security system installed, she thought, but knew she wouldn't. On the whole the thought of living in an electrically controlled prison conjured more nightmares than hearing footsteps on the stairs.

Josh rang her at work after lunch. 'Holiday time, chickadee. The prints won't be ready until Thursday morning.'

He put the phone down on her as she screamed, 'Wha-a-a-t!'

In quiet moments throughout the day she brooded about the delay. I ought to have gone myself. Why didn't I organise it?

She was still thinking about it as Charlie drove her to Coomb Abbey. She shook her

317

head. It was, after all, still the safest way. No one will think I've given the negatives to Josh, she thought. Why should they? Why hadn't she turned to Tommy Hung?

But who the hell knew what went on in that astonishing little man's head? Apart from the fact that he was one of the last people to see Jon Stanton before he was murdered.

She could be sure of Josh. Through and through. Marrow sure. He may be bonking Miss Rocket Launcher but that didn't mean she couldn't count on him.

'Look at that.' Charlie was slowing the car.

Coomb Abbey grew out of the top of a limestone outcrop, its jumble of battlements, square and round towers and crenellated chimney pots bronzed by a setting sun. 'The only thing that's missing is El Cid.' He changed down into second gear. 'My God, this hill is steep.'

'El Cid was Spanish,' Mitch said. Of their own accord her fingers were creeping across the handbrake to his black robe. 'I thought monks had to shave their heads. Or they had little tonsures.'

'Nuns shave their heads, too.'

'I'll never be a nun,' said Mitch. 'I'm too little.'

'Of all the reasons I've ever heard, that takes the biscuit.'

'Well, you live and learn. I've never tried on a habit before. You've got to be tall to carry one off.'

'And you'd have to do something about those eyes of yours.'

'What's wrong with them?'

He took a hand off the wheel and ran his forefinger down the nape of her neck. 'They're liable to get a feller unfrocked.'

'What am I going to do when I'm ninety?' moaned Mitch.

'Look at it this way. You've forty years to go.'

He began to follow the yellow parking arrows. She sighed and leaned back in the passenger seat. It was a soft evening. Through the open window she could hear the rush of breeze, the cawing of rooks settling in beech trees. 'Come on, Mitch. Stir your stumps.'

'Being a priest suits you,' she said, seeing the black figure straighten out by the driver's door. She clambered on to the gravel. 'In spite of my habit I feel absolutely naked. Couldn't I wear a teeny bit of make-up?'

'What? And lose that designer saint look? Just bang the door to. I'll lock up.'

'Good heavens!' Mitch caught sight of a diminutive Royal Navy captain. Hands clasped lightly behind his back, he was strolling through the car-park gates to the

319

Abbey. 'Tommy Hung. He looks absolutely splendid.'

'A Chinese version of Prince Philip.' Charlie was laughing.

'I wish I didn't have to be a nun. It doesn't suit me at all.'

'Of course it does. Brings out your hidden depths.'

'Pull the other one.' Mitch, stumbling, gathered up her skirts and followed Charlie. A stream of party-goers was heading up the incline to the crenellated five-storey gate-house. The studded doors stood open. A stone corridor led to an arch which formed the entrance to the inner courtyard. Feet echoed and re-echoed on paving bowed with centuries of use.

The huge courtyard was split into a lower and upper level by curving steps. To the right were Tudor buildings; ahead, on the upper level, the mass of the fourteenth-century banqueting hall, lemon and cerise roses rioting round the Gothic doorway.

Following Batman and a female Robin, Mitch and Charlie entered the two-storey hall. At the far end, on a wide stone dais, a long table had been set before a tapestry. Bottles and glasses were lined up in square battalions.

'Just what one likes to see,' said Socrates

coming up behind them. 'But you have to buy a drinks ticket to get a bottle. Fifteen quid. What a scam.'

'Digger! Let me introduce you to Charlie Collins.'

'I've been admiring the way you handle your frock,' Digger told him. 'I keep tripping over my skirts.'

'It's down to my admiration for the fair sex. I'm always watching the ladies. When you do that you learn a lot.'

'Not from me,' said Mitch. 'My hem is forever getting tangled round my ankles. God knows how my female ancestors managed.'

'Time to get the drinks in,' Charlie grinned, winking at Digger. 'Won't be long.'

'Turn round. Slowly,' Mitch ordered Digger. 'Oh . . . yes . . . You look scrumptious, honeypot. But so terribly decadent. You ought to have been Caligula.'

'Couldn't do with all those orgies,' said Digger. 'One doesn't just have to be dissipated. One has to be fit, too. I simply wouldn't be able to drum up the energy. Have you seen Freya?'

'She's not a nun, too?' Mitch asked. Her voice was rising.

'Well, she'd be a bloody sight more convincing than you. I can smell Chanel No.

5 from here. And a white habit! Really, blossom — '

'Oh, do shut up, Digger. I can be white if I like. Especially if you can be Socrates. Who is Freya?'

'Little Bo-peep.'

'I don't believe it.'

'And you'd better be nice to her,' said Digger. 'You're one of her sheep now. I've just heard she's got the station manager's job. Oh. Your new man's coming back.' He was casting a very critical eye over Charlie. 'Runs ten miles and then eats a breakfast of iron filings,' he decided. 'Aren't you the lucky one. Do try and live up to your habit. See you later, blossom.' Bending to hitch up his robe between thumb and forefinger, he trundled off.

'Have I frightened him away?' asked Charlie.

'He's doing his tour. Seeing if there's any talent. He can't be easy in any gathering until he's got that chore over and done with.'

'Chore?'

'Digger is a very conscientious man,' Mitch told him. 'Though I suspect he finds sex a frightful bore he feels he has certain obligations to society. It's his own variation of the Protestant work ethic.'

Charlie laughed. 'Can I just pour you a

drink and leave you for a couple of minutes? Nature calls. Hang on to the bottle, will you? Don't drink the lot.'

'Don't get kidnapped,' Mitch told him. Every now and then just looking at him redesigned her anatomy. Had she once felt this way about her husband Max? About Josh?

She supposed she must have.

At your age, too, she told herself as she watched him go. She consciously pulled herself together, straightening her back, lifting her head and shoulders.

I'll go and find Tommy Hung, she decided. But what can he have found out from Edna and Fred Cowley that I don't know already?

Tommy was in what had once been the kitchens of Coomb Abbey. He was kneeling and apparently worshipping a battered oak cupboard. 'See? The carving in these six tiny panels is perforated. Do you see that, Mitch? It's for ventilation. It's a dole cupboard. They stored bread in here and the poor lined up and got their rations.'

'How do you know that?'

'I read it up in a guidebook before I came.' He got up, dusting off his knees. 'Coomb Abbey has always been a tourist attraction. Queen Victoria came when she was a bright young thing. Horace Walpole. And I expect our Queen biffed along, too.' He moved his hands in a curious fashion, as if putting away a toy, and turned to her. 'Have you been able to get hold of Ann Wellesley?'

'No.'

'That's the damnedest thing I ever heard . . . '

'I've come to the conclusion that she did actually intend to talk to me — perhaps to discuss Robin Pemberton's death — but someone not only dissuaded her but did the job so well that she felt entirely justified in cutting me dead at the station.'

'Lygo Pim? Her boyfriend?'

'I wonder what his motive was? Do you want a drink?' She remembered the bottle she was carrying.

He shook his head. He was smiling. The smile got broader.

'You have found out something, haven't you?'

'Perhaps. The executive of Green for Good met last night. It was arranged that I should arrive when it was supposed to end — round about eight — and take Jeanie Campbell out to dinner. I arrived a little early and was in the men's cloakroom when the meeting broke up. One of the chaps left his papers on the bench while he popped out to the heads.'

'Heads?'

'WC. I managed to lift the papers. I didn't think it would cause too much alarm. The chap would simply suppose a colleague took them by mistake.'

'Oh, Tommy. Do get on with it.'

'Jottings mostly — a timetable of events apparently connected with Spencer Thumper's visit to Birmingham — '

'The Environment Minister?'

'My guess is that Green for Good are planning a demonstration. By the way, Radio Brum is mentioned.'

'Spencer Thumper's one of the guests in Digger Rooney's afternoon show. But nothing will happen at the station. Freya Adcock will use her influence to see it doesn't. She's just been made station manager. She won't want to foul her own backyard.'

'Well, I think we can be pretty sure that something's going to happen when the Minister comes to Birmingham.'

'Something awful enough to somehow involve the killing of two people?'

'I know, Mitch. Green for Good are famed for their non-violence.'

'As I see it, it has to be about individuals and not the group. I don't at all know where the photographs fit in but the only one who has a real motive for Jon Stanton's killing is his cousin Ann Wellesley.'

'But why kill Robin Pemberton?'

Mitch sighed. 'I don't know.'

'Is Ann Wellesley coming tonight?'

'No one seems at all sure. It appears to depend on whether she gets back from Edinburgh in time. There seems to be some kind of rallying of the troops going on. Oh, all right. That does fit in with your theory about some kind of demonstration when Spencer Thumper arrives. But can that really have something to do with the killings?' She paused and shook her head 'What we need are Sherlock Holmes's brains.'

'It certainly is one of his three-pipe problems,' Tommy said. 'Listen, I'll have a look round for the Wellesley woman and if she's here I'll tackle her.'

'That's one lady who isn't going to be thrilled if you tell her you're investigating Jon's death,' Mitch warned him.

'I'll think of something,' said Tommy. 'But I do find this fibbing hard going. Sometimes when I see Jeanie Campbell I go hot and then cold. It's not honourable, Mitch.'

'It's done in the best circles. Though top people call it being economical with the truth. I keep telling myself it's all right to fib as long as I don't lie to myself. But I know for a fact, Tommy, I'd have fallen on my sword long ago if I hadn't saved myself with a porkie now and then. Lies have their saving graces.'

He was examining her. He cupped rather than pulled his ear, almost as if he were trying to tune in. 'Why on earth did you choose a nun's habit?'

'It was chosen for me by my boyfriend. It happens to be one of Chaucer's left-overs.'

'Your boyfriend's rather got an eye for these things,' Tommy said. 'You look awfully nice in it. A naughty religious.'

'Men are extraordinary. What is so nice about an unholy nun?' But she was laughing. 'I suppose I must go and find Charlie. Have you ever been in love?'

'Unfortunately, no.'

'What's unfortunate about it? One can't deny there are some nice bits. Very nice bits. Marvellous bits. But you're not in control, Tommy. Somebody else is driving your car. And it can be so painful. Worse than having shingles.' She took a swig of wine from the bottle. 'Oh, well. Back to the fray, honey-pot . . .'

Sounds now blasted from the banqueting hall but in spite of following them Mitch managed to get lost in the maze of stone-flagged corridors. She found herself in a room which had sailed right out of a seventeenth-century galleon. She could almost hear the movement of cork between

327

the oak planks on the floor. The walls were plain panelled and a chequerwork wooden ceiling was painted in peeling greens and ivory. Stained glass emblems decorated two of the eight long lattice windows.

'Kiddo, it's you!'

Mitch turned to see Freya Adcock coming through the door. She was wearing a white dress with layered net skirts. The material was covered in baby hearts. There was a large heart on each sleeve and her baby-soft hair was held up by heart-shaped slides. 'Digger told me you were Bo-Peep.'

'If you ask me, Digger's nursery school education leaves much to be desired.' Freya rose on to her toes and swirled round. 'What do you think? OK? I thought that being a Good Fairy was going a bit far. The Queen of Hearts was something of a compromise but I think it works.'

'It's very . . .' Mitch reached out for a word, ' . . . dazzling.'

'One tries, kiddo.' Freya beamed. 'Actually, I'm looking for Quentin Plunkett. I have a message from his wife. It looks like she'll be stuck in Edinburgh with Ann. You've not seen him?'

'Who is he? Let me guess. Beethoven? Mozart? Brahms? Our musical maestro wouldn't stoop to Elgar.'

'I think he's a Coke can.'

'Quentin?'

'That's what he told me. Though he yelled it in that deafening way of his. He might have been telling me to mind my own business, kiddo.'

'That sounds more like it. Do you know the way back to the hall?'

Mitch followed her leader. The sounds became louder and louder.

'Give it, give it, give it to me baby ... Make me ... purr ... fect purrfect ... Give it, give it, give it ... ' roared the disco words, the beat of feet, the braying hall. 'Hey, honey. You honey. True honey ... make me ... create me ... sate me ... honey, honey ... ' Socrates, his skirts flying ever upwards, Batman, his cloak on end, Cinders grinding her bum, the black friar, both sandals off the ground, rope belt flaying Mary, Mary Quite Contrary. 'Give it, give it, give it to me baby ... ' Two heads bobbing and throbbing above frolicking Coke cans. ' ... Make me ... make me ... purr-fect ... '

Freya was yelling something in her ear, but Mitch couldn't hear her. Her feet had gone off on their own, rocking to the rhythm of the Coke can heads. Beyond the blasting beat, Mitch could hear another tune, a reedy whistle, and in her mind's eye she saw other Coke cans, all but one of them moving in a ghostly dance on the mantelpiece of Jon Stanton's flat.

'Hey honey. You honey. True honey . . . make me . . . create me . . . sate me . . . honey, honey, honey . . . ' Bettina's rat-plaits whipping her ears, Quentin's mane lifting off his beetroot head. The patterns of light suddenly resolved into a familiar wink of light beyond the dancing figures.

' . . . say hello to Lord Carr Lyons and then get hold of Quentin . . . ' Mitch caught the drift of Freya's words. 'There's Carrie.' Aladdin, his turban spinning on a raised golfing umbrella, was drinking from a champagne bottle as his pelvis jerked. 'Make me . . . make me . . . purr..fect.' The Queen of Hearts bounding, to the left and then the right, leapt towards him.

Mitch, resolutely turning her gaze from the flying black friar, found again the familiar wink of light. It hardened into the stud on Bettina's handbag which was sitting on one of the chairs lining the walls of the hall. Right, she thought, and seized her chance.

'Make me . . . create me . . . sate me . . . ' Her feet thumped as she rocked past sweating bodies. She dropped her own handbag on the chair and scooped up Bettina's. ' . . . Give it,

330

give it, give it . . . ' She mouthed the words triumphantly as she beat her retreat. 'Pur-rr . . . fect . . . ' rocked each of the timbers in the six-hundred-year-old hall. Through the door, Mitch raced past the cardboard arrows which pointed the way to the lavatories. Hurling herself into one of them, she slammed and locked the door. Her ear ever alert for the continuing beat, she opened the bag. She pulled out a diary. It was quite large, and, though it had only been in use for six months, well worn. She opened it and saw closely written pages. She stuffed the diary down her bra, opened the lavatory door and raced back along the corridor.

The beat was louder, faster, whipped up on a tide of clapping. 'Make me . . . create me . . . ' The chains of the chandeliers rattled, trophy displays of decapitated deer swayed, glasses bounced, mouths widened, feet hammered.

Mitch exchanged the bags.

Aladdin's hat fell off a rafter and capped an electric light bulb. A larger Coke can collapsed into a smaller one. Socrates' skirt fell down.

A diminutive navy captain, viewing all this from the entrance, turned on his heel and stalked away.

18

'For the classic country and western lyric you must have four elements. Your mother, your prison sentence, your lover and a train . . . ' Bettina Mayo was lecturing Quentin Plunkett. She was sitting behind his tape machine, his yellow leader round her neck. He was propped up against a nearby desk.

Mitch, waiting for a voice at the end of a telephone line, was watching this with some incredulity. You don't have to plan the downfall of those you dislike, she was thinking. Wait long enough and they'll land in the shit all by themselves.

'Right. Oh, definitely.' Quentin's hand appeared to be wandering around in mid-air but in reality it was moving towards Bettina's left leg. She seemed very bright, very sharp, honed. The rat-plaits, nestling on top of her head, were tied together with a white shoelace. She was wearing a bright green man-sized T-shirt over navy blue leggings, her shapely feet thrust in Jesus sandals. There was something about her which was — which was what? Cooking too fast? And there was, too, an over-familiar look about her. Mitch began to wonder if she were experiencing *déjà vu*.

She sighed and turned away. Because of Miss Smartie Pants she'd spent half the morning chasing a woman she knew who taught German when she should have been concentrating on Revell Ullman, Chancellor of the Exchequer, MP for Birmingham East.

The diary she'd filched last night was — wouldn't you know it? the frustration of it all was hot in her veins again — written in German. If it had been French Mitch might have stood a chance — even though it was more than her grasp of the Gallic subjunctive that left a lot to be desired. Bloody German, Mitch thought again and almost bared her teeth. You'd have thought getting a first in chemistry at Oxford was enough for most kids.

She glanced down gloomily at the pile of photocopied clippings about the Chancellor that News Information had sent her. If only I had as many brains as that rat-plaited kid, she mourned. Catch me horsing around with a dip-head like Quentin Plunkett. At least she'd been able to read the telephone numbers in the diary, thought that was all, for they had been preceded by what looked like mathematical formula. And she didn't know any maths teachers.

She glanced up. Bettina was twirling yellow

leader between her thumb and forefinger, aware Mitch was staring at her but apparently considering her presence so negligible that she need not acknowledge it. Mitch took a deep breath and, not without difficulty, detached herself from her frustrations. She'd a show to get out.

She looked down at the clippings. The Chancellor beamed at her. Like a tulip bulb, all his strength flowed from his belly; it fed up through a willowy neck to a lantern-jawed, Noddy head and down etiolated legs to policeman's feet.

She tried the phone again. 'Hello there.' Still no one at the end of the line.

She turned the sheets with her free hand. Revell Ullman was an Oxbridge man from London. It was his first wife, Helen Brierley, who had the Birmingham roots. She'd been born in Solihull and they'd met through her brother. It had apparently been love at first sight for they were married three months later. Two years after that, going home from a New Year party, the Rev had run his Rover into the side of a clothing warehouse. Helen, six months pregnant, had gone into labour. The child, stillborn, had arrived before the ambulance. The Rev had climbed out of the wreckage with barely a scratch; that talent for emerging unscathed from any wreckage, both in business and politics, had later stood him in good stead. Helen had been badly injured; she was unable to have any more children.

'Hello . . . ' she shouted down the phone.

Silence.

The Rev had moved into the chancellorship after the last Oxbridge man — a well-regarded figure who was considered as something of an intellectual — had walked the economy over a cliff. But if the British 'tightened their belts' and 'paid themselves less' and 'took their medicine' the Chancellor was sure the light would appear at the end of the tunnel. That's the next boom, Mitch thought, before the next bust, which would presage more hunting for light at the end of tunnels.

At last a voice. 'I'm afraid I simply can't reach Professor Klarner at the moment — '

Mitch slammed the phone down. 'Anyone seen Shaun?' she yelled.

'He's about somewhere. Editing. Freya rang for you again, Mitch. You'll have to go. Now. She's driving me mad . . . ' Trish, the secretary, told her.

'Not as crazy as she's driving *me*.'

'Oh, stress. Stress,' Digger Rooney crooned, fluttering his hands over his heart. His neck was rigid. He was balancing a polystyrene cup on his head.

'Oh, do shut up.' Mitch got up and coaxed her limbs towards the door. Even the small amount of disco dancing she'd done the night before had left her muscles quivering with indignation but, unlike Quentin, she could at least walk without a limp.

She managed to get herself to the station manager's door in reasonable order. There she paused. Today Freya had come in to work in her electric blue culottes and print jacket. Meeting her earlier in the cloakroom, Freya had commented on Mitch's attire. 'All these dresses and skirts . . . ' and she'd wagged a playful finger. 'I do believe you're changing your image.' Mitch had not been able to trust herself to reply. Now, feeling her anger rise again, she took a deep breath.

A job, after all, is a job.

But just how much is this job worth?

She nursed her limbs in.

The station manager's room was twice as big as that allotted to the programme organiser but, like all Radio Brum's management offices, had the same view of the dual carriageway in front of the building. Freya's desk was also bigger, and so was her chair. Her plant was so big a window sill was too small. It had to stand on the floor. 'Hi, kiddo. Take a pew.' In the latest approved management style she came round from behind her desk and dropped into one of the two chairs in front of it. 'What's on the menu?'

Mitch took the other chair. 'We've roughly divided the show into four strands,' she said, dragging her eyes away from the straining seams on the print jacket. 'Shaun's done wonders. One. We've got some local industrialists on tape giving their views. In the studio Professor Klarner will be picking up on the points they make with the Chancellor. Two. A tape from the consumer side, shopkeepers and the like. Joining Professor Klarner in the studio will be a woman from one of the financial houses. She's an undertaker specialising in little businesses — steps in when they go bust. That brings us to the six-thirty news bulletin. We go on a different tack then and look at women's issues. Tax relief on company cars, none on employing help to look after the children of working mothers . . . that sort of thing. Legion. A tape from women raising their points and Dr Ruth Clarke in the studio bearding Revell Ullman — '

'Clarke's an out-and-out feminist — '

'She's always been good value. She not only puts her points over well but with humour.'

'Keep a tight rein,' said Freya. 'And four?'

'Families and causes with individual gripes. We've got a mother of a chap who was

337

imprisoned in the Middle East. His salary was paid into a bank account while he was being held and now the Inland Revenue want their cut. If he had been working abroad he wouldn't be liable for tax — but, of course, he wasn't. He was chained to a central heating radiator. Then there's a woman from the hospital volunteer car pool. The pool ferry patients around. The Revenue want to tax their petrol expenses. There are three or four of these — '

'But the Chancellor will simply say he can't discuss individual cases.'

'I know. But most of the listeners will find the bulk of the programme heavy going. There's nothing like a bit of outrage to liven things up. And, of course, four isn't a stand-alone segment. We're lacing the stuff through the rest.'

'You're the ringmaster?'

Mitch nodded.

'Can you make them all perform?'

'That's my job.'

Freya thought about it. 'No suggestions. Sounds good to me. Make 'em jump, kiddo. Have you met the Chancellor before?'

'Once. He was Minister for Trade and Industry then.'

'Tricky man, by all accounts. Now. You're going to have your hands full doing your ringmaster stuff. I don't want you to self op. Shaun will drive the show. I'm going to bring Bettina Mayo in to do the running around — fetching glasses of water, fixing taxis, looking after coats — OK?'

Mitch nodded.

'You don't seem very keen. Bettina's got a lot of potential, you know. Good voice. Most young girls come to grief on S. They sound like demented swans. Not Bettina. She'll go far.'

'No doubt.'

'Hmm. Well. The set-up is this. Digger will move into Studio Two to do his 'Round and About' show which will leave Studio One free by four o'clock. I'll get Bettina to stick Radio Brum publicity stuff round the walls. The *Birmingham Sentinel* want to do some photos. And I'll get our in-house photographer to come along too. Just in case any of the nationals decide they're interested. Photo call five to six. That gives us ten minutes — I'll make sure the six o'clock news bulletin finishes on time. OK? I want just two on the photos. You and the Chancellor. We're not in the business of promoting leftie professors and feminists or even grey little creatures from financial houses. It's Radio Brum broadcaster with the king of the counting house. OK? Look businesslike. Make sure your headphones are on.'

Mitch nodded.

'The Chancellor and his entourage arrive at five thirty and they'll be shown up to this room. There'll be a decent sherry, one or two nibbles, nothing elaborate. Straight after the show the Chancellor is going off to a din-din at the town hall. One or two of our top brass will be here to show the flag. And, of course, I want you here, so make sure that everything is up and ready in Studio One by that time.'

'What about Shaun? He not only bagged the Chancellor but has produced some really good tapes for the show.'

'All right. He can come and meet. Tell him to go home and have a bath and get changed. He's to be nice and polite. Most of all he's to be invisible.'

'OK.'

Freya was now critically reviewing Mitch. 'Those light colours you're wearing should come up well on black and white photos,' she decided. 'But we're dealing with the Chancellor here. If you look like someone's secretary, Mitch, you'll get treated like that. You usually dress with such panache. It gives you presence.'

Mitch looked at all her panache in the presence before her and found herself robbed of speech.

'Find time after lunch to pop home, kiddo, and get yourself geared up for the occasion. Something with punch. But keep it light. Give me the vintage Mitch Mitchell. This is the first big Radio Brum occasion since I became manager. There're plenty of Brownie points to be grabbed. You and I together — won't we show 'em . . . ' and she winked.

After this Freya got up and — another trick learned in a management skills workshop? — started towards the door. Automatically Mitch found herself rising, found herself being shown into the corridor.

By then she felt like a performing monkey. Which, of course, is what a broadcaster is, she told her squeaking muscles as she tooled them back to the office.

'He wrote the lyrics in Normandy,' Bettina was lecturing Quentin Plunkett, now banished to a chaste distance and absent-mindedly rubbing calf muscles. 'He stayed in the same room as Proust. *Remembrance of Things Past*, right? Borrows heavily from the post-modernist deconstruction bag . . . the random wave formations . . . '

Mitch sank into her chair. Sighing, she got down to the early life of Revell Ullman as portrayed by the media. Before marrying Helen Brierley, it appeared that he'd never ventured further north than Oxford, where he'd spent his student days. During one of his earlier speeches it was evident that he'd thought the Black Country, the industrial belt to the west of Birmingham, was in Scotland. God preserve us from all politicians, Mitch thought gloomily, remembering the one and only time she'd been in the presence of a Prime Minister. She'd been working as a young reporter on a Manchester evening paper, covering a Harold Macmillan walkabout in some of the city's grimmer streets. The entourage had been passing a washing machine factory — domestic appliances had still been made in Britain in those days — when the siren went off. The Prime Minister had instinctively ducked. 'What's that?' As none of his advisers appeared able to answer, a member of his bodyguard had piped up 'It goes off when it's time for the workers to go home, sir.'

'Cheer up, Mitch. Come and have some lunch. You look like a professional mourner earning his crust the hard way.'

'Too much to do, Digger . . . Oh hell, why not? It's going to be a horrid day. I feel it. Deep in my aching bones. No need to look like that. You just wait. Some time soon you've got to get to grips with the Minister for the Environment.'

'All water off a duck's back, blossom,' Digger said. 'The secret is not to let the bastards get you down. Life is short. Politics go on for ever.' He had turned to gaze at Bettina, who was still lecturing Quentin. 'And you think you've got problems.'

After lunch Mitch went home to change. Her meekness worried her. When she was as biddable as this the left side of her brain was usually keeping the reasonable, conscious, rational right soothed while deep in unconscious dark it plotted revolution.

You aren't going to fire Freya Adcock. Don't even think it. Who would ever give you another job? You're unemployable. For God's sake, you're fifty years old.

Parking the TVR, she automatically looked towards her door step. Ever since Robin Pemberton's body had been discovered she expected a couple of detectives to appear on it. But still no sign of the police. Oh, if only she knew what was going on.

Probably nothing.

She bathed and changed into a silk top and baggy ochre yellow pants. The outfit was probably more suitable for an evening drinks party than a dust-up with the Chancellor but Mitch found she was out of patience with Freya. Sod her, she thought, and added long dangly ear-rings which had nothing discreetly

343

middle class about them.

She did think of getting through another half-dozen of the telephone numbers she'd found in Bettina's diary. She decided against it. Sufficient unto the day, she thought. She made herself a coffee, pretended she didn't want a cigarette — untipped, she was thinking, and king-sized — and drove back to the broadcasting centre.

'You look like a retired belly dancer,' Digger told her after looking her over.

'That's all right, then. Just as long as I don't appear to be someone's secretary,' and Mitch went to check Studio One.

The studio complex was on the opposite side of the corridor to the management offices. A door led into a box of space with two doors off. One was the entrance to Studio One, the other led into a long ops room. A door at the far end of this led into another box of space and off this was the door into Studio Two. This arrangement meant that staff had free access to the ops room even when the red lights were on and both studios were transmitting, either internally to other parts of the organisation or externally to listeners. Both studios had two windows, one overlooking the ops room, the other with a view of the broadcasting centre's inner courtyard.

344

Mitch entered Studio One. Shaun was already at the electronic desk, checking over the control panels. In a wire basket nearby were the pre-recorded elements of the programme — the taped interviews, some actuality from factory floors and city dealing rooms. The station's identity signal, trails for other programmes and the 'City Talk' signature tune were on separate cartridges. Records were stacked near them.

'Watcha . . . ' said Shaun. He was bent over the desk, fiddling with a fader.

'You look smart,' said Mitch.

'I look fucking unreal,' said Shaun.

'Certainly not at all your usual self.'

In the middle of the studio was a round table, centrally hung microphones unravelling down from their cabling. Shaun had put Mitch's notes in the place she would sit, opposite the window overlooking the inner courtyard, with a good view to the right into the ops room. Mitch studied the table. 'We'll have the Rev with his back to the wall facing the ops room,' she decided. 'Then when Bettina plasters the publicity material on the wall, that will form the background to the photos. We'll have the prof with his back to the courtyard window. That sound OK?'

'I feel like a little boy going to the birthday

party of some rich brat,' said Shaun. 'I hate dressing up.'

'You look handsome.'

'I look like a suit.'

'Never mind. You get to shake hands with a famous body. And your name is all over the recorded bits of the programme. That's not going to do your future any harm. Where're my cans?'

'Oh Lord. Didn't I get them?' Shaun got up.

'Don't bother. I'll — '

'No, no. I've ants in my pants. I hate this waiting about. Leave it to me.'

Mitch began to check through the tapes. A microphone spoke. 'They're arriving,' Trish, who was helping out in the ops room, told her. 'Freya has just buzzed through. She wants you in the manager's office.'

'We're off, then.'

'Good luck.'

Mitch, wrenching her shoulder pads forward, discovered the sudden pump of adrenalin had magicked away her muscle fatigue. She was able to march into the fray.

The organisation's local top suits were already gathered in Freya's office, and were being waited on by a couple of secretaries from Admin. As men who had been broadcasters in some previous incarnation, they allowed themselves all that was avant-garde in ties; one wore scarlet-rimmed glasses, another conveyed his artistic temperament by having a centimetre more hair than his colleagues. Mitch's presence was acknowledged with a few ritual words of greeting. That done, they turned their backs and spent their time confirming their status. 'Of course, as I told the DG . . . ' 'The VIT found out soon enough — naturally, he apologised to me . . . ' 'When I was on Captain Bob's yacht . . . ' When they were not letting each other know how important they were they eyed the secretaries' legs and breasts and giggled.

They did not eye Mitch. Now she'd turned fifty most men totally disregarded her. Those who didn't, she chose to regard as connoisseurs.

Holding her head high, she marched over to the station manager's desk and got herself a glass of Freya's good sherry. It tasted so sour she almost pulled a face. Was it some kind of wine vinegar? she wondered. Perhaps introduced by management to keep all programme contributors sober — at least for the duration of the broadcast?

Even before the door opened a quiver went through the top suits and they spread out in V formation to welcome Britain's Chancellor to their bosom. At first Revell Ullman was indiscernible, surrounded by a swarm of his own henchmen. Slowly, he emerged, first the bulbous stomach, then the bald, nodding head and lastly the policeman's feet. 'Are we really on time?' he was asking an aide, his famously bushy eyebrows stretching into the stratosphere. 'Good Lord! What's gone wrong?' The aide and others who overheard the quip laughed heartily. But when the Chancellor became serious again, so did the aide, so did the others.

Wine vinegar or no, Mitch, in desperate need of a drink, downed it and got another.

'What a lot of wankers.' The whisper dropped in her ear. She turned to see Shaun, all spruce and glittering, regarding his superiors with the wide eyes of the very young.

'You'll join them,' Mitch predicted.

'Will I? What a way to spend the only life you've got.'

'Everyone says that. At the beginning. But when you've got a wife, a kid and a mortgage it's the only game in town.'

'No way.'

'No?'

'The Chancellor is asking for you.' The electric blue-breeched Freya was bearing down. 'Photo call four mins. Shaun. Check the publicity stuff is thick on the walls. Tell Bettina to keep an eye on the *Birmingham Sentinel* photographer. Make sure he doesn't get too pushy. Hop to. Mitch, for God's sake, put that glass down . . . ' and Mitch found herself being swept towards the magic circle.

'My dear,' beamed the Chancellor, beamed the aide, beamed the organisation's top suits. 'And what kind of a ride is one going to get?'

'A mystery tour, of course.'

They all laughed.

'I hear you're quite the old hand. 'On Report', was it? Good programme, that. My wife watched when she got the chance.'

' 'Fair Play', actually.'

'Really?' The Chancellor's eyebrows made their climb. 'Good for you . . . ' showing appreciation for a programme Mitch realised he'd probably never heard of until now. 'I must watch the Ps and Qs, mustn't I, my dear?'

'I would say you always did that.'

'Would you now?' And the Chancellor looked at her for the first time, his round, rather protruding eyes, fully open. He'd never been a man to be caught on the hop. 'A mystery tour, eh? I thought those had gone quite out of fashion.'

'Did you?'

An aide was whispering something into

Revell Ullman's ear. 'Seems we're on parade, my dear. The photographers await. After you. After you . . .'

And so it was that Mitch led Britain's Chancellor into the studios, Freya and the organisation's top suits trundling behind Revell Ullman's men.

Professor Klarner was in the ops room, already stripped down to his shirt-sleeves and popping broad bright red braces. His horn-rimmed glasses rested in his woolly hair. He was like a champion motor-bike rider. When he was ready to go into action those glasses snapped down on to his nose. Vroom. Vroom. At these moments Mitch swore she could hear his brain hotting up. 'Whatcha there,' he called to her now. 'Good evening, Chancellor.'

'Evening, Ronnie. Jacket off already?'

'All tooled up and ready to go.' Ronnie Klarner smiled his cherub's smile. He eased his plump buttocks back, relaxing his leg muscles, and then limbered up. 'One hell of a day. Rush. Rush. Rush. Sorry you couldn't reach me earlier, Mitch.'

'No problem.'

'There's an old dear waiting in reception for you.' Bettina had come up behind Mitch. 'Says it's urgent. She wants to talk to you.'

'Who is it?'

Bettina shrugged. 'Grey-haired. Print frock. Reception has the name.'

'Madeleine Stanton? Oh hell. Show her up to my office, will you? Get her a cup of tea or something.'

'If we could just have the Chancellor and Mitch. In Studio One now, please. Mitch and the Chancellor. Photo call,' and when Freya's hands said 'Chop chop' even Britain's Chancellor showed a fair turn of speed. They found themselves swept through the tiny cupboard of a corridor through the door into Studio One. Shaun was already at the electronic desk, ready to drive the show. He was gossiping with the two photographers lounging against the ops room window. They picked up their cameras as the party came in.

'How goes it?' said Greg Jones, the *Birmingham Sentinel* man. 'This will be over in a jiffy. We'll try a shot across the table, mike in the foreground. Heads closer together. No big black gaps. Closer . . . good. Relax into it, you guys . . .'

'Where are Mitch's cans?' asked Freya.

'Here.' Bettina was there, turning so Mitch could see the crossed cricket bats on her bright green T-shirt. Mitch was still looking at the motif as she took the cans.

'Just a quickie.' The photographers were already snapping. 'Smile. You're enjoying yourselves. Life's wonderful. Smile there. Smile.'

'Don't forget Mrs Stanton,' Mitch told Bettina. 'Make her comfortable.'

'Put the cans on, Mitch!' Freya was shouting.

Mitch looked down at the earphones. They were Jon Stanton's. She looked back at Bettina but the girl had disappeared.

'Mitch!'

The cans weren't heavy. No, not at all. They were light. But they weren't light enough.

Still holding them in her left hand, Mitch felt for the tubular shaft which supported the back cushion on the studio chair. She jerked the chair off the floor.

'Christ, girlie!' the Chancellor yelled, whacked in the stomach by a wildly revolving chair seat. Mitch flung her arm back. The chair wobbled in the air. She brought her arm down, letting the chair go. It crashed through the studio window into the courtyard below.

'Mitch!'

Her spine arched as her arm shot back again. She hurled the earphones through the hole the chair had made.

Silence.

No one was breathing.

Light bathed the studio. It was bluish,

pretty. The walls shifted a little, white dust shook out of plaster. Mitch felt her body rising on a wave of noise. There was a jarring thud as she landed into a universe of grey and white pin-stripes. She was aware of opening her mouth as she doubled in pain. 'Town hall . . . ' the Chancellor was mumbling. 'Tow-n-n-n . . . ' Through her agony Mitch's brain clattered on. He's dead. Am I dying? She was aware they had both been blown back against the studio wall. He had keeled over sideways. She was sitting, his torso her back-rest. She leaned forward again, bending into the pain, teeth gritting, nails digging into her palms.

As the pain ebbed she looked up, blinking the grit of plaster out of her eyes. She began to make out Greg Jones, the photographer. A piece of the ceiling was wedged between his raised arm and neck. Blood from his ear was running into it. His eye was in the view-finder, the camera clamped firmly between steady hands.

Smile.

Relax into it . . .

No big black gaps.

And yet she was slowly sinking towards one.

She became aware of something else as the pain began to flood back. Her buzzing head.

One shaking hand moved upwards. A forefinger pressed, released, pressed her ear. And then she bent into the agony.

When she opened her eyes again she became acutely aware of pink cabbage roses on a Liberty print frock and a jumbo-sized water pistol in capable female hands. The gun was aimed at Mitch and then aimed a little higher. 'Helen!' The Chancellor's yell dislodged a large lump of plaster half hanging from the ceiling. It hit the round table in the centre of the studio; grit ricocheted off walls.

Helen's mouth, pink as one of the cabbage roses, grew wide on a cough, wide enough to receive the muzzle of the turning gun.

The world was suddenly full of electric blue breeches. There was a champagne cork pop and Freya was rolling on the floor, howling.

Helen lifted the gun again.

Not at me. At the Chancellor, Mitch realised. She forced her body up through pain, the better to protect Britain's treasury.

But the gun was turning inwards, a meal for Helen's ever-widening mouth. Unseen hands were grappling with her from behind. A Liberty print sleeve was slowly tearing away from the bodice. Shaun was flying through the air. He took her legs from under her in a rugby tackle.

Pop.

Pop. Pop.

The gun?

A camera?

'We'll be late again!' The Chancellor's yell was turning into a sob. 'Oh sweetie. Late, late, late. Tell them.'

'Tell them yourself!' Mitch's lips were rounding. She clamped her teeth down on her shriek. When she opened them again she wondered, Have I broken my back? 'Oh shit,' said the Chancellor. 'Is that really Helen?'

19

She was sitting up in her hospital bed, a peach bed jacket slung round her shoulders, two little plastic slides holding back wings of baby soft hair. Mitch was relieved to see that — as far as was discernible — Freya Adcock wore nothing remotely resembling anything in her wardrobe.

' . . . after the explosion? Ah. Well. She was there with this thing in her hand. A Walther PPK, right? Sometimes used by Luftwaffe aircrew in World War II? I read that in *The Independent*.'

'But did she aim the gun at the Chancellor — ' an off-vision interviewer prodded.

'At one of my broadcasters! I thought this woman was going to shoot Mitch. I was already going for her when I saw her turn the gun on herself. Christ! The way she was waving it about. I had to get the thing off her.'

'You made a dive for her and that's when you got hit?'

'Too right, kiddo. The bullet passed right through me. Missed my spine by a fraction. I'm lucky to be mobile. I'm lucky to be here at all. Really. Don't I know it. Even the starch in these sheets feels super.'

'When you were hit you lost consciousness? Or did you — '

'I hit the deck. And that's it. That's all I know.'

'Going for someone with a gun . . . that was very brave.'

'No one's going to start taking pot shots in my studio. No way. I couldn't believe it. First this huge explosion and then there's this woman with a pistol in her hands. On my radio station . . .'

'But was she going to gun down the Chancellor?'

'The last thing I remember seeing was her turning the gun on herself. I tried to wrestle it off her and got hit. But if you are looking for the person who really saved the day don't look at me. That was one of my broadcasters. Mitch chucked the bomb out of the window. It's all down to Radio Brum. Plenty of bottom. The lot of them. I'm told that Shaun O'Neill took the legs from under the woman with the Walther. A pretty good show all round if you ask me. Mind you, I think the security people could do more. Plastic explosives seem as easy to get one's hands on as elastoplast. And how the hell did that woman get hold of a German pistol?'

357

Mitch, hobbling over to the television on her crutches, switched off the lunchtime news. Tears started to run down her face. She turned as Josh Hadley came into the room with a tray of coffee. 'Oh, what a mess. What an awful mess.'

'Stop wailing. Sit down and drink your coffee.'

'You'd wail if you were in as much pain as I am. You'd wail even more,' sobbed Mitch. 'I know you w-w-would . . .'

'This is a time for celebration, chickadee. Half a dozen people owe their lives to you. It was your quick thinking that saved the day.'

'I saved my skin. That's what I did. Same as anyone else would have d-done.'

'Come on. Come on, chickadee. You're shaking like a leaf. Come and sit down.'

'For God's sake don't be kind to me. That'll make me h-h-howl even more.'

'There. Lift that leg up on the couch. Do you need another cushion behind your back?'

'Please.'

'There you go.'

'He completely took me in, Josh. I just couldn't believe my luck. This guy made me feel twenty again. Better than twenty. Oh, he was lovely. Lovely. I couldn't get enough of him. And all the while — ' She dashed away the tears. 'The bastard cold bloodedly set me up.'

'He also fooled Bettina Mayo. One day that young kid is going to wake up in gaol and wonder what happened to her life. From all accounts she was into peace movements before she fell in love with Charlie Collins. Or whatever his real name is. If you were an inexperienced twenty year old instead of fifty you might be in her shoes.'

'At times I'm glad I broke my leg. I almost wish I'd broken my back. I want the p-pain,' she wailed.

'Stop being ridiculous. Here. Drink this coffee.'

She took it. The spoon began to rattle in the saucer.

'Drink it.'

She spluttered. 'What have you put in this stuff?'

'Brandy.' He grinned. 'Put a bit of iron back into your soul.'

'My eyes must look frightful. I must look a helluva mess.' Then, as if she suddenly expected cameras to invade the room, she abruptly turned her face to the back of the couch. 'That damned phone is still off the hook, isn't it?'

'Of course it is.'

'Telly chat shows indeed. As if I'm just

another freak to be wheeled on to a chat show!'

'By the way how much did the *Sun* offer you?'

'Twenty thousand.'

'Will you do a deal?'

'Have you gone mad? Can't you see the headline? BOMBER BONKS BROADCASTER. What about my daughter? What about Cassie, the poor lamb. What about what's left of my dignity? Listen, I'm saying nothing. Nothing at all. No comment.'

'Just how did you know those earphones contained explosives? I still don't understand that.'

'For a start they weren't my cans. Oh, they looked like mine all right. They looked like half the cans on the station. But they were Jon Stanton's.'

'How could you be sure?'

'Fiddlers know their fiddles. And, of course, they felt wrong in my hands. They wouldn't to most people. Perhaps only an ounce or two difference in weight. But if you've been using the damned things day in and day out for over twenty years — '

'But that still doesn't add up to a bomb.'

'You forget I'd been investigating Jon Stanton's death. What you don't know is he took some photographs of Bettina and a man just before he died and sent them to a painter friend of his called Robin Pemberton. Before he opted out Pemberton worked for MI5.'

'And the man in the pictures was Charlie Collins?'

'Yes. It suddenly occurred to me where the negatives were. When I saw them I couldn't make out the figures though there was something about the set of one of the heads . . .'

Josh got up and walked over to the window. He had his back to her when he asked, 'What really happened when you saw Robin Pemberton?'

'He was dead by the time I got to him. He'd been shot in the head.'

'Who do you think did it?'

'I don't know for sure. Perhaps we'll never know if Bettina and Lygo Pim carry on keeping mum. But I think my — Charlie Collins did it, didn't he? First Jon and then Robin Pemberton. The bastard set up Robin's death in such a way that I thought I'd be implicated. I made sure the body was hidden from sight. I hoped to get to the bottom of what was behind it all before events caught up with me — '

'Oh my God. No wonder you looked so awful that day I saw you at the furniture warehouse.'

'I think this whole thing started by chance when Bettina Mayo met and fell in love with Charlie. She was already working for a southern radio station and in her spare time campaigning for Green for Good. It was known months ago that Sackville Thumper, the Environment Minister, would be in Birmingham this summer for a conference. I think he was the intended target. I think what happened was that when Charlie heard the Chancellor was coming he simply switched targets. Everything was set up, ready. All he did was change the target and move up the date. It must have seemed a heaven sent opportunity.'

'The thinking is that Charlie converted Bettina to the terrorists' cause? But where does Lygo Pim fit in?'

'Apparently he was used as a front man. Like Bettina, he wasn't known to the security forces. Charlie kept well in the background because he was known. That's why those photographs were so important. If those had fallen into the right hands the game would have been up.'

'The whole thing was a wolf in sheep's clothing operation?'

'What could be more ideal than an organisation like Green for Good which is known for its non-violence? For being harmless? It's not going to attract any attention from the security forces, is it? And from Charlie's point of view — that bastard would see a certain macabre fitness. The security chap told me that Charlie's head of an Irish splinter group called Green Action — named for the Emerald Isle. He's probably spent months laughing up his sleeve. Green subverting green.'

'So he is an IRA man.'

'No. He's apparently head of a breakaway group set up for the sole purpose of targeting politicians, judges, people in public life.'

'But where on earth does the Chancellor's ex-wife fit in?'

'She doesn't. When the police searched her place they found a diary. It seems she's been plotting to kill her ex-husband ever since she learned his new wife was going to have a baby. She seemed to cope with the divorce but when she learned he was to become a parent . . . She'd had a miscarriage after a car accident and after that she couldn't bear a child, you see. He was the driver. He got off scot-free.'

'But how did she know he'd be on the station that night?'

'The *Birmingham Sentinel* prints schedules of our programmes. And because it was a special edition of 'City Talk' there have been

363

one or two stories in the papers too. She knew she could use me to get on the station and so I suppose she thought an ideal opportunity had presented itself. I thought Madeleine Stanton had come. I actually asked Bettina Mayo to show her up.'

'Christ.' Josh was suddenly grinning. 'Who'd be in the Chancellor's shoes?'

'Who would be in Helen Brierley's shoes, don't you mean?' Mitch shuddered. 'When she saw her husband — her ex-husband — she said she realised that he was a stranger. She'd not known him for years. He was somebody she'd made up. It was then, she told the police, that she knew that she had not been plotting his death at all. She'd been organising her own. 'I'm the corpse,' was what she actually said. 'It's as plain as day. Every time I look in the mirror. That's what I see. Me.' '

'Jesus,' said Josh.

'The police said her diary was an ABC of different methods of doing it. Killing, I mean. And what is even more . . . well, she'd researched decomposition. She'd pictured what happens to the body after death 'almost gleefully' — that's what a sergeant told me. He was horrified.'

'What will they do with someone like that?'

'They've bunged her into a psychiatric

364

hospital. I suppose it must be doubtful if she'll ever stand trial.'

'But I still don't really know what made you realise you were holding a bomb and not Jon's earphones.'

'It all flowed from Bettina Mayo. For one thing, I'd stolen her diary. Against the phone numbers were no names but what looked like mathematical formulae. Except for one. The symbol there appeared to be crossed cricket bats. It was a Dublin number. Nothing in that, of course. But it did put the word Irish into my head.

'Nothing hit me immediately. I'd seen Bettina earlier in the office and I was — well, I was uneasy. But I didn't know about what. I thought it was just some form of *déjà vu*. It wasn't until we were in the studio that I realised the bright green T-shirt she was wearing was the same one I'd seen Charlie Collins in. And the motif on the pocket wasn't crossed cricket bats at all but lacrosse sticks. Of course, I knew then. He was Bettina's boyfriend. He was the man in the photos. And a bit of that old Irish revolutionary song came into my head. You know. About 'the wearing of the green' . . . I was also holding Jon's cans, cans I'd later seen in Bettina's flat.

'My God, did I panic. I wanted to throw

the damned thing out but, of course, the studio window doesn't open. I had to hurl a chair through the window to make a hole before I could toss the bomb out. But it shouldn't have gone off then. Apparently the wiring had come adrift. They reckon it actually exploded before it hit the ground which was why the force of the blast affected the studio so badly. The bomb people think the cans were rigged so that the bomb would go off as soon as the electric current hit the wires. We'd all have been killed, Josh. Everyone in Studio One. The b-b-bastard . . . ' She gulped some more coffee.

'They'll get him. They collared Lygo Pim last night, didn't they? How did they know he was involved?'

'He more or less gave himself away. He lost his nerve. Made a break for it. I think the police have already tied him in with Charlie. To be honest it seems that Charlie regarded them — like me — as expendable. It seems he was away long before the bomb went off.'

'They'll get him. His mug is plastered over all the newspapers. And television.'

Mitch shook her head. 'The bastard'll be out of the country already. Back on his foreign travels. They think he was once a priest. I find that almost — incomprehensible. He was here the night before the explosion.' Her eyes opened wider as if she were trying to see him. 'He made love to me . . .'

'We'll see you through, chickadee. All of us. Look at Freya. My God. She risked her life for you.'

'She's truly weird.'

'Is that all you can say about her?'

'No. No. I'm sorry, Josh. I feel . . . well, I won't trust my judgement about people again ever. I mean, how could I fall for that bastard?'

'Oh, come off it, Mitch. Who hasn't been deceived?' He turned back to the window.

'I keep remembering the way Bettina Mayo looked at me that morning before the Chancellor came. What am I saying . . . ?' She shuddered. 'I wasn't there for her. She knew I was going to die and she'd already stopped acknowledging me.'

'Look at that! There's a hell of a fuss going on by the gate. Seems to be . . . yes, there's a policeman searching a bouquet . . .'

'Are the reporters still there?'

'Yes. Oh wait — there's a chinaman, too. A little chap in a blazer.'

'Tommy Hung! I must see him, Josh. Please. Go down to the gate and rescue him for me. Oh Lord. He can't see me like this. He'll expect me to have a stiff upper lip.

You've no idea. He thinks we're all some sort of impossible heroes. I must wash my face. Help me up!'

'Here we go then. Where's the crutch? Good. OK? Who the hell is Tommy Hung?'

'He thinks he's a detective. He thinks I'm a detective too — '

Josh was going to say something but Mitch winked a swollen red eyelid. He grinned. 'OK. There's my girl . . . '

'The Chancellor sent me roses,' said Mitch as she hobbled before him through the door. 'See. On the hall table. Three dozen.'

'I should bloody well think so.'

'No doubt he'll put it on his expenses claim. I got lilies from the top suits at the broadcasting centre. That'll certainly go down on exes.'

'Who are these from?'

'Lilac? Mrs Stanton. She put her cheque in. You know, in settlement of her bill,' and Mitch was sobbing again. 'T-that poor l-lad.'

'Are you going to make it up those stairs?'

'Of c-course I am. I travel on my bum.'

'Why not use the downstairs cloakroom?'

'My make-up's upstairs. Time I p-put my face back on, honeypot.'

'That's it, chickadee.'

'Did I tell you? My daughter's flying from Japan tomorrow. She'll be so horrified. I never was like the other mothers. I was always in some kind of hot water. I'm always embarrassing that poor k-kid.'

'Cassie is proud of you.'

'Only when my purse is open and she's got a new dress in her hands.'

'Rubbish. She's a good kid. Now, I better rescue your chinaman before there's a punch up.'

When Mitch — by way of a bum shuffle she'd last seen her daughter use at the age of two — arrived back at the bottom of the stairs, she'd bounced herself into a very different mood. For one thing she was wearing her electric blue culottes and print jacket — why the hell should she let herself be chased out of her own clothes? But she hadn't broken her new rules about make-up. She wore very little. Anyone with eyes to see could observe the sign of recent weeping. She'd wept for the deceiving tenderness of Charlie's flesh, for pride's sake, for shame's sake, for the sake of all her hurts. She wasn't afraid now of anyone seeing that because she'd found she could still lift her head.

To hell with the bastard.

She was going to be all right. She was going to *make* herself all right.

From the kitchen came the sound of

clattering pots. 'Josh is cooking you lunch I believe,' said Tommy from behind a huge basket of peonies. 'The dear chap rescued me from the arms of the law.'

'Oh Tommy, you shouldn't — '

'Of course I should. The table here, do you think?' and it wasn't until he'd dumped the basket of flowers that she saw his face. He was beaming. 'We couldn't have made a better start, Mitch. We must name our agency immediately. Before you get interviewed on television and interviewed by *The Times*. My dear girl. We'll be known worldwide before we've hardly begun. What about Mitch Mitchell Investigations?'

'Are you serious?'

'Are you?'

Mitch thought about it. She hobbled towards the window before turning. 'Damn it all.' She was amazed. 'I think I am.'

'And you wouldn't mind? Naturally, I'd keep well in the background . . . I'd . . . '

Before she really realised what she was saying it was out. 'Tommy. We'd be in it together or not at all.' A brush with death had certainly made her view her life in a different way. But you haven't thought any of this through, a small voice in her wailed. What do you think you're up to?

'Mitch Mitchell Associates?'

'Mitchell Hung certainly won't do,' and she thought about it.

'Mitchell and Orient?'

'But isn't that some not very good football team?'

'Are you thinking of Leyton Orient? I was thinking about what must be your favourite train.'

'The Orient Express?' He beamed. 'Mitchell and Orient. Of course we shall keep ourselves small. We shall be very exclusive.'

'Don't let your hopes rise too much.'

'What you did, Mitch, is as good as having a 'by appointment to Her Majesty, suppliers of . . . ' Mark my words. You were . . . you were . . . well, jolly good. Jolly good. I'll finance our little venture. A good address. The right stationery.'

'Nothing too plush.' Mitch, alarmed, suddenly saw acres of inch deep carpet improbably seeded with Corinthian columns. 'Remember Philip Marlowe's joint — ' Suddenly she was laughing.

Josh popped his head round the door. 'Anyone who can get Mitch to laugh gets invited to lunch. Can you stay, Tommy? We're having a cheese soufflé, a little salad and some new potatoes. Nothing grand.'

'I'll be honoured,' said Tommy.

'Do you know, I still haven't found out

about Ann Wellesley,' said Mitch as they went through to the dining room. 'I still can't understand why she made that appointment to see me and then simply cut me dead.'

'Lygo Pim's doing,' Tommy deduced. 'After all, he was her boyfriend. She probably told him and he laid down the poison. After that, they probably cooked up what happened at the station between them.'

'I don't suppose we'll ever know.'

'Oh, I wouldn't go as far as that,' said Tommy. 'A great deal more will come out when Bettina Mayo and Lygo Pim stand trial.'

'But they won't catch the man who should be in the dock. They won't get their hands on Charlie.'

'We're going to forget that bastard and have our champers,' said Josh. 'This is a celebration lunch. Impromptu, certainly. But those are the best ones.'

'We'll drink to Mitchell and Orient,' said Mitch.

'Who the hell are they?' asked Josh.

★ ★ ★

It was six months later when a post card came. It arrived the same day as the buff

372

envelope. It was the day Mitch saw stockbroker Willie French and learned what a Rights Issue was. She was investigating the affairs of the financier Arno Czinner.

She opened the buff envelope first. It was a Witness Order. It read: *That (if notice is given you to that effect) you attend and give evidence at the trial of Bettina Mayo and Lygo Pim at the Crown Court at Birmingham.*

She was warned: *Failure to comply with this order may render you liable to imprisonment for three months or a fine.* She also got a small orange leaflet telling her what to expect.

The postcard was from Rio de Janeiro. On the front was a picture of the Sugar Loaf Mountain.

Lots of swimming. Lots of wine, women and song. Miss you, though. You're special. Till we meet again. It was signed by a pair of crossed lacrosse sticks.

Oh, hell, thought Mitch. But she didn't cry. She no longer cried over Charlie Collins.

She went out into the snow. Her mind was already thinking of money-man Arno Czinner, who had told her the night before: 'Czinner Enterprises fights armed with Christian principles, Miss M. No fucking around.'

But as she took out her car key her fingers quivered — just a little — as she fitted it into the lock of the TVR.

THE END

ABERDEEN
CITY
LIBRARIES

We do hope that you have enjoyed reading this large print book.

Did you know that all of our titles are available for purchase?

We publish a wide range of high quality large print books including:
Romances, Mysteries, Classics, General Fiction, Non Fiction and Westerns.

Special interest titles available in large print are:
The Little Oxford Dictionary
Music Book
Song Book
Hymn Book
Service Book

Also available from us courtesy of Oxford University Press:
Young Readers' Dictionary
(large print edition)
Young Readers' Thesaurus
(large print edition)

For further information or a free brochure, please contact us at:
Ulverscroft Large Print Books Ltd.,
The Green, Bradgate Road, Anstey,
Leicester, LE7 7FU, England.
Tel: (00 44) **0116 236 4325**
Fax: (00 44) **0116 234 0205**

Other titles in the
Ulverscroft Large Print Series:

THE UNSETTLED ACCOUNT

Eugenia Huntingdon

As the wife of a Polish officer, Eugenia Huntingdon's life was filled with the luxuries of silks, perfumes and jewels. It was also filled with love and happiness. Nothing could have prepared her for the hardships of transportation across Soviet Russia — crammed into a cattle wagon with fifty or so other people in bitterly cold conditions — to the barren isolation of Kazakhstan. Many did not survive the journey; many did not live to see their homeland again. In this moving documentary, Eugenia Huntingdon recalls the harrowing years of her wartime exile.